YAWAR FIESTA

The Texas Pan American Series

Yawar Fiesta

JOSÉ MARÍA ARGUEDAS

Translated by Frances Horning Barraclough

 University of Texas Press, Austin

Copyright © 1985 by the University of Texas Press
All rights reserved
Printed in the United States of America

First edition, 1985

Requests for permission to reproduce material
from this work should be sent to:
  Permissions
  University of Texas Press
  Box 7819
  Austin, Texas 78713

Library of Congress Cataloging in Publication Data
Arguedas, José María.
  Yawar fiesta.

  (Texas Pan American series)
  Translation of: Yawar fiesta.
  1. Puquio (Peru)—History—Fiction.   2. Quechua
Indians—Fiction.   I. Title.   II. Series.
  PQ8497.A65Y313   1985   863   84-19625
  ISBN 0-292-79601-3
  ISBN 0-292-79602-1 (pbk.)

Translated from *Yawar Fiesta*, © Editorial Losada, S.A., Buenos Aires, 1941

"Puquio: A Culture in Process of Change" translated from "Puquio, una cultura en proceso de cambio," published in *Estudios sobre la cultura actual del Perú*, © Universidad Nacional Mayor de San Marcos, Lima, 1964

The Texas Pan American Series is published with the assistance of a revolving publication fund established by the Pan American Sulphur Company.

Contents

Translator's Note

The novel *Yawar Fiesta* describes the social relations between several classes of people in the Peruvian highland town of Puquio in the 1920s and 1930s. It is the story of the different ways the upper class, mestizos, and Indians reacted to the national government's attempt to suppress the traditional Indian-style bullfight. It reflects the degree to which the actions of each group are derived from its Indian or Spanish heritage, and how each reacts to social change. The author, José María Arguedas, also meant to show that the Indians could accomplish great deeds when they worked together, as in building a highway through the high Andes to the coast, and even capturing and killing one of their demigods, the bull Misitu.

There are many different terms, both respectful and derogatory, for these groups of people; names by which they call themselves and names by which others call them. Some of these terms I have translated into English; others have been left in their original language, as no English equivalent exists. The following outline may help the reader to sort them out. For further explanations see the glossary.

THE CAST

The upper class of Puquio
As they call themselves:
    las autoridades (the officials)
    los principales (the important people, the leading citizens)
    los señores (title used to address a notable; used in the sense of "lord" or "master")
As the Indians call them:
    la autoridad (the authority)

werak'ocha (the name of the Incas' supreme god; today it is the equivalent of *señor*, a respectful title of address)

mistis (although this is the Quechua word for "white," it is used by Indians for upper-class people of both white and mixed ancestry)

niñas (the "girls"; corresponds to a Quechua term for unmarried women)

k'alakuna (a derogatory Quechua word meaning "the peeled or naked ones"; the persons referred to have no ties of mutual obligations with the Indian community; this could be applied to the upper class or to the mestizos)

"extrangueros" (the foreigners, outsiders, or strangers)

The mestizos (persons of mixed Indian and white ancestry)
As they call themselves:

los señores

los vecinos (a term from the Spanish colonial period, it originally meant people who owned house lots, had a right to pasture cattle on the town common land, and were permitted to vote; in this book they are called town citizens, townsmen, or townspeople. Townsmen, as used here, does not include the Indians who live in the town. *Vecino* is not a racial term.)

As the upper class calls them:

los vecinos

los mestizos

los cholos (a derogatory term for mestizos or Indians who have adopted the speech and dress of the Western culture)

As the Indians call them:

tumpa-mistis (half-*mistis*)

"chalos" (the Indian pronunciation of the word *cholos*)

The Indians
As they call themselves:

Varayok' Alcalde (the Chief Staffbearer, the head of the Indian civil-religious hierarchy, the mayor of the Indian community)

varayok', varayok'una (staffbearing Indian leaders, members of the hierarchy in which a man proceeds upward by performing successively more difficult duties; higher ones have been called *"selectmen"* here)

naturales (natives, "for they never call themselves Indians")

runa (a man); *runakuna* (people)

punarunas (puna-dwellers, people who live on the high, bleak uplands)

punacumunkuna (puna community members)

tayta (father; Indian equivalent of *señor*, sir, or sire; *taytacha*,
   "honored sir," is sometimes mistakenly transposed into Spanish *padrecito*, "little father")
mama (mother); *mamacha* (lady or ma'am)
k'ari (a brave man)
As others call them:
indígenas (a polite term meaning indigenous people)
comuneros (members of an Indian community)
concertados (Indians who have left their community and serve
   in their *misti*'s house all their lives in exchange for food,
   clothing, and a small annual salary)
colonos (serfs, Indians belonging to a hacienda)
gentiles (heathens)
indios (Indians)
cholos, "*chalos*"
guanacos (animals similar to llamas)

In the original novel the Indians speak a strange kind of Spanish based on their own language, Quechua. To be faithful to the author's intent, I tried to reflect this to some extent in their English dialogue. Arguedas writes of his own difficulties in determining how they should talk in the article that follows: "The Novel and the Problem of Literary Expression in Peru."

The novel *Yawar Fiesta* was first published in 1941. The article "Puquio: A Culture in Process of Change," which is included in this volume, was written by J.M.A. from an anthropological and musicological point of view and describes the same town as it existed more than a decade later, showing changes that resulted from the building of the highway to the coast.

For encouraging me to translate the Puquio article I wish to thank John V. Murra as well as Patricia Netherly, who clarified several anthropological and linguistic points. I also acknowledge the skillful assistance of Celia and Felix Palacios and of Fredy Roncalla, who explained Quechua terms, Peruvian turns of phrase, and Andean social situations. Finally I am grateful to Martin Wolf, Claire Eisenhart, and Margaret Adams for making many useful editorial suggestions.

F.H.B.

Preliminary Note

The novel *Yawar Fiesta* (*Bloody Fiesta*) is the culmination of a search for a style in which the ancient Quechua language could pass over into Spanish and become an instrument of expression free enough to be able to reflect the heroic deeds, the thought, the loves, and the hatreds of the Andean people of Hispano-Indian descent— not only of the multitude who speak only Quechua, but also of the heirs of the Spanish conquerors, who for centuries have been influenced to the core by the Andean universe that is alive and pulsing in the native language.

In this novel the reader will be able to feel, to scent, and even to intermingle and become thoroughly familiar with the deepest and most original confluences and conflicts between the European and the oldest Andean civilization. Those confluences and conflicts are vividly portrayed in the singularly heroic events described. Equally extraordinary are the agents that unleash those adventures.

The author spent part of his early childhood and adolescence in Puquio, where the novel takes place. When he visited the four *ayllus*[1] that make up the town of Puquio eighteen years after the book's publication, he was elated to find how in *Yawar Fiesta* the mestizos,[2] the landowners, and the tense relations between them, as well as the majestic, wild, and extremely rugged, yet tender landscape were described as if they had been interpreted and sung in the

1. An *ayllu* is an Indian neighborhood or community and its members are called *comuneros*.—Trans.

2. A person of mixed Indian and white ancestry. (See glossary for Spanish and Quechua words not explained in the text. For the most part, I have followed the author's original spelling of Quechua words and place names, although it varied over time and does not always agree with present-day orthography.)—Trans.

onomatopoetic Quechua language. Its syllables contain almost the material essence of things and the manner in which man has ever poured out his life on those matters. I should also warn that this tale may disenchant those who love the great formal conquests of the modern novel. The work is original in style and language, and in the revelations it may offer about the so intricate, so little known Andean universe, there where it is most ancient and most densely populated.

For the readers' information, the editor of the collection published in Chile in which this novel appears has wisely chosen to include as a prologue an article I wrote in 1950 on how and why we consider this novel to be the culmination of a real struggle that a Quechua-language author had to undergo to transform Spanish into a free and sufficient means of expression. These lines are a sort of prologue to that prologue.

J.M.A.

June 17, 1968
Santiago, Chile

The Novel and the Problem
of Literary Expression in Peru[1]

HUMAN CHARACTERS IN THE ANDES

The distinguishing features of the peasants in the countries descended from the Inca Empire and Spain have mainly been determined by cultural factors; for that reason the peasant in those countries is called by a proper noun that expresses all of this complex reality: Indian. From that noun other adjectives have been derived that have found wide acceptance in art, literature, and science: *indigenista, indianista,* and Indian.

Thus people speak of the *novela indigenista,* and my novels, *Agua* and *Yawar Fiesta,* have been called *indigenista* or Indian. And that is not the case. It's a matter of their being novels in which Andean Peru appears with all of it elements, in its disturbing and confused human reality, of which the Indian is only one of many different characters.

Yawar Fiesta is the novel of the so-called "big towns," the capitals of the highland provinces;[2] *Agua* is the story of a village, of a district capital.

There are five main characters in the "big towns": the Indian; the tough-minded, hardhearted landholder, heir to a centuries-old tradition that inspires his actions and serves as a foundation for his beliefs; and the new landowner, who engaged in shady lawsuits, plays politics, and is the national authorities' servile flunkey. Then there is the town mestizo who, for the most part, does not know where he is

1. *Mar del Sur, Revista Peruana de Cultura* (Lima, Peru), yr. II, vol. 3, no. 9 (January–February 1950): 66–72. Version revised and corrected by the author.—Trans.

2. Peru is divided politically into departments, which in turn are divided into provinces and districts.—Trans.

going; he serves the landowners and takes brutal action against the Indians, or sinks down into the crowd, bustling around in it to stir people up and discharge his aggressions, or else could identify himself with the Indians and generously sacrifice his life to defend them. The fifth character is the provincial student who has two residences—Lima and his hometown—for the most part a Messianic type whose soul smolders between love and hatred. This human element—so noble, so tenacious, so self-denying—is soon swallowed up by the implacable forces that sustain the social order against which his courage has been wounded and wasted. Over these five basic characters float the national authorities; they ride roughshod over them; and often, depending on the wickedness, indifference, or occasional good intentions of such elements, the towns are moved to march off in different directions, at a violent or routine pace.

Another recent Peruvian character who appears in *Yawar Fiesta* is the provincial person who migrates to the capital. Lima's invasion by men from the provinces began quietly; when the highways were built it took the form of a headlong invasion. Indians, mestizos, and landowners moved off to Lima, leaving their towns drained or less active, bleeding. In the capital those Indians and mestizos have lived and are still living through a painful initial adventure, eking out a poverty-stricken existence in districts where there are no lights, no water, and scarcely any roofs, to go on "entering" the city, or turning their shapeless shantytowns into a city, while transforming themselves into day laborers or ordinary white-collar workers. To what extent have these squatters wrought a change in the capital's traditional spirit?

The novel in Peru has been, thus far, a narration of the adventures of towns rather than of individuals. And it has been predominantly Andean. In the highland towns the romance, the novel of individuals, has been blotted out, buried by the drama of the social classes. The social classes also have an especially heavy cultural base in Andean Peru; when they clash, and they do it barbarically, the struggle is not impelled by economic interest alone; other spiritual forces, deep and violent, fan the flames, arousing the factions relentlessly, with unceasing and inevitable urgency.

There are scarcely any Indian names in *Yawar Fiesta*. It tells the tale of several heroic deeds performed by Puquio's four Indian communities; it is an attempt to portray the communities' soul, the light as well as the dark side of their being, to show how people are constantly being disconcerted by the ebb and flow of their day-to-day destiny. Such a tide, under a definition of limits that is only apparent beneath the surface, forces them to make a constant effort to accommodate, to readjust to a permanent drama. How long will the tragic duality of Indian and Western endure in these countries descended from Tahuantinsuyo[3] and from Spain? How deep is the current that separates them? A growing anguish oppresses whoever contemplates the future from the inside of the drama. These adamant people—the Indians—who transform everything alien before incorporating it into their world, who will not even let themselves be destroyed, have demonstrated that they will not yield to anything but a total solution.

And what about the other faction, the other current? That is even more complex, intricate, murky, and changeable, of a variable and contradictory disposition in the so-called "big towns." The traditional landholders—old in spirit—are serene and have no pangs of conscience; their behavior patterns have not been disturbed; they drive their fists, brandish their canes, and sink their spurs hard; they are the masters. The students and so-called progressives view them with a bright and clear hatred; they, the masters, may perhaps sometimes fear this hatred, but they never hesitate or yield to it. In the same faction—the same in relation to the Indian—there are other different kinds of people, and they are often inimical to one another, from the unstable mestizo who has barely emerged from the Indian mass to the revolutionary militant. These characters are myriad, and their different souls can only be defined through the novel. We have already stated this in the beginning.

Is a novel that deals with the adventures of all these characters an Indian novel, one that is merely Indian or *indianista*? It is probable, or more than probable, that the Indian may appear as the fundamental hero in these novels. As a result of a cherished misadventure, my childhood and part of my adolescence were spent among the Lucana Indians; they are the people I most love and understand. But those who take the trouble to read *Yawar Fiesta* and get to know Julián Arangüena and the police sergeant who appear in that novel will see that I have written about the lives of all the characters of a "big town" in the Peruvian highlands with a clear conscience, with a clean heart, insofar as it is possible for a human heart to be clean. As for *Agua*, that was really written with hatred, with the fury of a pure hatred, the kind that springs from universal loves up there in the regions of the world where two factions confront each other with implacable cruelty—one group that bleeds and another that squeezes out the last drop of blood.

3. Quechua name for the Inca Empire, meaning "Four Regions."—Trans.

For the tales in *Agua* contain the life of an Andean village in which the characters of the traditional factions are clearly defined, portrayed, and made to confront each other. Only two classes of people live there, and they represent two irreducible, implacable, and essentially different worlds: the landowner, convinced to the marrow of his bones, by the action of centuries, of his human superiority to the Indians; and the Indians, who have maintained their cultural unity all the more tenaciously precisely because they have been subjected to and confront such a fanatical and barbaric force.

And what is the fate of the mestizos in those villages? Today they prefer to leave, to go to Lima, to support themselves in the capital at the cost of the most difficult of sacrifices; that will always be better than becoming the landowner's overseer, beneath the silence of the highest of skies, suffering the encompassing hatred of the Indians and the equally staining contempt of the owner. There is another alternative that only one in a thousand chooses. The struggle is fierce in those worlds, more so than in others where it is also fierce. To stand up, then, to both Indians and landowners; to place oneself like a wedge between them; to fool the landowner by honing one's ingenuity to an incredible sharpness, squeezing even more out of them, and at times conspiring with them in the deepest secrecy, or showing only the tips of the ears, so that the owner may learn of it and be induced to yield, whenever necessary. Who will change this social "equilibrium" that has already prevailed for centuries—an equilibrium that is profoundly horrible—and destroy it, to enable the country to roll more freely and catch up with other nations—of the same age but with less human potential—that have already left such a shameful period behind?

But I was referring to the hatred with which I wrote the stories in *Agua*. My childhood was spent in several of those villages where there are 500 Indians to each landholder. I would eat in the kitchen with the Indian "lackeys" and servants. And for several months I was the guest of an Indian community.

To describe the life of those villages, to describe it in such a way that its pulse would never be forgotten, so that it would beat against the readers' conscience like a river! The characters' features were clearly pictured in my memory; they were living with demanding realism, scorched by the great sun, like the church façade in my hometown, in whose vaulted niches bouquets of flowers lie slowly dying. What other kind of literature could a man born and brought up in the interior villages write then, and even now? Could he speak of the revulsion felt by those defeated by whatever monstrosities man has accumulated in the big cities, or toll sleep-inducing bells?

But there was a perplexing hindrance to the realization of that burning desire. How to describe those villages, towns, and fields; in what
language could I write about their placid and at the same time dis-
quieting life? In Spanish? After having learned, loved, and lived it in
the sweet and pulsing Quechua language? It was a seemingly insolu-
ble situation.

I wrote the first tale in the most correct and "literary" Spanish at
my command. Later I read the story to some of my writer friends
from the capital and they praised it. But I came to detest those pages
more and more. No, they were not like that—neither the men, the
town, nor the landscape I wished to describe, I should almost say to
denounce! Under the spurious language, an apparently contrived
world—marrowless and bloodless—was shown; a typically "literary" world in which the word had consumed the work. While in my
memory, deep within, the real theme went on smoldering away untouched. I rewrote the story and finally understood, once and for all,
that my Spanish would be inadequate if I kept on using it in a traditional literary fashion. In those days I was reading Vallejo's *Tung-
steno* and Güiraldes' *Don Segundo Sombra*. Both books lighted
my way.

Could I perhaps be advocating the Indianization of Spanish? No.
But there is a case, a real case, in which the man from those regions,
feeling ill at ease with the Spanish he has inherited, sees the need to
use it as a raw material that he may modify, taking from and adding
to it, until he transforms it into his own means of expression. This
possibility, which has already been realized more than once in literature, is a proof of the limitless qualities of Spanish and of the highly
evolved languages.

We are not referring, in this case, to the clearly differentiated Spanish spoken by the people in some countries such as Argentina, but
to the literary expression of the American countries in which the
dominant survival of the native languages has created the complex
problem of bilingualism. Each case presents a different problem: in
the former it is a matter of linguistic fait accompli, which the writer
may or may not take up, make use of, and re-create. In the latter case,
he must solve a more serious problem but, in exchange, may count
on an advantage especially sought after by the artist: the possibility
of, the necessity for a more absolute act of creation.

In contrast to the solution of these particularly critical situations
in literary expression, there has always been the problem of univer-

sality, the danger of a regionalism that contaminates the work and constrains it. This is the danger that the latest introduction of foreign materials into an already clean and perfect means of expression always implies! But in such cases one is not primarily concerned with universality; instead it is a matter of simply being able to achieve self-realization. To realize oneself, to translate oneself, to transform a seemingly alien language into a legitimate and diaphanous torrent, to communicate to the almost foreign language the stuff of which our spirit is made: that is the hard, the difficult question. The universality of this rare balance of content and form, a balance achieved after nights of intense labor, is a thing that will come as a function of the human perfection attained in the course of such a strange effort. Do the real features of the human being and of his sojourn exist in the depths of this work? It does not matter if those features are painted with unfamiliar colors—such an outcome could lend greater interest to the picture. Just so the colors are not a mere tangle, the grotesque tracks of the movements of a powerless being, that is what is essential. But if the language, so charged with strange essences, lets one see the depths of the human heart, if it transmits to us the history of his passage over the earth, the universality may be a long time coming but nevertheless it will come, as we all know that man owes his preeminence and his dominion to the fact that he is one and unique.

In my personal experience the search for a style, as I have already stated, was long and anguished. And one of those days I began to write, for me, as fluidly and luminously as water slips through millennial channels. I finished the first story in a few days and timorously laid it aside.

I had already written "Warma Kuyay," the last story in *Agua*. The Spanish was docile and appropriate for the expression of my intimate moments, my own history, my romance. Here was the story of the first love of a highland mestizo, of a mestizo of the most culturally advanced type. Frustrated and impossible love for an Indian girl, with the saddest, most ill-fated ending. I know now that even in that story the Spanish is imbued with the Quechua soul, but its syntax is untouched. The same construction, the Spanish of "Warma Kuyay," acclimated as it is, was of no use to me in the interpretation of the community's struggles, the epic theme. As soon as my spirit mingled with that of the Quechua-speaking people, the desperate search for a style began. Was it simply a matter of an elemental lack of knowledge of the language? And yet I have no complaints about the style of "Warma Kuyay." While I was deeply immersed in the community's home I did not have the same command of Spanish, could not use it as naturally and properly. Many of the essences I felt to be best and most legitimate could not be diluted into Spanish terms of familiar construction. It was necessary to discover subtle ways to disarrange the Spanish in order to make it into the fitting mold, the adequate instrument of expression. And since it was a case of an aesthetic discovery, it was made in an imprecise, dreamlike fashion.

It was made naturally for me, the seeker. Six months later, I turned to the pages of the first story in *Agua*. There was no longer anything to complain about. That was the world! The small village burning beneath the fire of love and of hatred, of the great sun and of the silence; amid the singing of robins that had taken shelter in the bushes; beneath the highest and most avaricious of skies, beautiful but cruel. Would that world be transmitted to others? Would they be able to feel the extreme passions of the humans who dwelt therein? Their great lamentation and the incredible, the transparent joyfulness with which they were wont to sing in moments of calm? It seems they did.

Yawar Fiesta is still within the stylistic limits of *Agua*. For five years I struggled to tear out the Quechua idioms and make literary Spanish into my sole means of expression. I rewrote the first chapters of the novel many times and always came back to the starting point: the labored, anxiety-laden solution of the bilingual writer.

But some day the two worlds into which these countries descended from Tahuantinsuyo are divided—the Quechua and the Spanish—will be merged or separated definitively. Until then the bilingual artist's Way of the Cross will continue to exist. With reference to this grave problem of our destiny, I have tentatively cast my vote in favor of Spanish.

What language should the Indians be made to speak in literature? For the bilingual person, for one who first learned to talk in Quechua, it seems impossible to have them suddenly speak Spanish; on the other hand, whoever has not known them throughout childhood, from deep experience, can perhaps conceive of them expressing themselves in Spanish. I solved the problem by creating for them a special Spanish language, which has since been used with horrible exaggeration in the work of others. But the Indians do not speak that Spanish, not with Spanish speakers, and much less among themselves. It is a fiction. The Indians speak in Quechua. All of the southern and central highlands, with the exception of some cities, are completely Quechua-speaking. People from other regions who go to live in the southern towns and villages have to learn Quechua; it is an unavoidable necessity. So it is false and horrendous to present the

Indians speaking the Spanish of Quechua servants who have become accustomed to living in the capital. I am just now, after eighteen years of effort, attempting a Spanish translation of the Indians' dialogues. The first solution was to create for them a language based on the Spanish words that have been incorporated into Quechua and on the elementary Spanish that some Indians manage to learn *in their own villages*. The realistic novel, it seemed, had no other road.

Excising the Quechua words is an even longer and more arduous feat than taking out the Quechua turns of phrase. It is a question of not losing one's soul, of not being completely transformed by this long, slow undertaking! But care must be taken and one must be vigilant and work to retain the essence. As long as the source of the work is the world itself, it should glow with whatever fire we succeed in kindling; our use of the other style, for which we are unrepentant despite its strangeness and its native elements, should be infectious.

Was and is this a search for universality through the search for form, for form alone? For form insofar as it means a conclusion, an equilibrium reached through the necessary mixture of elements seeking to constitute themselves into a new structure?

I do not doubt—and may I be pardoned for expressing this conviction—I do not doubt the value of the novels published in this book[4]—their value in relation to the one I am writing at the present time. To have attempted to express oneself with a sense of universality through the steps that lead one to master another language, to have attempted this in midleap, that was the reason for the neverending struggle. I aspired to and sought a universality that would not disfigure, would not diminish the human nature and terrain I attempted to portray, that would not yield one iota to the external and apparent beauty of the words.

I believe that in the novel *Los Ríos Profundos*, this process has come to an end. It could only have one ending, the use of Spanish as the legitimate means of expressing the Peruvian world of the Andes: noble whirlwind in which different spirits, as if forged on antipodal stars, struggle, attract, repel, and mingle with one another amid silent snows and lakes, frost and fire.

It is not a matter, then, of a search for form as it is superficially and customarily understood, but rather a problem of the spirit, of the culture, in those countries in which alien currents meet and for cen-

---

4. This essay was to be used as a prologue to the second edition of *Agua* and *Yawar Fiesta*, a project of Editorial Huascarán, Lima, that was not completed.—Trans.

turies do not blend, but instead form narrow zones of confluence, while in the deepest and widest places the main currents flow on, unyielding, incredibly.

And why should the literature that shows us the disturbed and misty features of our people and of our own countenance in such a tormented fashion be called *indigenista*? It is quite evident that it does not deal solely with the Indians. But those who classify literature and art frequently fall into imperfect and misleading conclusions. Nevertheless we should be grateful to them for having obliged us to write this kind of self-analysis, or confession, which we do in the name of all those who must and do suffer deeply from the same drama of literary expression in these regions.

JOSÉ MARÍA ARGUEDAS

YAWAR FIESTA

1. Indian Town

Amid fields of alfalfa and patches of wheat, broad beans and barley, on a rugged hillside lies the town.

From the Sillanayok' Pass one can see three streams that flow closer and closer together as they near the valley of the great river. The streams plunge down out of the punas[1] through steep channels, but then spread out to cross a plain uneven enough to hold a small lake; the plain ends, the river's course is broken again, and the water goes tumbling down from one waterfall to another until it reaches the bottom of the valley.

The town looks big as it follows the slope of the mountain; from the banks of a stream, where eucalyptus trees grow, the tiled roofs rise up to the top of the ridge; at the top they come to an end because Girón Bolívar, the street where the leading citizens live, is on the ridge, and there the roofs are white, of corrugated tin. On the mountain flanks, almost without streets, amid barley fields, with large corrals where cushion plants and leafy pepper trees grow, the houses of the *comuneros* in the *ayllus*[2] of Puquio resemble an Indian town. Indian town, on the mountainside, by a stream.

From the Sillanayok' Pass one can see three *ayllus*: Pichk'achuri, K'ayau, Chaupi.

"Indian town!" exclaim the travelers when they reach this summit and spy Puquio. Some speak contemptuously; on the summit the coastal people shiver with cold and say:

"Indian town!"

1. High, bleak regions of the Andes.—Trans.
2. An *ayllu* is an Indian neighborhood or community, and its members are called *comuneros*.—Trans.

1

But on the coast there are no mountain passes. They do not know how their towns look from afar. A mere inkling of it they get on the highways because the roads widen when a town is close by, or from the look of the façade of a nearby hacienda, from the joy of the heart that is familiar with distance. To see our town from a pass, from a mountaintop where there are magic heaps of stones the travelers leave, and to play an arrival *huayno*[3] on a *quena* or *charango* or on a harmonica! To look down upon our town, to gaze at its white tower of stone and lime, to see the red housetops along the slopes, on the hill or in the valley, where roofs glitter with wide streaks of lime; to watch the kestrels and black hawks soaring in the sky over the town, and now and again a condor who spreads his great wings to the wind; sometimes to hear the crowing of roosters and the barking of the dogs who watch the corrals. And to sit for a while on the mountaintop to sing with joy. This is something those who live in the coastal towns cannot do.

Three *ayllus* can be seen from Sillanayok': Pichk'achuri, K'ayau, Chaupi. Three towers, three squares, three Indian neighborhoods. Because they are pretentious, the Chaupis roofed their chapel with tin. From Sillanayok', one can see the Chaupi chapel; next to a big stone, it looks long and gleaming, with its squat white tower.

"Atatau!" say the *comuneros* from the other neighborhoods. "It looks like a *misti* church."[4]

But the Chaupis are proud of their chapel.

"Better than a *misti* one," they say.

Coming in by the Sillanayok' road, the town begins on the banks of Cullahora Creek with the *ayllu* of Pichk'achuri. There are no real streets anywhere; the *comuneros* have put up their houses any place that suited them: on a little slope, in a good place, with a round or square corral, but with some sign by which they can recognize it from the mountains. On the outside a whitened wall, a low door, a window or two, sometimes a stone bench built against the wall; inside there is a porch with stubby pillars resting on white stone bases; at one end of the porch a dividing wall for the kitchen. By the corral

3. Indian song and dance of Inca origin.—Author
4. *Atatau* is an exclamation of disgust.—Author
Misti is a term used by Indians to designate a person of the aristocratic class, of Western or near-Western culture, who has traditionally dominated the region (politically, socially, and economically) since colonial times. Although *misti* means "white" in Quechua, by now, naturally, none of them is of the pure white race or of pure Western culture. (See Puquio article, p. 150, for further explanation.)—Trans.

wall, beside the house or in the middle of the patio, a leafy pepper tree gives shade in the morning and in the afternoon; the hens fly up into the pepper trees at midday and drowsily inspect themselves for fleas. The house roofs are always made of tile, tiles made by the K'ollanas and the K'ayaus; the roofs are streaked with lime and in the middle of each rooftop there is an iron cross. That's how the K'ayau and Pichk'achuri neighborhoods are, from Girón Bolívar to Cullahora Creek. Coming in from the coast one enters the town through these *ayllus*.

"Indian town!"

The whole slope is full of houses and corrals; occasionally the traveler comes upon winding streets, wide in one place, narrow in another; the street disappears where it is cut off by a bean or barley field and reappears farther along. The traveler climbs the hill, now and then leaping over irrigation ditches lined with sorrel and green grass. Once he nears the top of the hill there are narrow cobbled lanes with white stone sidewalks, little shops with display counters resting on mud brick benches. On the counters there are bottles of sugarcane liquor, mounds of bread, bras in assorted colors for the Indian women, white shirt buttons, candles, soap, and sometimes lengths of shirting and coarse cotton cloth. It is the mestizos' place; it's not for Indian *comuneros* or prominent citizens; that is where the "*chalos*"[5] live; the shops belong to the half-caste women who wear percale clothing and straw hats.

All of a sudden, on reaching the top of the hill, one comes out onto Girón Bolívar.

"What?" the strangers exclaim in surprise.

For this is the street of the taxpaying property owners, of the leading citizens. A long, narrow, well-kept street with sidewalks of polished stone. Girón Bolívar begins at the Plaza de Armas, goes on for three or four blocks, and then drops down into a wide ravine and stops at the square of the Chaupi community. At that end of Girón Bolívar there is a big fountain with four water taps; beyond that is the Chaupi *ayllu* square with its tin-roofed chapel. There are "Alberto," an Indian statue made of *alaymosca* stone, and the huge rock, Makulirumi, which is the neighborhood's totem. Farther along, right out in the open fields, is the Indian town of Chaupi. From one corner of the Chaupi square Calle Derecha takes off; it's like a pro-

---

5. *Chalo* is a derogatory term for a person of Indian or mixed blood who has adopted the speech and dress of the Hispanic culture; it is the local Indian pronunciation of the word *cholo.*—Trans.

longation of Girón Bolívar, but Calle Derecha is an Indian street.

On the other side of Girón Bolívar, on the far slope of the hill, lies the community of K'ollana. K'ollana cannot be seen from Sillanayok'; the hill hides it. Like Pichk'achuri, K'ollana ends at a stream, the Yallpu. The town begins and ends with streams.

On Girón Bolívar the important people make their homes; there they live all year around. The other solid citizens' houses are also on Girón Bolívar; there are the bars where they get drunk; that's where the billiard parlor, the pharmacy, and the stores are located.

"What?" say the strangers as they come out onto Girón Bolívar.

Well, it suits the *mistis'* tastes. The doors are green, blue and yellow; almost all of the houses are two stories high, with balconies that shade the sidewalks. The streets are narrow; at night, when they chase one another, the cats leap across from one roof to another. But the streets are straight; the steep ones and the level ones are all straight; and the ditches that run down the middle of the streets are well-paved with stone; from all the entry ways little channels run out to these ditches.

The Plaza de Armas also belongs to the prominent citizens, even more so than Girón Bolívar. But the Plaza de Armas is not in the center of town. At one end of Girón Bolívar is the Chaupi square, at the other the Plaza de Armas; beyond the Plaza de Armas there is no more town. On the Plaza de Armas stand the best houses in Puquio; that's where the *misti* families who have friends in Lima live— "foreigner," the Indian *comuneros* call them—the showiest, lightest-colored girls. On the Plaza de Armas are the main church, with its squat tower of white stone, the Subprefecture,[6] the headquarters of the Civil Guard,[7] the Court of First Instance, the Public School for Boys, the Town Hall, the jail, the pen for stray cattle; all the authorities who serve the leading citizens; all the houses, all the people with which they make themselves respected, with which they command.

In the middle of the Plaza there is a concrete fountain, and around the fountain a circular garden with grass, yellow flowers, and green flax. At the foot of the Town Hall steps is another water fountain.

Beyond the Plaza de Armas there is no more town; Girón Bolívar comes to an end at the Plaza.

---

6. Office of the Subprefect, an official appointed by higher authorities to administer the provincial government. A Peruvian province is similar to a county.—Trans.

7. The Peruvian national police force.—Trans.

That is why Girón Bolívar is like a snake that cuts the town in two; the Plaza de Armas is like the head of the snake; there are the teeth, the eyes, the head, the tongue—jail, animal pound, Subprefecture, Court—; the body of the snake is Girón Bolívar.

Day and night, the important people live on Girón Bolívar; there they seek one another out, stroll, look one another in the eye, fall in love, get drunk, hate each other, and fight. On Girón Bolívar the citizenry yell at election time; there they go around in gangs, jeering at their political opponents; sometimes they get so angry they kick one another and even pull the cobblestones out of the ground and crack each other's heads with them. When the young people show off their clothes, when they are happy, they ride their horses from one end of Girón Bolívar to the other, with their bodies erect, their heads held high, reining in the horses sharply and making them rear at every street corner.

Girón Bolívar is also the first place to which the important people from other districts come. They ride from one end of the street to the other, jingling their silver spurs, putting their coastal steeds through their paces. After delivering presents to the Subprefect and the Judge, the district personages get drunk on "fine" liquor at the pool hall and in the girls'[8] stores.

In the evening, the *mistis* congregate in the billiard parlor; there they play casino, dice, and seven-and-a-half; they talk until midnight and get drunk.

The *mistis* ride up and down that street, raging and growing fat, from the time they're born until they die.

Puquio is a new town for the *mistis*. About 300 years ago, give or take a little, the *mistis* came to Puquio from other towns where they had mining business. Before that all of Puquio was an Indian town. In the four *ayllus* nobody but Indians lived. From time to time, the *mistis* would come in search of peons for the mines, seeking provisions and women.

The other towns around Puquio are on mountainsides full of mine shafts; along all of the streams that bring water to those towns old ore mills are tumbling down; the old-timers milled silver there. Those towns are named for saints; their streets are wide; their Plazas de Armas are quite square and are in the middle of town; the churches are large, with arched portals; the high altars of the churches are sometimes made of carved wood, and their gilding is still visible. On the mountains around Puquio there were no mines; that's why the

8. Indians address non-Indian women as "girls" to avoid calling them "women," which they would consider derogatory.—Trans.

mistis would arrive suddenly, have their party with the Indian women, recruit people willingly or by force for the mines, and go away for a time.

But the mines gave out; mining was no longer profitable; then the *mistis* scattered to all the Indian towns of the province. Their towns, which had been named after saints, were almost emptied of gentlemen. Now those little towns are tumbling down like the old ore mills; their streets are being obliterated; the churches are also collapsing, the altars are losing their gilt and are covered with dust.

Most of the *mistis* fell upon Puquio, because it was a big town, with plenty of Indians for servants, with four irrigation ditches, one for each *ayllu*, to bring water for their crops. Big town, in a good place.

The *mistis* went with their priest, with their "foreigner" Child God; they made their Plaza de Armas on the edge of the town; they ordered a church to be built for them with arched portal and gilded altar; and from there, from their Plaza, like someone who is digging a ditch, they went on building their street, with no respect for the ownership claims of the *ayllus*.

"So what!"

It had to go in a straight line. *Misti* street is always straight.

In a short time, as soon as there were houses with balconies on Girón Bolívar, as soon as they could fit a few lanes onto one or the other side of Girón Bolívar, they moved the provincial capital to their new town.

And the plundering of the *ayllus* began. With the authorities' backing, the *mistis* began with the K'ollana neighborhood. K'ollana had good corn, barley, and wheat fields. The judges and the notaries signed papers of every description; that sufficed. After K'ollana came K'ayau. The lands with the most water were in those districts and they were closest to town. Next came Chaupi and Pichk'achuri. That's why Chaupi and Pichk'achuri own more land. In former times, it was the other way around.

From so much going into offices, from so much running to and fro about the documents with which their lands were being taken away, the Puquios learned to defend themselves in lawsuits, buying judges, court clerks, and notaries. Each Indian community rose up as a whole to defend its members. Every Sunday there would be council meetings in the *ayllus*; every Sunday the *comuneros* would come together to make decisions. And they put a stop to land-grabbing in the valley. By that time, the *mistis* had already become the owners of almost all of the cropland; by then, the K'ollanas and the K'ayaus were reduced to being mere field hands for the important people.

6

But the *ayllus* would not let go of the water.

The Indian staffbearers[9] schedule the irrigation water allotments, each in his own community, the same as in former times.

For that reason, at dawn on the days the water is being distributed, the *mistis* of Puquio go into the Indian communities to ask for water to irrigate their crops. Still shivering with cold, hiding their chins in their scarves, the prominent citizens go into a huddle with the neighborhood Indians and raise their hands and shout:

"Don[10] Gregorio! For my little patch of corn!"

In the early morning their blue and black overcoats, their straw hats, their "foreigner" cloth hats look like alien garb amid the red, yellow, and green ponchos of Puquio, among so many vicuña-colored Indian hats.

Sometimes the sunlight has reached the mountaintops and the staffbearing water distributor is still hearing:

"For my little wheat field in K'ellok'ello, for my corn patch at K'erok'ocha, for my barley at Cullahora! Don Gregorio!"

How many times have the *mistis* gone to the water distribution place, cracked their bullwhips, and taken the staffbearing leaders off to be shut up in the jail! But while the Chief Staffbearer was straining on the bar, the four *ayllus* would be all astir; Indians from K'ayau, from K'ollana, from Pichk'achuri, from Chaupi would go around to all the houses to notify the people. From Makulirumi Rock they'd sound the *wakawak'ra*[11] trumpets. Puquio would become as still and silent as it is in the darkness of the night.

On every street the *mistis* would fire their little bullets; on every street they'd get drunk and threaten the *comuneros*. They'd go into one house after another, kick the little children, and bloody the Indians' noses, mouths, and foreheads.

"Don't matter!"

You think *misti* knows how to irrigate? You think *misti* knows how to put up a wall? You think *misti* can weed wheat fields? Does *misti* mend road, make tiles and adobe bricks, slit sheep's throat? Well, who'd build the water intake points, who'd dig the ditches, who'd mend the dikes; who'd set the floodgates during the flash-floods of January and February, when the freshets that come down out of the mountains wash out the canals and fill up their intakes with stones, clods, and sand?

9. Indian community leaders, or *varayok's*; they carry long staffs as symbols of authority. The highest rank is held by the *alcalde indio*, a Spanish term meaning mayor of the Indian community.—Trans.

10. Spanish respectful title of address.—Trans.

11. A trumpet made of bull's horn.—Trans.

"Jajayllas!"[12]

Not even bullets, whipcracking, or the pleading of the *tayta*[13] Vicar could make the *comuneros* leave their *ayllus*.

"My eye first he'll take out! Like thieving sparrowhawk my eye first he'll eat! *Cumun yaku*[14] *jajayllas!*"

The Puquios knew that.

Then the *mistis* would be the first to humble themselves. In their minds they were really weeping with rage, but they'd get cane liquor from all the stores and with that they'd plead with the staffbearers and the elders. They'd go to the communities, whichever ones their property was located in, and enter the houses, sweet-talking, pledging friendship.

The *"chalos"*[15] sometimes side with the townsmen,[16] sometimes with the Indian communities, according to where their interest lies. They do not live on Girón Bolívar; their houses are on the lanes that come out onto the *misti* street. But whether they like it or not, the *mistis* also classify them by *ayllus*. They are Chaupi, K'ollana, K'ayau, Pichk'achuri mestizos. The Prefect appoints one of the "chalos" from each *ayllu* to be its Lieutenant Governor.

At night the mestizos gather in the doorways of the pool hall and the bars to watch the *mistis* gamble and see what they drink. Sometimes they go into the stores and stand with their backs to the walls so as not to bother anyone, looking on.

Each townsman has three or four trusty *"chalos,"* and he sends them anywhere at all, sometimes just to do him a favor. On rainy days the townsmen call any mestizo on the street who is a friend of their household and send him to fetch their overcoat, their umbrella—they order them to do any old errands. It is from amongst these people that the gentry select their overseers. These halfbreeds, who follow the prominent citizens around like dogs, are called *k'anras*[17] by the *comuneros*; probably there's not a dirtier word in the Indian speech.

12. Quechua expression of scornful derision.—Trans.

13. Father; also used as an affectionate and respectful form of address.—Trans.

14. Community water.—Trans.

15. Mestizos.—Author

16. Throughout this book the word "townsmen" is used for *vecinos*, a Spanish term meaning town citizens who own house lots, pay taxes, and have voting rights. The term "townsmen," therefore, does not include everyone living in the town.—Trans.

17. Disgustingly filthy persons.—Author

But some of the mestizos are workers; they do business with the coastal towns, taking cheeses, sheep, and wheat down and bringing back bootleg rum, candles, and soap.

Many of the mestizos become friendly with the Indian communities and speak up for their members. In the *ayllus* they are called Don Norberto, Don Leandro, Don Aniceto . . .

The Indians speak to them respectfully. But at fiestas they dance with them, equal to equal; when there is trouble, the mestizo friend gives them good advice and defends the *ayllus*.

That's how life is on Girón Bolívar and in the neighborhoods. That's how the *misti* strangers came to Puquio.

But when the Puquio people look down from above, from Sillanayok' Pass, from the top of Tayta Pedrork'o, when they see Girón Bolívar gleaming like a snake's back among the tiled roofs of the *ayllus*, they exclaim disgustedly:

"*Atatauya* Bolívar, street!"

When the Indians look down and speak that way, in their eyes another hope is glowing, their real soul is shining forth. They laugh loudly; they may be furious, too.

From the mountain peaks four streams descend and flow near the town; in the cascades the white water is calling, but the *mistis* do not hear it. On the hillsides, on the plains, on the mountaintops the yellow flowers dance in the wind, but the *mistis* hardly see them. At dawn, against the cold sky, beyond the edge of the mountains, the sun appears; then the larks and doves sing, fluttering their little wings; the sheep and the colts run to and fro in the grass, while the *mistis* sleep or watch, calculating the weight of their steers. In the evening *Tayta Inti*[18] gilds the sky, gilds the earth, but they sneeze, spur their horses on the road, or drink coffee, drink hot pisco.

But in the hearts of the Puquios, the valley is weeping and laughing, in their eyes the sky and the sun are alive; within them the valley sings with the voice of the morning, of the noontide, of the afternoon, of the evening.

18. The sun—Author

2. The Dispossession

In the olden times, all of the mountains and fields on the puna [1] belonged to the *comuneros*. In those days there were not many cattle in Lucanas: the *mistis* did not covet the grazing land. The great high, bleak region was for everyone. None of the pastures were enclosed by stone walls or barbed wire. The big puna had no owner. The Indians lived free everywhere: in caves in the rocks, in huts they built in the hollows, at the base of the mountains, near the springs. Occasionally the *mistis* would go up onto the puna to hunt vicuñas or to buy meat from the little Indian farms. And also from time to time, out of pure cussedness, they would carry off ten or fifteen sheep, four or five scrawny cows; but like the erratic hailstorms, they would come to the puna for a little while, do their damage, and go away. The puna really belonged to the Indians: the puna with its animals, with its grass, with its cold winds, and its showers of rain. The *mistis* feared the puna and let the Indians live there.

"For those savages the puna is good enough," they would say.

Each of the Puquio communities had its own grazing lands. These were the only boundaries on the punas: a brook, the brow of a hill marked the claims of each *ayllu*; and there were never any lawsuits between the communities over land. But the Pichk'achuris were always the real *punarunas, punacumunkuna* [2]; they even had villages in the highlands: K'oñek, Puñuy, Tak'ra, twenty or thirty huts in the bottom of a valley, behind a hill, near the blackish *k'eñwa* [3] thickets.

---

1. In many places these grazing areas are above 3,500 meters.—Trans.

2. Puna people, puna community members; *kuna* is the plural suffix in Quechua.—Trans.

3. A low, coniferous tree with scaly red bark.—Trans.

On the high puna, beneath a cloudy sky, in the great silence, whenever the rainstorm begins and black clouds strike fear and make the heart tremble, or when the white gulls fly singing in the high, limpid sky and the traveler's eyes gaze into the distance, pensive in the vastness of the silence, at any time at all those stone huts with their blue smoke, with the barking of their little dogs, with the crowing of their roosters, are a consolation to those who walk the wild puna. In those towns the staffbearing Indian leaders command; there's no Lieutenant there; there's no Governor; there's no Judge. The staffbearer is authority enough. In those towns there are no disturbances.

Only when the *mistis* went up onto the punas in search of meat and fired their guns and cracked their bullwhips to herd the sheep together so they could pick out the best stud rams, only then was there any commotion. Because sometimes then the *punarunas* would get angry and gather together. Signaling to one another from house to house, from farm to farm, with whistling and *wakawak'ras*, they'd come together in anger, surrounding the important people and the bullying *chalos*; then the *mistis* would run away or be stoned, right there beside the herds of sheep. After that would come the deterrent: uniformed police on the puna killing old Indians, women, and little children, and then the plundering. For a time the farms and hamlets would be left in silence. But before long the *punarunas* would return to their hollows; they would light the fires inside of their stone huts and the blue smoke would swirl round the rooftops; at dusk the dogs would bark in the doorways of the houses; and early in the morning the sheep would baa contentedly, lifting their muzzles skyward, beneath the sunlight reflected from the snowy peaks. Years later the old Indians would give children the shivers telling them the story of the deterrent.

The Pichk'achuris have always been real puna-dwellers. The other *ayllus* also had little farms and community members up in the high bleak areas, but most of their people lived in town; they had good croplands near Puquio and did not want the punas, almost fearing them as the *mistis* did. Pichk'achuri was, and still is, an *ayllu* shared by Puquians and *punarunas*.

All of a sudden, there was a great demand for cattle on the coast, especially in Lima; then the *mistis* began to take over the Indians' wheat fields to plant alfalfa in them. But that was not enough; from the coast came more and more calls for cattle. The *mistis* who took beef cattle to the coast came back loaded with money. And the important people were almost frantic; they ran the Indians off to grab their land, and once again they made the judges, notaries, and court clerks sweat. . . . Amongst themselves there were often beatings and shootings, too. "Out with the wheat! Out with the barley! Out with the corn! Alfalfa! Alfalfa! Get out of here, Indians!" Like madmen they ran back and forth to the towns near and far from Puquio, buying, swindling, and sometimes rustling bulls, steers, and calves. Well, there was real money in it! Nice new bills! And they'd go frantically from the Court to the town cattlepen, to the court clerks' offices, to the pastures, even at night, with bullwhip in hand, revolver in belt, with five or six of their overseers coming on behind. Then they remembered the punas: "Grass! Cattle! Brutish Indians black with cold. Let's go up there!" And the whole lot of them would run racing, racing for the puna. They began to make a clean sweep, once and for all, of the stone huts, of the hamlets; they began to put up stone walls and fence off the free puna with thorn bushes and stones.

Year after year, the important people would draw up papers, all kinds of documents, swearing that they were the owners of this spring, of that grazing land, of the fields with the best pastures, nearest the town. They would appear suddenly on the puna, by any road, in a great cavalcade.[4] They would come with harp, violin, and clarinet, men and women, singing, drinking wine. They would order their lackeys and farmworkers to build a stone hut rapidly, or would go into some cave, evicting the Indian who was living there while tending his cattle. With the *mistis* came the Judge of the Court of First Instance, the Subprefect, the Provincial Chief of Police, and some local policemen. In the hut or in the cave, men and women would get drunk; they'd dance, shouting and stomping the ground furiously. They would have a *fiesta* on the puna.

The Indians of the grazing lands would warn one another, running from farm to farm; they would come together fearfully, knowing the *mistis* never came up onto the punas to do them good. And the community members from the puna would go out to greet the "Ductur" Judge, *tayta* Priest, the "Governments" of the province, and the *werak'ochas*[5] who were the leading citizens of Puquio.

Taking advantage of the Indians' presence, the Judge would order the ceremony for taking possession; the Judge would go out onto the grass field, followed by the townspeople and the officials. On the dry yellow grass, to the silence of Indians and *mistis*, he would read a

---

4. From *cabalgada*, a Spanish word used in the sixteenth century for the Conquistadores' expeditions to capture Indian slaves and find gold and other booty.—Trans.

5. Werak'ocha was the name of the Inca's supreme god; today it is the equivalent of *señor*, and is used when speaking of upper-class men.—Trans.

paper. When the Judge had finished reading, one of the *mistis*, the new owner, would cast some dirt into the air, toss some pebbles anywhere at all, and thrash around on the hay. After that men and women would shout, throw stones, and laugh. The *comuneros* would watch all of this from a distance.

When the hubbub had died down, the Judge would summon the Indians and tell them in Quechua:

"*Punacumunkuna*: Señor Santos is the owner of these grasslands; all of it—hills, dales, springs, and all—belongs to him. If the animals of anyone else—be he Indian or townsman—come in here, it's a stray. If he wants to, Señor Santos can rent this land out, or else put his own cattle on here. So that . . . Indians! *Werak'ocha* Santos is the owner of these grazing lands."

The Indians stared fearfully at the Judge. "Grazing lands now belongs to Don Santos, Indians!" Well, yonder is paper; well, yonder is *werak'ocha* Judge; yonder is policeman, yonder is girls; important people with their harp player, with their clarinet player, with their bottles of beer. Well, yonder is *tayta* Priest!

"Don Santos is owner."

"If there's Indian animals on these grasslands, they're 'strays'[6] and . . . to the cattle pound, to Don Santos' corral, to die of thirst or increase the herd of cattle Don Santos will take, year after year, to 'foreign' land."

The Priest put a wide silk scarf over his arms, as he did for baptisms, looked off into the distance in every direction, and then prayed a while. Presently, as the Judge had, he addressed the Indians:

"*Cumunkuna*: By law Don Santos has proven that these grazing lands belong to him. Now Don Santos is going to be respect; he's going to be boss of the Indians who live on these lands. God in heaven also respects law; law is for everybody the same. *Cumunkuna*! Let's see you kiss Don Santos' hand!"

And one by one, hat in hand, the *comuneros* went up to the new owner and kissed his hand. Out of respect for *tayta* Priest, out of respect for *Taytacha*[7] God.

"By law Don Santos has proven that he's owner of the grazing lands."

"*Taytacha* in heaven also respects law."

And now where? Where, then? On its return the cavalcade disappeared over the next pass, beyond the yellow grass that whistled in

6. Such "strays" may be confiscated by the legal landowner.—Trans.
7. Great Father.—Trans.

the wind; it vanished amid shouting and the bursting of rockets. And the *punacumunkuna* looked lost; suddenly they seemed like orphans.

"*Taytallay tayta! Mamallay mama!*"[8]

The Indian women clung to their husbands' legs and wept. They already knew that soon after that cavalcade had left, three or four horsemen would come to round up the "strays" on those grazing lands, to drive them to the town cattlepen with rifleshots and whip-cracking. Wouldn't they? There was nothing one could do about it now. The "Governments" of the province was the friend of all the important people and loudly berated all the Indians who went to his office to recover their cattle. Sometimes the Indian claimant would end up like a thief instead, painfully straining in the stocks or hanging from the bar. In the Subprefect's office the *misti* is an important person; with his chest sticking out, with his commanding voice, he is the master.

"Señor Subprefect, that Indian is a thief," is all he says.

And when the town notable lifts his finger and points at the Indian, saying "thief," a thief he is, a downright thief, a recognized cattle rustler. And for the cattle-rustling Indian, there's the bar in the jail; for the thieving Indian who comes to reclaim his "strays," there's the stocks.

And meanwhile, the *punacomunero* is suffering in jail; meanwhile he sings through tears:

Sapay rikukuni	How alone I find myself
mana piynillayok',	with no one, no one at all,
puna wayta jhina	like a puna flower
llaki llantullayok'.	with only my sorrowing shadow.
Tek'o pinkulluypas	My *pinkuyllu's*[9] voice
chakañas rikukun	sounds hoarse now;
nunaypa kirinta	its beauty has been marred
k'apark'achask'ampi.	by so much sobbing.
Imatak's kausayniy,	What kind of life is this,
maytatak' ripusak'	where am I going to go?
maytak' tayta mamay	Where are my father and mother?

8. "Father, my father! Mother, my mother!"—an expression commonly used in difficult or distressing situations.—Author

9. A giant, five-holed flute the southern Indians of Peru play at community celebrations.—Author

14

¡illiusi tukukapun!　　　　　Everything's come to an end!

While the "cattle rustler" is singing in the jail, Don Pedro, Don Jesús, Don Federico, or anyone at all is making sure he is sentenced, in collusion with the shady lawyer whom the court appoints to defend *cholos*; and they drive the puna-dwellers' little herd of cattle off to the "foreign land" or winter them in the K'ollanas' alfalfa fields to sell later.

The *punarunas* knew this very well. As the years went by the important people kept pushing the K'ayau, Chaupi, and K'ollana herders higher and higher, right up to K'arwarasu, up to the mountaintops and the high plains where the dry grass is coarse and stunted and sticks to the ground like cattle ticks. That's why, when the *mistis'* cavalcade had vanished beyond the hill that concealed the cave or the stone hut, the Indian women would cling to their husbands' legs and wail with grief; the men would say,

"*Tatallaya!* Screwed! Screwed!"

The crowd of Indians, the *punarunakuna*, would immediately look for another cave or build another hut, farther up, next to the snow, where the grass is coarse and stunted, there they would take their cattle. Then the struggle would begin; the llamas, the cows, the wooly horses, the sheep would always run off seeking their former haunts, looking for tall tender grass. But down there would be Don Santos', Don Federico's *concertados*—the notables' hirelings, "*chalos*," hungry half-breeds. One by one the Indians' cattle would go, falling as "strays" to swell the boss's beef herd.

Thus, little by little, the herders from the Chaupi and K'ayau grazing lands were finished off. The *comuneros* who no longer had any animals, huts, or caves came down to the town. They entered their community like strangers, carrying their pots, their pelts, and their children. Well, they were *punarunas*, herders; they went to town only for the big holidays. Then they used to enter the communities with new clothing, happy faces, and "a whole lot of money" for "drink," for cakes, and to buy colored cloth on Girón Bolívar. They would enter their *ayllu* proudly and were fêted. But when they came in so poverty-stricken, fleeing from the *mistis*, they came with their bellies bare to the wind, black with hunger and cold. They would say to anyone:

"Well, here we are, *papacito!*[10] Right here, little brother!"

The *ayllu's* staffbearing leader would receive them at his house.

10. Little father; this is Quechua-ized Spanish for "great or honored father," from *taytacha*.—Trans.

15

Later he would summon people to a houseraising, and the neighborhood *comuneros* would put up a new house in seven or eight hours for the *punaruna*.

And in Puquio there would be one more hand to work the prominent citizens' field crops, or to be "hooked" to go to Nazca or Acari, to work on the coast. There they would make good bait for the malarial mosquitoes. The hacienda owner would keep them bound to him for five or six months after their contracts had expired, and put them into the cotton fields, shivering with fever. On their way home, they would find eternal rest in the sun-scorched sands, on the slopes, or up on the puna; if they ever did get as far as the *ayllu*, they would walk the streets jaundiced and sickly, exciting all the *comuneros'* pity; their children were also like the malaria victims—lacking souls. But many of the puna people, by working hard, with the protection of the *ayllus*, first taking service as lackeys and hired hands in the *mistis'* houses to get together a little money, and later by getting a little cropland to work on shares, managed to lift their heads. From *punarunas* they transformed themselves into town-dwelling community members. And now that they lived in Puquio, in the *ayllu*, their hatred of the notable who had taken their land was even stronger. In the *ayllu* there were thousands and thousands of *comuneros*, all together, all equal; there no Don Santos, or Don Fermín, or Don Pedro could take advantage of them so easily. The puna-dweller who had wept in the hayfield, the *punaruna* who had strained in the stocks, who had beaten his head against the jail walls, that "Endian" who had come down with fear in his eyes, once he became a Chaupi, K'ollana, or K'ayau *comunero*, was emboldened to look directly into the eyes of the townsmen who came into the Indian communities to ask a favor.

That is how the community members had come down from the K'ayau, K'ollana, and Chaupi punas some time before. There were only a few of them left up there. A few, near K'arwarasu Mountain on the summits, herding their cattle together and defending them from the gentry, beneath the rain, beneath the thunder and lightning storms, beneath the black clouds of January and February. And up there on the wild puna, looking out for themselves from dawn til dusk, running through their sheep and counting them every hour, making the dogs bark all around the flock, they began to grow silent. And they didn't even come down into town for the holiday. On the heights, close to the hailstorms, enveloped in the dark clouds that hide the mountain peaks, little by little the puna would cast its spell over them. And they would become wild creatures.

16

Others, in order to remain in their favorite haunts near their animals, would sell their cattle to the new owner of the grazing lands, receiving ten, fifteen soles a cow, three or four reales a sheep.[11] They'd bury their money at the foot of some large enchanted rock, or on the mountaintops. And when they were completely destitute, without a single lamb to console them, they would stay on as herdsmen for the boss; they'd declare themselves the orphan children of the notable who had appropriated the grazing lands, and every time the *señor* came to visit his lands they would cry,

"Here we are, *papituy, Taytituy!*"

Like sick puppies they would cringe in the doorways of their stone huts.

"My little father! Little boss!"

They'd wring their hands and run round and round the boss, whimpering. They would show him the herd of nondescript sheep, cows, and horses and say,

"Yonder is your little sheep; yonder is your cows. All, all there, *taytay.*"

At dusk, as the boss went riding off into the distance, followed by his overseers, all of the *punarunas* would watch them go as they clustered together in the doorway of the hut. The sun would be shining on their faces, the golden sun. And the *punarunas* would still be trembling; as in a wound, the blood would be aching in their hearts.

"Yes sir, boss!" they'd say, as the cattlemen's white hat disappeared over the brow of the hill, or beyond the *k'eñwa* woods.

But that was nothing. From time to time, the boss would hire men to go up to the little farms to round up the cattle. The hirelings would cut out the piebald, the brindled, the spotted bulls. Then the *punarunas*, with their families, would give a send-off to the bulls that were going down to the valley to increase the herd of cattle the boss would take to "the foreign land." Then they really would suffer. Neither death nor frost caused the highland Indians more suffering.

"Pinto, brindly, spotted one for the herd!" the hirelings would command, at daybreak.

The kids and the women would get all excited. The kids would run to the young bulls, who all this time had been sleeping in the corral. With their arms they would caress their wooly muzzles.

"My little spotted one! Where they gonna take you, *papacito?*"

The spotted bull would stick out his rough tongue and widen his

11. In the early 1930s a Peruvian sol was worth about U.S. $.40; one sol was equal to ten reales.—Trans.

nostrils; he would let the boys pet him, gazing at them with his big eyes. And afterwards the children would cry; they'd wail with their high-pitched, goldfinch-like voices:

"My little spotted bull! Little Spot!"

And just then the cattle-drivers would arrive; they'd crack their whips over the boys' heads:

"Enough, enough, damnit!"

The herdsmen would crash in and cut the chosen ones out of the herd by cracking their bullwhips.

Then came the deepest sorrow. The family would gather in the doorway of their stone hut to sing farewell to the bulls that were leaving. The oldest man would play the *pinkuyllu*, his sons the *wakawak'ras*, and one of the women a small drum.

Vacallay vaca	My cow, cow
turullay turu	my bull, bull
vacachallaya	my little cow
turuchallaya.	my little bull.

The *punarunas* would be shouting out their song; meanwhile, the cattle-drivers, by cracking their bullwhips, were rounding up the piebald, the spotted ones . . . and were riding off into the distance, leaving the little farm behind.

Vacallay vaca	My cow, cow
turullay turu . . .	my bull, bull . . .

The *pinkuyllu* whistled loudly over the puna, the *tinya*[12] cord rasped on the leather; and in the hollows, in the rocky places, across the puna lakes, the voices of the *comuneros*, of the *pinkuyllu* and of the *tinya* lapped the *ischu* grass, and rose up into the sky, scattering their bitterness over all the puna. The Indians on the other farms crossed themselves.

But the children suffered the most; they cried the way they used to do when they woke up alone in the stone hut on a dark night; as if they were going to die, they wept; and from that time on, hatred for the gentry grew in their hearts, as the blood swells, as the bones grow.

That is how the Indians were dispossessed of the puna of K'ayau, Chaupi, and K'ollana.

12. A small drum.—Trans.

3. Wakawak'ras, Trumpets of the Earth

On the puna and on the mountains surrounding the town they were now sounding the *wakawak'ras*. When they heard the *turupukllay*[1] on the country roads and in the wheatfields, Indians and townspeople spoke of that year's bullfight.

"Damn! Pichk'achuri gonna stand its ground. Pichk'achuri winning saddlecloth, leaving widow in big bullring," said the *comuneros*.

"K'ayau community says they're gonna bring the bull they call Misitu[2] down from K'oñani plain. They say staffbearers have sworn to bring Misitu."

"Nonsense! Misitu's with the devil. When the hell they ever bringing Misitu? No man's brave enough to stand up to Misitu from K'oñani."

"Even if some of 'em dying, too, K'ayau says they're gonna turn Misitu loose on twenty-eighth."[3]

"You think Pichk'achuri dumb enough to believe that? K'ayau are lazy slugs. When they ever winning *turupukllay*? Grandfathers, too, never has seen K'ayau leaving widow on twenty-eighth. Nonsense!"

"Sure. Now Pichk'achuri gonna be man in *turupukllay* too."

In all four communities, people were talking about the bullfight. Pichk'achuri won year after year; the Pichk'achuri bullfighters watered the ring with their blood. Where were there men to equal the

---

1. Bullfight, and also special bullfight music played on *wakawak'ras*—Author

2. *Misitu* means "little cat," or "great cat" in the Indians' Quechua-ized Spanish.—Trans.

3. July 28 is Peru's national holiday.—Author

capeadores[4] from the largest *ayllu*? Honrao Rojas had torn off his shirt and vest only the year before. Don Nicolás' brindled bull had tossed him into the air like a ball. While the girls were trembling on the balconies, and the Indian community men and women were shrieking on the barriers, on the walls, and on the housetops, Honrao got right up again; after having been buried in the dirt, after having had his belly trampled, and clawing, clawing the ground, Honrao stood up. Blood was oozing from his vest and shirt.

Saying "Goddam little bull!" he had torn off his vest and shirt to bare his gored ribs.

"*Atatau yawarcha!*"[5] he screamed.

He had made his blood spurt out onto the ground as if from a fountain.

"I Pichk'achuri *runakuna, k'alakuna!*"[6] he had said.

The four *ayllus* already knew that. No one could compare to the brave men from Pichk'achuri. But that year, they said, K'ayau would be first in the arena.

Ever since June they had been playing *turupukllay* all over the puna and on the mountains surrounding the town. The *wakawak'ras* were already announcing the bullfight. Hearing the music high up on the puna, the young boys would feel afraid, as if the brindled or tawny bulls who had roared around the Pichk'achuri ring, pawed the earth, shaken the barriers, and gored Honrao Rojas' chest might spring right out of the *k'eñwa* thickets at them. Up on the punas and along the roads, rain or shine, at dawn or at dusk, the *wakawak'ras* kept announcing the bullfight. Out in the open, the sound of the *turupukllay* breaks one's heart, conquering it as if it were a baby's: the voice of the *wakawak'ra* sounds deep and slow, like the voice of a man, like the voice of the high puna with its cold wind whistling through the mountain passes, over the lakes. Hearing the trumpets, the young girls from the *ayllus* and from all the little farms would be whimpering.

"Well, now it's the twenty-eighth," they'd say. "For Misitu the *fiesta* is; they say they're gonna take him to the big bullring; his rage sure gonna fill it, drawing blood from Puquio Endian!"

"*Ay taytallaya!* They say K'ayau has taken a notion to toss K'oñani Misitu into bullring on twenty-eighth."

---

4. Amateur bullfighters who challenge the bull with their capes or, in this case, ponchos.—Trans.

5. Little blood.—Trans.

6. "I'm Pichk'achuri person, you outsiders."—Trans.
K'alakuna is a derogatory name for the leading citizens.—Author

"Well, who'll it be, my little mother? Well, who'll be widow? Well, who'll be weeping in graveyard on twenty-eighth?"

On all the mountains the *wakawak'ras* were singing, announcing the *yawar fiesta*. Indians from K'ollana, from Pichk'achuri, from Chaupi, from K'ayau were playing at dawn, at mid-day, and while they were coming down to the roads in the evening. At night, too, from the Indian quarters, the *wakawak'ras'* song rose up to Girón Bolívar. Trumpeters from the four neighborhoods began to compete with one another. But Don Maywa of Chaupi was the best horn player. Don Maywa's house was next to Makulirumi Rock, on the square. In the evening, while it was still early, the community leaders and some of the Indians who lived nearby would enter Don Maywa's house. There they'd chew coca leaves, and sometimes Don Maywa would get out his bottle of cane liquor and treat them. A tallow-burning clay lamp with a wick lighted the room from a cowhide shelf. Between drinks, Don Maywa would raise his *wakawak'ra* and play bullfight music. The *wakawak'ra's* voice would fill the room; the walls resounded with it. The *comuneros* would gaze upwards; it gripped them, oppressing their chests; there was no music for dying like the *turupukllay*. From time to time the other *ayllus* would reply.

From the four quarters, as the night began, the bullfight music would rise up to Girón Bolívar. From the Chaupi square, straight up to Girón Bolívar, the *turupukllay* rose on the wind. In the shops, in the pool hall, in the notables' houses, the girls and townsmen would hear it.

"At night that music sounds like it's coming from the graveyard," they'd say.

"Yeah, man. It troubles your mind."

"That's not it! It's not the music," explained one learned gentleman. "It's that we associate that melody with the bullfights in which the Indians have the bulls destroy them, to the beat of that little tune."

"Yeah, man. But it troubles your mind. They shouldn't be allowed to bother us that way at dinnertime."

"Faggots! I like that tune. On a single horn—how well those Indians play!" someone replied.

The girls and the ladies complained too.

"Such penetrating music! It's hateful to hear that tune at this hour. The Civil Guard should be asked to forbid them to play that tune at night."

"Yes. And we've already had the Civil Guard here for several years now."

"Those Indians will be working up their courage from now on. How ugly that trumpet sobs!"

"Makes me think of the bullfights."

"That *cholo* Maywa is the worst of all. His music goes right down to the depths of my soul."

The sound of the *wakawak'ras* interrupted the *mistis'* conversation under the lamps on the corners of the Girón Bolívar; it disturbed the peace of the diners in the houses of the leading citizens. In the Indian neighborhoods, the boys would gather when Don Maywa played.

"Sounds like it's already bullfight time!" they'd shout.

"Bull, bull!"

And they'd make good use of Don Maywa's *pukllay* to play at bullfighting.

Sometimes Don Maywa's trumpet was heard in the town when the Priest was saying the rosary in church with the ladies and girls of the town and with some of the women from the Indian neighborhoods. The bullfight music was dispiriting to those pious souls; the Priest, too, would pause for a moment when the melody came in to him. The girls and ladies would look at one another uneasily, as if the brindled or tawny bulls were bellowing from the church doorway.

"Devil's music!" the Vicar would say.

Sometimes, late at night, once the town was silent, they'd play the *wakawak'ras* from some high mountain. Then the *pukllay* resounded in the valley, from rim to rim, from hollow to hollow; it would come into the town, at times quite clearly, at times rather muted, according to the strength of the wind.

"You hear?" they'd say in the *mistis'* houses. "Like deep sobbing it is, like people's voices."

"Full of the valley that *turupukllay* is! Why can it be? It oppresses my heart," the girls would say.

"What wretched music! It's soul-wracking!" said the prominent citizens.

In the *ayllus*, the Indians would hear it too, and they also commented.

"Still sounds like Don Maywa! That sure is *pukllay*!"

"Must be Pichk'achuri *comunero* playing. Wild bull'll sure be raging, hearing it."

With the wind, at that hour, the bullfight music would flow out over the mountaintops and swirl through the passes, reaching the little farms and villages. On a bright night, or in the darkness, the *turupukllay* would come down as if from on high.

4. K'ayau

On the first Sunday in July, in the afternoon, four staffbearing leaders from K'ayau community went to Don Julián Aranguena's house. The sun was warming the white paving stones in the courtyard. Don Julián's servants were seated on the stone bench along the kitchen wall.

"Morning," the hands greeted the staffbearers.

"Morning. Where's *tayta* boss?"

The girl, Julia, came out onto the veranda.

"Morning, missy. K'ayau community members looking for *tayta* boss."

"Father! Staffbearers from K'ayau," called the young woman.

Don Julián came out onto the veranda in his vest, a newspaper in his hand.

"Well, you always standing up for K'ayau, *taytay*," said the Chief Staffbearer. "Since your alfalfa and field crops, too, grazing lands, too, on K'ayau *ayllu* land, Don Jolián."

"Certainly."

"That's why we're going in after Misitu bull from K'oñani, for twenty-eighth."

"What?" Don Julián looked startled. "Misitu's wild. Nobody can get him out of the woods."

All the staffbearers laughed.

"Nothing's impossible for *ayllu*, *tayta*. Might even be carrying big mountain down to ocean sea, too."

"Nothing's too much for *ayllu*."

"Like puppy dog we're gonna drive Misitu."

"By God! Like a hound dog he's gonna come along, sniffing the road."

"Some of your foolishness. Nobody can drag that wild beast out of his haunts. Even I haven't been able to do it."

"Well, that's so, boss; that's how Misitu of K'oñani is."

"Magic, magic, Pichk'achuri's saying, *taytay*! Isn't any magic, Don Jolián. Every year Pichk'achuris winning in bull-ring. Pichk'achuris have lots of grazing land in highlands; plenty of *sallk'a*[1] on Pichk'achuri community's grazing land. That's why winning on twenty-eighth."

"Now K'ayau gonna put Don Jolián's bull, Misitu, into ring. That's a lie about magic. Misitu's nothing but a big savage, mad right down to his heart. That's why we're wanting him for *turupukllay*."

"K'ayau gonna be first on twenty-eighth!"

"All right, all right. I won't oppose it. But I'm telling you—that bull's going to rip the guts out of all the Indians you send to bring him down from K'oñani."

"Nothing but dog for K'ayau *comunero*."

The Chief Staffbearer drew a bottle of cane liquor from one of the pockets of his rough woolen jacket.

"*Taytay*, to your Misitu you'll have a little drink," he told Don Julián.

"To your *ayllu*, K'ayau, then, Don Jolián!" urged the staffbearer who maintained order in the community's planted area.

"Okay, okay, but just one."

The Chief Staffbearer filled the little enamel cup the Indian selectman handed out to him. The selectman passed the cup to Don Julián.

"Good luck to you! I hope God protects you. Poor things!"

Overhearing the staffbearers' request, Don Julián's *concertados*,[2] who were in the courtyard, commented:

"Well, K'ayau sure wanting Misitu."

"*Jajayllas*! Where they taking Misitu?"

The three *concertados* went over to the veranda. One of them, Don Fermín, said:

"You can't do it, *taytay* Chief. When Misitu of K'oñani gets mad he fights the woods, too; he gets furious at his own shadow, too. No one can stand up to Misitu."

The Chief Staffbearer drained his little cup of cane liquor before replying.

1. Savage; this name is used for wild mountain bulls.—Author
2. Indians who have left their communities; they are lost souls who serve their *misti* all their lives in his house, receiving in exchange food, clothing, and a small annual salary.—Author

"You think we're sending *concertados* to get Misitu? K'ayau community gonna be sent." The Chief Staffbearer was drunk by this time. "Just looking at Misitu will make *concertado* cry; like dog, howling, he'll run away! But *comunero* raging for Misitu. Damnit! You think Indian community's scared of a dumb bull?"

"Excuse him, boss. Damning *concertados* for being lazy slugs. He's already high, you see," the selectman continued, raising his voice. "*Atatau concertado!* Fooling around."

"All right, all right! We're done talking. I'll donate Misitu to the *ayllu*. And you may go."

"Why not, boss!"

"Thanks, Don Jolián."

"You just standing up for K'ayau *ayllu*!"

"Like always, for your *ayllu*!"

Hats in hand, they went down the steps, crossed the courtyard, and reached the entryway.

"Like a dog, we're gonna bring your Misitu, Don Jolián," said the Indian selectman.

Don Julián watched the staffbearers leave, pityingly.

The Chief Staffbearer was the first to step out onto Girón Bolívar.

They put on their hats and went out into the street, proceeding down the middle of the road. The shop girls and the town notables stared at them.

"I hear tell K'ayau is going to bring in Don Julián's bull, Misitu, this year."

The staffbearers greeted the girls, pushing back the brims of their hats with their hands. The four of them walked along together sedately. With long strides they reached the second street corner.

"Chief! Is it true you're going to bring in Misitu for the twenty-eighth?" asked Don Pancho Jiménez from the doorway of his store.

"Of course, we are, *tayta*!" The four of them stopped in front of the store.

"Don Jolián just now donating Misitu."

"Good! I want to see that, staffbearers. Boy, bring four bottles of cane liquor."

"I'll present you with twenty-five quarts if you get Misitu down here. Here's your advance."

"Thanks, boss! Like dog, Misitucha gonna come for you."

The Chief Staffbearer accepted the bottles.

"Ok, then, get going. Council meeting will be waiting."

By this time, several *mistis* and some "*chalos*" had gathered by the store. The staffbearers doffed their hats in farewell, drew the corners of their ponchos over their shoulders, held their heads high, and continued down the street. They came to the third corner and turned left, toward K'ayau *ayllu*.

On Girón Bolívar, the *mistis* went on talking about the K'ayaus' boast.

"The tigers! If those Indians manage to bring Misitu down here there'll be a worse uproar than ever in the bullring."

"That'll be something to see. I've offered them twenty-five quarts of firewater. Last year only one Indian died in the arena. But on the twenty-eighth, if they bring Misitu . . ."

"No, Don Pancho. The uproar's going to be up on K'oñani. The *ayllu*'s determined to go after Misitu, even if it takes 500 Indians to do it. The bull's going to have his heyday up there on the puna. What a gutting there's going to be!"

"When the Indians have their minds made up there's no stopping them. Didn't you see how they built the road to Nazca in twenty-eight days?"

There were more and more people on Don Pancho Jiménez's corner.

"That's because there were more than 10,000 Indians working, too."

"They got road fever. You should have seen them. They looked like ants."

"And they'll bring that bull in. You'll see. It's true that it's only one *ayllu*, but there's 2,000 of them. He might be dead, but they'll put him in the bullring."

"The Puquio Indians have determination, whatever else."

"No doubt about it. Those Indians are really stubborn."

"Up on K'oñani's where the fight's going to be, the real bullfight. I just might go."

"At today's council meeting they'll decide who's to go and they'll set the day. We'll soon find out."

On the edges of the crowd people were talking.

"K'ayau *ayllu* says they're going to bring Misitu down for the twenty-eighth."

"Misitu's the bull they say they're going to bring for the twenty-eighth."

"It's going to be a great bullfight, like in the olden times."

"Nuts! Not even the son of Christ'll get that wild beast out of the *k'eñwales*."

From one side to another, the length of Girón Bolívar, the news spread.

"They shouldn't allow it," said some ladies. "It's barbaric! Poor Indians! They're heathens. You think I'm one, too? I'm not going. I'm not one for savage customs."

"Are you going to go?" the girls asked one another, from that day on.

"I don't know, child; it'll be something to see. But I'm scared."

"Misitu or no Misitu!" said one of the old men. "I've seen some really savage bulls, *macho* bulls, after their legs had been mangled by dynamite, chasing the Indians and still bellowing! Misitu! How can he be so great? There won't be any more bulls like the ones we old men have seen!"

The whole *ayllu* met on the K'oro slope. K'ayau holds their meetings in an open field on the hillside, amid the houses of the Llana harpists and of the *comuneros* from Kaychu and Chamochumpi. Almost in the middle of the big field there's an *alaymosca* rock that's a foot and a half high. The whole community of K'ayau lies along the Tok'to slope, among bluffs and ravines; there's not a straight street in the neighborhood; it's an Indian town. That first Sunday in July, the entire *ayllu* was at the council meeting. From all of the little farms and even from the mountain grasslands the K'ayaus had come down into the town.

When the staffbearing leaders appeared on K'oro Hill, the Indians got all excited. There were more than a thousand of them. They spoke to one another in loud tones.

"Move, make way! Damnit!"

"Make room, damnit!"

They all craned their necks.

The Chief Staffbearer stepped up onto the rock. All the K'ayaus tilted their faces upward.

"Don Jolián Arangüena donating Misitu to *ayllu*. . . ."

The Chief Staffbearer spoke in Quechua; he informed the meeting of their interview with Don Julián.

"That's the way, damnit!"

"Now you're talking, damnit!"

"Misitucha! Now you're talking!"

The sun was now passing through the center of the sky; it blazed down on the whitened walls, on the lime-streaked roofs. The rocks atop the mountains surrounding the town seemed blacker at that hour; there were no longer any clouds in the sky; high overhead soared kestrels and white-breasted hawks, circling slowly.

"Whole *ayllu* will be sent," proclaimed the Chief Staffbearer.

"Certainly, *tayta*!"

"Sure!"

"Misitu, damnit!"

"By God we'll show the *mistichas*. Important people will be frightened by Misitu."

"Certainly!"

"You're not fooling!"

"K'ayau'll be first in bullring!"

"Maybe Misitu only gets mad in high country. Maybe with dynamite he'll be scared as a little dog."

"Saddlecloth liable to scare him."

Indians were arriving from all the *ayllus* to observe the K'ayaus' council meeting. Women and children, as well, looked on from the harpists' corner. In the other *ayllus*, council meetings had already ended and they came to K'ayau to find out what was happening. In the square at Pichk'achuri, the *comuneros* were all excited, watching the hillside.

The K'ayaus all spoke loudly. From afar one could hear them yelling in the meeting.

"Misitu'll come in all tied up!"

"Whole *ayllu*'ll be sent!"

From the middle of the square in Pichk'achuri, a rocket shot up into the air; smoking, it rose up into the sky and passed over the council meeting; it went way up, crossing the sky over K'ayau, and burst high above Tok'to Mountain. The empty rocket came straight down like a *liwi*[3] and landed on the edge of the community, in the mountain grass. The K'ayau Indians watched the rocket, from its takeoff until it hit the ground.

"Damn, filthy people."

They turned around to look at the Pichk'achuri square. The Pichk'achuris were leaving the square by all four corners; many were raising their arms to throw the corners of their ponchos over their shoulders.

"*Jajayllas*, rage!"[4]

The K'ayau staffbearers and *comuneros* looked at one another.

"First on twenty-eighth will be K'ayau *ayllu*!" they exclaimed, almost shouting.

That Sunday the *wakawak'ras* thundered in the four Indian neighborhoods all afternoon and into the night. Although it was well into its waning phase, the moon came out and shone brightly, because the sky was clear. The mountain wheat fields were plainly seen from the town; the eucalyptus trees appeared in Pichk'achuri and the pepper

---

3. Three stone balls connected by a thong or cord that bring down quarry by entangling limbs.—Trans.

4. The K'ayaus meant to say "Get mad and get going." The Pichk'achuris were making a belligerent gesture.—Trans.

trees in the corrals; one could even count their branches. In K'ayau, in K'ollana, in Chaupi they kept playing the bullfight music.

The moon shone down on the tin roofs on Girón Bolívar; the pepper trees swayed darkly in the yards and fields of the Indian neighborhoods; the wind howled on the mountains, making the wheat and the eucalyptus branches bow down. The *ayllus'* mongrel dogs despaired, and through the highest part of the sky, stronger than the wind and the voices of the dogs, the *wakawak'ras* thundered like the voices of bulls sobbing on the mountain peaks and in the depths of the valley surrounding the town.

From that Sunday on, in the townspeople's houses and in the neighborhoods, in the streets and in the tilled fields, people were discussing the bullfight, the competition between K'ayau and Pichk'achuri; which *ayllu* would bring in the bravest bulls, which *capeadores*, while working with their chests close to the horns, would fell them with dynamite in the arena.

Chaupi *ayllu* and K'ollana, too, would put up four bulls each, as they did every year. But the only way in which Chaupi surpassed the other *ayllus* was by having more blacksmiths, more carpenters, and hatmakers; that is, by having master craftsmen. K'ollana excelled with its stonemasons and ritual dancers. Almost all of the leading citizens' houses were the work of the K'ollanas. But on the twenty-eighth they just weren't up to it. *Ayllu* members and town citizens would be trembling in the stands when the fighters from K'ayau and Pichk'achuri, ponchos in hand, taunted the brave bulls from a distance. *Cholas* and girls would be trembling while the brindled or piebald bull was turning round and round in front of the barriers, with Juancha or Nicacha hanging from his horns, sometimes by the belt, sometimes by the groin. Honrao Rojas would enter the bullring with a stick of dynamite in hand, its wick smoldering; he'd motion with his arm for the spotted or the piebald bull to come closer.

"*Chascha*! *Turucha*,[5] damnit!"

The pied animal would be pawing the ground, his tongue lolling out.

Meanwhile Don Maywa and the Pichk'achuris would be playing *turupukllay* on the *wakawak'ras*, and in the arena the sandy ground would be scorching.

"Goddam *chascha*!"

From a distance, the bull would start to rush forward. Honrao Rojas would already be aware of that. Laughing, he'd be waiting.

5. "Dog! Little bull . . ."—Trans.

"Jajayllas turucha!"

Just as the bull was about to gore him, Honrao Rojas would fling the dynamite. The bullring would resound, a whirlwind of dust would rise up from the ground. Honrao Rojas would walk backwards toward the barrier. Sometimes the bull would be kicking, his back on the ground; or he'd be running like crazy, with blood spurting from his chest; at other times, when the dust lifted, the bull would catch sight of Honrao; bellowing, he'd leap forward, but by then it would be too late; Honrao would be reaching the barrier, laughing.

"Jajayllas turucha!"

That's how the K'ayaus and the Pichk'achuris were in the bull-fights. That's why Chaupi and K'ollana did not even consider competing with the bullfighters from the other *ayllus*. But on the twenty-eighth and on important holidays, K'ollana and Chaupi would put their ritual dancers on the streets. On all the street corners and in the squares, the K'ollana *danzak's* were the masters. No man could equal the Tankayllu[6] and *tayta* Untu from K'ollana. Tankayllu went out dancing with Nicanor Rojas as his harpist and Jacinto Pedraza as violinist. His pants and his vest, mirror and golden sash, varicolored beads gleamed; on his large felt hat he'd wear a hawk's body, beak forward; his steel scissors could be heard three blocks away. When Tankayllu went out dancing, people gathered from all four *ayllus*, and when he entered Girón Bolívar clicking his shears, the girls and the *mistis* came out onto the balconies.

"That Indian is an artist!" they'd say.

But the *danzak'* competition was not like the bullfighting one. With the brave bulls, it was a great contest before all the people from Puquio and the country districts. However, when the Tankayllu came out onto Girón Bolívar clicking his shears, the girls and the *mistis* pressed close together on the balconies to get to see him. Then there was no K'ayau, nor Chaupi, nor K'ollana; the whole populace, the Indians from all the neighborhoods rejoiced, filling the *mistis'* streets; their eyes sparkled as they watched the townspeople's faces.

"He's an artist. They ought to take him to Lima!" they'd say on the balconies.

"He might be an Indian . . . but how well he dances!"

"How horribly elegant."

Watching the citizens' faces, the *comuneros* from the four *ayllus*

6. This mirror-bespangled ritual dancer carries large steel scissors that he clicks. His name, Tankayllu, is the Quechua word for a large, heavy-bodied, buzzing insect that flies through the fields sipping honey from the flowers.—Trans.

had a ball; the rejoicing was the same for all the Indians of Puquio. And inside themselves they were taunting the *mistis*:

"What are *mistis* having? With their little Nazca horse, with their silver trappings, with their little necktie they're showing off. With nothing but rag. Where they having man to equal Tankayllu?"

That's why the K'ollanas were relying on the Tankayllu and on *tayta* Untu for the twenty-eighth. In the Indian quarters they said that the Tankayllu was going to show off different clothing and a new felt hat that year.

Meanwhile, in Pichk'achuri and in K'ayau they were getting ready to bring the fiercest bulls from all the punas into town. The Indian bullfighters were bragging.

"I'll be, I am *k'ari*."[7]

The town citizenry were also talking about the bullfight in all their meetings. When they met on the roads on the way to their tilled fields, or returning to town; while they were drinking beer and pisco[8] in the stores; whenever they gathered to chat beneath the lamps on the street corners, they'd lay bets on K'ayau or Pichk'achuri, for Misitu or against him, Don Pancho Jiménez against Don Julián Arangüena.

"The Indians'll drag your Misitu in," Don Pancho yelled at him.

"I'll make you a bet!" answered Don Julián. "I left him in the *k'eñwa* thickets and didn't put a bullet in him, because all the people from the puna and from the other towns are talking about my bull. Because he's the boss of the high country! I've donated Misitu to K'ayau community so the bull can feast on the Indians. It's a present for Misitu, really!"

And his whole body shook with laughter.

Don Pancho Jiménez and Don Julián Arangüena made a wager of ten dozen bottles of beer.

But on the balconies of the Subprefecture, the bull was discussed even more than in the *ayllus* and on the corners of Girón Bolívar.

The Subprefect was from Ica; he'd never seen a *turupukllay*. At noontime and in the evening, the Subprefecture balcony was always full of *mistis*. All of the leading citizens would talk to the Subprefect about the bullfight in Puquio; they'd interrupt one another, because each would want to tell the most important thing, whatever was most sensational according to the townsmen's way of looking at things.

7. A brave man, like a North American Indian brave.—Trans.
8. An alcoholic drink made by fermenting and distilling grape juice.—Trans.

"You're going to enjoy it, Señor Subprefect. It's something phenomenal."

"You know the square in the Pichk'achuri district: it's bigger than the Plaza de Armas in Lima. A gang of Indians from each community closes off one corner with a barrier of eucalyptus logs. We watch the bullfight from Don Crisóstomo Bendezú's balconies and from a box the Indians put up on the wall, by Don Crisóstomo's house. The Indian mob finds places on the rooftops, on the barriers, and on the walls. You'll soon see how it is! Ten, twelve bulls are fought. It's a big square. They don't make a special barricade for the bullfighters to hide behind; they just dig a pit in the middle of the square. The Indians are wilder than the bulls and they come in, taunting them. They fight the bulls with their ponchos; and when they get scared they all run and pile into the pit. The bull stays up on the side of the pit, snorting with rage. But not all of the Indians run well, and the bull catches some of them; he hooks them in the crotch and rips them up like rags. . . ."

"That's nothing!" said another; they all wanted to make themselves heard by the Subprefect. "That's nothing! There are four saddlecloths for the bravest bulls; the most important young ladies of our town donate them; they are silk saddlecloths, with silver coins and sometimes gold ones on the corners and in the embroidery. The saddlecloths are paraded around by us on horseback, to the sound of bursting rockets and to the music the band makes on those *wakawak'ras* the Indians play. You should see it! They sew the saddlecloths onto the wild bull's back, starting from the hump of muscle on his neck. The Indians go crazy over the saddlecloth; they enter in droves to tear off the saddlecloth. And that's something to see, Señor Subprefect! Because the Indians are also like wild beasts. . . ."

"Lord! That must be hard to take."

"It's elegant!"

"But I didn't believe it was so savage. We'll soon see. Only perhaps that's not very Christian. . . ."

"Don't say that, Señor Subprefect; your predecessor was of the purest Lima stock and he enjoyed it just as much as if he were getting paid to watch it. You'll pardon the expression, but he was happier than a hog watching it. You should have seen him!"

"The civil guards also say they've never seen anything more thrilling."

"Just the same, I don't agree with those savage customs."

"Don't say that, Subprefect! Without a bullfight the twenty-eighth wouldn't be a holiday."

"There wouldn't be anything."

"What about the Tankayllu?"

"Ah, my dear Subpre! The Tankayllu is an Indian ritual dancer who's really worthwhile."

"All there is for the twenty-eighth is the bullfight, the Tankayllu, and the schoolchildren's torchlight procession."

"But the bullfight is the strong point. The rest is for the birds, rubbish. Without the *turupukllay*, the twenty-eighth would be like any other day."

"I'm already seeing our Subpre turning yellow with excitement when K'encho comes out against Misitu, dynamite in hand."

"Because they're going to bring Misitu, Señor Subprefect! Our Indians are determined. Don't think they're like those little Indians from the other towns. Before, in the olden days, our grandfathers had to work their hides off to keep those Indians down. And they gave them more than one scare! Now we more or less get along with each other. And these *cholos* are really something!"

"Yes, sir!"

"Now you know the road you came on was made by the Indians in twenty-eight days. The market place was built by the *ayllus* in two months. They were working like ants."

"And these Indians are contagious. In those days, when they were building the market, even I, who have laziness in my blood, felt an itch to go in with them."

"That was something to see, Señor Subprefect. On community projects they work very hard, although they fall asleep in the fields when they're working for the leading citizens."

"Well, Señor Subprefect! They're going to drag Misitu in by the ears."

"And with Misitu we'll have a bullfight like in the olden times."

"I hope so, gentlemen! I see you like those bullfights more than the Spaniards do their Joselito and their Belmonte."[9]

"It all depends, sir. We have our *cholos* here who are really smashing, too."

At noontime and in the evening, the notables who had gone out to their tilled fields would arrive. Some of them would go straight home; others knew that at those times one could chat with the Subprefect on the balcony outside his office, and they'd head for the Plaza. Once they were in the little park, they'd pull back on the reins to show off their swift little horses, so the townspeople and the leading official would look at them. They'd dismount at the door of the police headquarters and go running up the steps to the Subprefec-

---

9. Famous Spanish bullfighters.—Trans.

ture. Those who had already arrived would draw closer and closer, surrounding the Subprefect.

"You will carry away with you an undying memory of our town. This is going to be a great bullfight."

"I hope so, friends. Although I don't like these savage customs very well."

"Then what would you have said about the bullfights of twenty years ago, when they used to tie a condor to the back of the wildest bull, to make him even more furious. With the condor pecking him, the bull would roll the Indians around as if it were nothing at all. And then the townsmen would go in on horseback and kill the bull just by jabbing him with their lances. At the end of the *fiesta* they would sew streamers onto the condor's wings and turn him loose, amid shouting and singing. The condor would take off with his streamers trailing; he looked like a black comet. Months and months later, up in the high country, that condor would still be flying from snowy peak to snowy peak, trailing his streamers."

"In November, Señor Subprefect, I found a condor with his streamers on. It was something to see !"

The townsmen pressed closer. Everybody wanted to say his part, to tell something new.

"You don't know about our great mountain, Señor Subprefect. El Misti of Arequipa is a little heap of dirt alongside of our snowcapped mountain, K'arwarasu. It has three peaks covered with pure snow. And how can it be? Black crags stick right up out of the snow."

"Yes, my Subpre! On one of those crags was the condor. I shot into the air near him with my revolver. And the little animal flew away from the rock. He flew off over those three peaks, trailing his streamers. I followed him with my eyes until he disappeared into the clouds that are always there on top of K'arwarasu."

Sometimes the Subprefect would tire of hearing them talk, hour after hour, about the bullfights, the wild bulls, the Indians. . . .

"Gentlemen, we'll go for a little walk."

And they would go down to take a turn around the little park. There the Subprefect would say goodbye and go to visit the girls' shops. But they, too, liked to talk about the bullfights and the Tankayllu.

"The devil!" he would say, once he was alone. "They talk to me so much in this town about that dancing Indian that I'm beginning to want to see him."

But the Judge and the Captain (the Provincial Chief of Police), who were also from the coast, told him confidentially:

"That Tankayllu is a filthy Indian like all the rest of them, but he does some pirouettes and calls attention to himself. As for the bullfight . . ."

"It's a savage custom, just as you think it is. And what those dumb Indians do is more disgusting than amusing."

And while the authorities and townspeople talked on Girón Bolívar and in the Plaza de Armas, while, in the pool hall, in the drugstore, in the eating places, and in the shops people recalled the bullfighting of yesteryear, in the four Indian neighborhoods and on the mountains, the *wakawak'ras* were sounding. Some nights from K'ayau and from Pichk'achuri rockets would rise up over the *mistis'* street and burst.

5. The Edict

One Wednesday morning in the middle of July, the Subprefect sent for the Mayor and the eminent citizens of the town.

The Subprefect received the townsmen in his office. As they came in, he showed each one to a chair so he could be seated. By eleven o'clock, the townspeople had already occupied all of the chairs and benches in the office. There were about fifty of them.

The Subprefect stood stiffly with his back to the table, a paper in hand, and began to speak.

"Your Honor and worthy citizens, I have some bad news for you. I have received an edict from the Ministry prohibiting bullfights without trained bullfighters. To those of you who have talked so much about the bullfights in this town, this is a fatal blow. But I think this prohibition is for the good of the country, because it puts an end to a custom that was a savage survival, as you yourselves have informed me, because the bulls caused deaths and injuries. As you must realize, I have to enforce this order. And I'm letting you know in good time, so you can hire a professional Spanish-style bullfighter in Lima if you want to hold a bullfight for the national holidays. The edict will be posted on the main street corners."

Not to have a bullfight in the Pichk'achuri square? Not to have a hole in the ground in which the Indians could conceal themselves? Not to parade the saddlecloths around with rockets and *wakawak'ra* music, mortar explosions, and firecrackers? Not to toss dynamite at the bravest bulls? Would the *cholos* from Pichk'achuri and K'ayau no longer be able to enter the ring to use their ponchos as capes and stand their ground firmly before the wild bulls of K'oñani and K'ellk'ata? What would the bullfight be like, then? Where would it be held? Would the Puquians all gather in Pichk'achuri—Indians and townspeople—just to watch one little professional making passes at the K'oñani bulls in the neighborhood's open field?

Don Pancho raised his arm, as if to point to the Subprefect's seat.

"Sir," he said. "How's that possible? There's a bet on this year between the neighborhoods of K'ayau and Pichk'achuri. And the K'ayau Indians are going to bring in Don Julián's bull, Misitu."

"Although it may be for next year, since they're prohibiting the bullfight."

"All of us citizens will get together and file a formal complaint."

"And besides, the professional bullfighter surely won't know how to fight bulls in Pichk'achuri."

And all the important people who were friends of Don Pancho spoke in turn. Once Don Pancho had begun, not one of them remained speechless.

But in the end, the group of citizens who were most prominent and were friends of the official raised their voices loudly, when they saw the Subprefect looking at Don Pancho Jiménez angrily.

"No Señor Subprefect! We citizens who are really aware of the situation are on the side of the authorities. The Puquio bullfight is a disgrace to our town. It makes us look like African savages, and we enjoy seeing these *cholos* put themselves between the bulls' horns, without knowing how to fight bulls, and drunk to boot," said Don Demetrio Cáceres, going up to the Subprefect's table. He pretended he was furious. "I've been to Belmonte's bullfights in Lima and I've enjoyed his artistry. Here the people must be taught how to watch bulls and civilized bullfights. All of these gentlemen around me are the ones who go to Lima; they're the ones with the most education. And we support the national government. Yes, sir."

And he went on talking for a long time, since the Subprefect kept nodding his head in approval. And all the townsmen, beginning with the largest property owners, went up to join him at the official's table. By the time Don Demetrio Cáceres stopped talking, Don Pancho was far away, near the outer door; there with him were the least important Puquians who were not such good friends of the Subprefect; they were jostling one another to get closer to the notables, but the latter were looking at Don Pancho as if they were disgusted with him, elbowing one another and trying to make the Subprefect see they were on Don Demetrio's side.

"Señor Subprefect!" Don Pancho called out from a distance, "I may have shown a lack of respect for authority, but that's no reason for them to crowd you and push me to the door. Now, Don Demetrio is well read, and he stays in Lima for months on end; Mayor Antenor, Don Jesús Gutiérrez, Don Gregorio Palomino, Don Jorge de la Torre

. . . they're also the most important people in Puquio. But, if truth be told, they enjoy themselves just as much as we do at the Pich-k'achuri bullfights; they're tickled to death when the bull rips some drunken Indian's pants to shreds. You think they're not? We've all been raised the same way in this town, but they understand authority first of all. Well, who isn't gonna obey the national government? But this year, K'ayau's gonna bring Misitu, and there's a bet on between the two neighborhoods; a great bullfight it's gonna be; that's the only reason I've been begging to have it, and the other people too. But so far as obeying the authority's concerned, we're all obedient, Señor Subprefect. And there's nothing to get angry about!"

"That's right, Señor Subprefect."

"You see just how it is!"

All those who were near the door spoke out, clamoring, showing their obedience.

"Very well, gentlemen. We're all in agreement," said the Subprefect. "Let the provincial council take whatever steps are appropriate with regard to the bullfight, in conformance with the edict. I have nothing more to say. And now you may go."

"Not yet!" said Don Pancho. "Señor Subprefect, since we're all here together, we could at least have a drink of beer!"

"Champagne will be drunk, Señor Subprefect!" yelled Don Demetrio, as if he were putting Don Pancho and his followers down.

"All right, Don Demetrio. It's nothing to get hot about. Each man treats according to the state of his pocket."

"Señor Subprefect, would you be so kind as to accompany me to the billiard parlor?"

"Certainly, Your Honor! There are no conveniences here."

The Subprefect, Don Demetrio, and the Mayor walked to the door; the townsmen made way for them. And they followed the official out.

In the Plaza, in front of the headquarters of the Civil Guard, a group of mestizos and Indians had gathered. As the townsmen came out onto the balcony of the Subprefecture, the *cholos* and Indians broke up into little groups, and they watched the townsmen cross the Plaza and enter Girón Bolívar.

"Hey! Something must be happening for sure," said one of them.

Stealthily, in groups of three and four, the mestizos took the lead and headed for Girón Bolívar. The Indians came on behind, in a herd.

The townsmen entered the pool hall, but Don Pancho and a group of prominent citizens stayed outside in the street, since the store could not hold all of them.

"Señor Subpre! To your health we'll go drink some beer in my store. You're in good company here," Don Pancho called out.

"Go right ahead, gentlemen. I'm sorry not to be with you," answered the Subprefect.

And then some of those who were already inside the pool hall came back out to go with Don Pancho. Thus, the town's citizens were now divided into two factions—one with Don Demetrio Cáceres and the other with Don Pancho.

Inside the pool hall, Don Demetrio began to speak.

"Sometimes, Señor Subprefect, we have to yield to the wishes of the more backward people of Puquio. But with an official like you, now, it's another matter. We feel you support us and set us on the right road to civilization."

"Yes, yes! Of course, of course!"

"That's the truth."

"That's the way it is."

"With twenty Subprefects like you, Peru could be civilized in a hurry. We need officials who'll come and teach us, and who are determined to impose the culture of the foreign countries. In these towns, Señor Subprefect, we're still living in darkness. No use even talking about our backwardness! And here every good custom is ruined by the environment, by the *cholos*, and by some citizens who are Indian on the inside. Don't you see how the bullfight is? Here they hold it with *wakawak'ras*, with dynamite and lances, in a bullring that's a big field. How about that! There aren't any two-steps, or marches, or crimson capes, or *banderillas*.[1] It's pure Indian! *Huaynos, ayarachi*.[2] And drunken *cholos*. And seeing all that, Señor Subprefect, tell me who wouldn't come to a bad end? And that's how all the holidays are, religious or patriotic. Just the same. That's why an official like you is our salvation."

"Of course!"

"Well, then, you see how it is, Señor Subprefect!"

"Okay, okay! Fortunately, on the coast there's no longer anything like that. Down there, civilization is now a fact. And I shall help you with all my heart. I know there'll be difficulties; obscurantism is hard to overcome. Don't you see that other group is more recalcitrant? Now they'll get drunk and cry over the bullfight."

"Don't pay any attention to them, sir. They're ignorant and cowardly. But they'll obey, peacefully."

---

1. Rounded dowels two feet long, covered with colored paper and with a steel harpoon point, that are placed in pairs into the bull's withers.—Trans.

2. Literally the Quechua word *ayarachi* means "corpse-making"; it is a kind of lugubrious funeral music.—Trans.

"I know, I already know that. But I see they're more like back-woodsmen."

"Have them serve the champagne! Hurry!" Don Demetrio rapped on the counter.

Don Norberto became alarmed when he heard them call for ten bottles of champagne.

In Don Pancho Jiménez' store, there was more noise than in the pool hall. The majority of the townsmen were crowded in there, all talking at once. Outside the door, almost filling the street, *"chalos"* and *comuneros* were listening, and they were talking too.

"What kind of bullfight is it gonna be without K'encho?" yelled Don Pancho." So Honrao, Tobias, Raura[3] aren't going in? What's it gonna be like if there isn't any dynamite, if there isn't any saddle-cloth? All balled up, that's what! What lousy little Spanish bull-fighter's gonna go into the square at Pichk'achuri? Like a *tankayllu* he'll dance around the square; like a grasshopper he'll be lost in there."

"You see? Pichk'achuri square is big enough for one hundred, two hundred Indians to go in and fight bulls. Playing *wakawak'ras*, setting off dynamite. How's a white guy gonna go into the Pichk'achuri bullring? The Indians would laugh so hard they'd piss."

"No! No! We'll send a telegram to Lima. We'll plead with the Ministry."

"And doing it now, yet. Just when K'ayau is crazy to bring Misitu."

"That's what really bothers me."

"And Don Demetrio acts like a foreigner. Surely his soul is crying for the bullfight. 'Ai, how's it gonna be without Honrao?' he's saying down inside. But in the Subprefect's office he looks like somebody from Lima who's being held prisoner in Puquio."

"Why do they have to be such brown-noses and faggots?"

"And now, goddamnit, the K'ayaus are going to find out, and they might not even go after Misitu."

"Don't say that."

"A pisco, you *k'anras*!"

"What do you mean, pisco? Cane liquor! I want a real drink."

"Cane liquor!"

"Why must they meddle in town affairs? But if you ask for something legitimate for the town with a written petition, they won't even look at the paper!"

"Hey, Don Pancho! Maybe we won't be able to do it."

3. The name K'encho means "Brings Bad Luck," Honrao means "Honored," and Raura, "Burn."—Trans.

"Maybe there won't even be a bullfight!"

The "*chalos*" and *comuneros* were listening. By now, they were all jostling one another by the doorway.

"What must have been?"

"Government must have commanded not to hold bullfight."

"*Tayta!* What's boss Don Pancho saying? There's no bullfight, he says?" asked one *comunero*.

Don Pancho went to the doorway of the store. From there he spoke to them.

"The bet with K'ayau's off! There's no need for Misitu, nor for bulls from K'oñani. Instead steers must be brought for the little bullfighter from Lima. Government says it doesn't want natives bullbaiting. Just now remembered, it says, its native who suffers in the bullfight on twenty-eighth. Hell! Now there's no bullfight, nor saddlecloth, nor barricades, nor dynamite. Bring steer, milk cows; professional toreador must be brought from Lima. On our little ears we'll wear carnations to go to the bullfight on twenty-eighth."

While he was talking, the other townmen came out of the pool hall. When they saw the Subprefect, the mestizos took off, almost running down the street. The Indians stood with their backs pressed to the wall.

"Here comes the Subprefect!"

"The Subprefect's coming!"

The townsmen inside of Don Pancho's store became excited. Don Pancho went up to the counter.

"Why's everybody trembling? More cane liquor!"

The Subprefect found Don Pancho with half a glass of firewater in his hand.

"What's going on here? What's all the uproar about?" he asked.

By this time Don Pancho was drunk. Lined up behind the Subprefect were the Mayor, Don Demetrio, Don Jesús Gutiérrez . . . the eyes of all of them stared at Don Pancho as if he were a dirty dog.

"There isn't any uproar, Señor Subprefect. I'm just here notifying them that a professional bullfighter from Lima is going to fight the bulls, that our government is taking pity on its natives."

"Who ordered you to notify people?"

"Well, I'm not notifying them! I'm just letting them know. We're saying goodbye to our Puquio bullfight with a little cane liquor. That gringo, Don Cáceres, has toasted the little toreador from Lima with his champagne. It's nothing to get hot about. We each do what our conscience tells us to do."

"No insults! I won't stand for it, Señor Subprefect!" said Don Demetrio, who went up to the doorstep of the store, stopped beside the

Subprefect and, leaning over, looked in at Don Pancho.

"Goddamn mongrel! Ass-kisser!" Don Pancho grasped his glass firmly and dashed the rotgut rum into Don Demetrio Cáceres' eyes. The drink splashed in the townman's face, ran down onto his shirt, and dripped onto the ground. The Subprefect stepped up into the store and gave Don Pancho a shove.

"Go ahead and hit me, Señor Authority. With you I'm not gonna quarrel," the latter said calmly.

He covered his face with his arms. The other townsmen slipped out of the store. In the street, people were running toward Don Pancho's doorway. Two civil guards arrived, opened a path for themselves, and entered the store.

"Take this *cholo* off to jail!" ordered the Subprefect.

As the guards were dragging Don Pancho out the door, Don Demetrio gave him a kick in the rear. The Subprefect shouted from the doorway:

"And clear out, you guanacos![4] Out!"

All the people ran, up the street and down the street.

"Stupid *cholos*! Savages!"

"Yes, sir! They're a bunch of brutes."

"A bunch of savages!"

"The shame of Puquio!"

Don Antenor Miranda, Don Jorge de la Torre, Don Jesús Gutiérrez . . . talked rapidly; they also stuck out their chests the way the Subprefect did, and looked with loathing at the people who were rushing along Girón Bolívar and crowding into the side streets.

The two guardsmen dragged Don Pancho off by the arms. The *cholos* and some of the town citizens watched this with frightened, rather questioning looks.

"For defending Puquio I'm going to jail."

"Shut up!" the guards yelled at him.

And they shoved him into the jail yard. In the yard the Indian "cattle rustlers" and the *cholos* who had been accused of murder, rape, and contempt for authority were sunning themselves. They all stood up when they saw a *misti* prisoner come in.

"Hell! I'll tangle with that ass-kisser's guts! Some day!"

Along the now-cleared street, the Subprefect and the prominent citizens returned to the Plaza. By all four corners, Indians, townspeople, and some "*chalos*" were entering it, but when they saw the Subprefect in front of the police headquarters, they left again as if

4. Wild animals with reddish-brown wool, related to the llama; *guanaco* is also used as a derogatory term.—Trans.

42

they were being chased. Others stood peering around the edge of the corner at the Subprefecture for a while and then dodged back out of sight.

"These towns are dumps! No wonder the Chileans beat us. They stare at us like guanacos," said the Subprefect.

"Yes, sir! The Indians' cowardice gets into one's blood."

"That's true, Señor Subprefect! The Yankees did well to exterminate the redskins."

Just then the Judge came out of the Courtroom with two law clerks; seeing the townsmen assembled in the little park in front of police headquarters, they went over to the group.

As the Judge was greeting the citizens, a loud cry came from the doorway of the police station:

"I shit on Demetrio Cáceres, goddamnit!"

"That Pancho Jiménez is the only one who has a mouth. Sergeant! Make that man shut up or I'll beat his brains out."

They waited there for a while. Don Demetrio wanted to hear whether Don Pancho was groaning. "Now they're probably kicking him. They must be knocking him down," he was saying to himself.

"Very well, gentlemen. I'll be leaving you. I suppose the council will meet this evening."

The Subprefect bade them all farewell and set off for his office.

Once alone, the townsmen glanced at one another mistrustfully, each trying to figure out what the others had on their minds. Don Antenor spoke first:

"Seriously, our bullfight is a backward custom. But that mob of Indians is going to be hard to convince."

"But the town has to respect the law and prohibit the bullfight in Pichk'achuri. The national government is the national government!"

"Of course!"

"Of course!"

"Who says it shouldn't?"

"The Subprefect will see that it's all arranged."

"I'll have the meeting called for 9 PM It would be well if all the town's citizens went and the Reverend Father, too," said the Mayor.

"Yes. So that all the citizenry may commit themselves to supporting the edict."

"Until then, gentlemen."

"So long."

They all lived on Girón Bolívar, but they separated. They had nothing more to say to each other. And one after another, they reached Girón Bolívar.

At night a gasoline lantern illumined the balcony of the Town Hall. The streetlamps on the corners of the Plaza barely brightened the limed walls; in that light, the people looked like shadows. The kerosene streetlamps increased the darkness in the middle of the Plaza. The light from the Town Hall passed overhead, as if it were coming out of a window, and shone on church tower and rooftop; the iron cross on the church was clearly visible; the white cloth that hung from one of its arms was fluttering in the wind.

The townsmen went up both sets of steps to the Town Hall, coming in from the Girón Bolívar corner and from the K'ayau quarter. Some of the townsmen were chatting on the balcony, beneath the lamp. From the Plaza one could even see the color of the ties and kerchiefs they wore round their necks. They waved their little arms; now and again they turned round as they talked and then stood facing the others, sticking out their chests and paunches. Don Antenor went in and out, from the balcony to the town meeting hall.

When the Vicar came up onto the balcony, Don Antenor shook his hand, bowing. They all entered the meeting hall.

Puquio's meeting hall is large, fifty chairs can fit into the length of it. At the head of the room there is a raised platform, and that's where the town office is. There is a cedarwood table and the Mayor's seat, which is a large, thronelike, leather-covered chair. And to the right and left of the town armchair are other smaller, leather chairs for the councilmen. A portrait of the President of the Republic hangs on the headwall; to the right of this portrait there is a symbolic picture of the war with Chile, painted by Don Narciso Cueva, an Indian from the interior towns.

The Mayor and the councilmen seated themselves in their leather chairs and the other townsmen took the wooden chairs, facing each other, the length of the hall. One of the councilmen surrendered his seat to the Vicar and went down to sit among the citizenry.

Two gasoline lamps lighted the room brightly.

The Mayor stood up and began to speak:

"Honorable councilmen, Reverend Vicar, worthy taxpayers: You are all aware of the edict from the Ministry prohibiting bullfighting without trained personnel. We have convoked this council meeting in order that all of you may commit yourselves to following the edict and also to reach an agreement on the bullfight. We also want to hear the advice of an outsider, our Vicar.

"I ask for the floor."

"The worthy citizen, Señor Cáceres, has the floor."

"Our national government, gentlemen, heeding its call to protect the helpless native with his backward-oriented brain, has dictated this intelligent measure. We cannot disagree with this edict, by which a barbaric custom of our town is extirpated to the very root. I request the council to send a telegram thanking His Honor, the Minister of the Interior, for this order which protects the natives' lives. And frees Puquio from a barbaric custom."

Don Demetrio gave all of the townsmen a scornful look. And he sat down.

The townsmen applauded him.

"We want to hear the counsel of our Vicar," requested the Mayor.

The Vicar arose, and, hiding his hands in the sleeves of his cassock as if he were in the pulpit, spoke.

"Your Honor, worthy citizens: Well, you know that I have been a Karwank'a Indian. The saintly Bishop of Ayacucho took me in as an act of charity and sent me to the Seminary. But in my heart I go on loving the Indians like brothers. Now the Pichk'achuri bullfights have always been an offense to the Lord. The worthy citizens, if you'll pardon my saying so, have been enjoying a Satanic feast. Where else has anyone ever seen drunken Indians sent in against wild bulls in hopes of having the pleasure of seeing a Christian disemboweled? In that way, people living here, in our towns, have been offending our Lord, the Child Jesus, the patron of the town. For that reason, the Government's prohibition is holy."

"But Don Pancho Jiménez wants the bullfight!" yelled Don Demetrio Cáceres.

"Let us forget the wicked sons. Sooner or later, he'll come to understand his blindness. But the town council should approve Señor Cáceres' request. That is my opinion as a priest."

"Long live Doctor Salcedo!"

"Vivaáá!"

"Señor Cáceres, do us the honor of drafting a telegram," the Mayor requested.

Don Demetrio stepped up onto the dais and took the Secretary's place.

As Don Demetrio was writing, Don Julián Aranguëna asked a question from the rear of the hall:

"Your Honor, is there going to be a bullfight or isn't there?"

"Yes, sir. The council will hire a professional bullfighter from Lima."

"And what's the bullfight going to be like? Aren't the Indians going to do anything but watch it? What about the saddlecloths? And the dynamite? And the *ayllu* of K'ayau? Is the bullfight just going to be held in silence?"

"Don Julián! I beg you not to contradict the Ministry!"

"What do you mean, contradict? I'm not Don Pancho Jiménez. I'm speaking sense here. I've donated my bull to the *ayllu* of K'ayau and I want to know."

"The *ayllus* are going to bring in the bulls, same as always, Don Julián. But the bullfight is going to be held in the modern way."

Don Julián laughed so loudly the hall resounded.

"You don't say, Your Honor! If, by some miracle, they do bring Misitu in, how can a little toreador stand up to him? Let's see, what do you say, fellow citizens?"

Don Demetrio arose and walked over to the edge of the platform.

"Your Honor, we must put these backward ways behind us. There aren't any bulls for a Lima bullfighter. Misitu is a poor pussycat compared to the real Mala bulls."

"You've seen those bulls in Acho. In the first place, Don Demetrio will piss when he sees Misitu. And my bull'll rip the guts out of any little toreador. . . ."

"Señor Arangüena!" answered the Vicar, realizing what Don Antenor and Don Demetrio had on their minds. "That's the toreador's business. But the town has a legal obligation, and would do very well to hire a professional. Let Senor Cáceres go ahead and read us the telegram. And I beg you all to keep calm."

"All right, all right! What must happen will happen." And Don Julián shrugged his shoulders.

Don Demetrio read aloud:

"The Mayor, Vicar, and notable citizens of this city thank and congratulate you for measure against bullfights without trained bullfighters, to protect helpless indigenous population."

"It doesn't convince me," muttered Don Julián; some of the townsmen were nodding their heads in approval of what Don Julián was saying. But they all signed the telegram.

They signed and left hurriedly. In the square, by the steps, they encountered a populace of Indians, "*chalos*," and schoolchildren.

"*Taytay, taytay!*" the Indians called out. But the town worthies ran down the steps and made their way through the crowd rapidly, as if they were fleeing.

When Don Julián came down, the Indians from K'ayau moved closer to the stairs. They managed to line up on the bottom step. Behind the K'ayaus the Pichk'achuris, K'ollanas, and Chaupis were talking in the darkness. The lamp on the street corner was useless; its light did not even reach the fountain in front of the jail. By now the mob of Indians extended as far as the big fountain; standing up on the iron pipe and on the concrete base, they were watching the meeting hall doorway; they were milling around in front of the Mayoralty the way they did during the Corpus Christi procession. . . .

"Damnit! Won't be!" they were saying.

"There isn't any *pukllay*!" they said. "Won't be!"

Don Julián descended the steps, put on his hat, and calmly walked away; other prominent citizens came back when they heard the Indian mob.

"*Taytay patrón*! Letting us know! Governments don't want, they say, *turupukllay* in Pichk'achuri," they told Don Julián, questioningly.

"*Arí*!"[5]

"Won't be, Don Jolián!"

The K'ayau staffbearers went up a step.

"Misitu'll come, Don Jolián. There'll always be *pukllay, werak'ocha*."

"With foreign bullfighter it'll be; foreign toreador gonna come with his *banderilla. Taytay* Mayor will bring him for twenty-eighth," answered Don Julián.

"Won't be, Don Jolián! Misitu is for K'ayau *ayllu*!"

"*Kank'am pukllay*! (There'll be a bullfight!)" Don Antenor shouted from the Town Hall doorway. He came down the steps and looked at Don Julián beseechingly.

"They must be told that there's going to be a bullfight, Señor Arangüena. Bullfight same as every year. Don't you know these Indians are a bunch of savages?"

"*Cumunkuna*!"

Don Antenor spoke for a long time in Quechua.

"It's all right, *Taytay* Mayor!"

"It's all right!"

"It's all right!"

By the K'ayau corner, filling the street like a drove of cattle, the Puquios left the Plaza.

The *mistis* looked at one another.

"Nothing, nothing, Don Antenor!"

"You'll just have to conform to it, gentlemen. You mustn't get discouraged. It'll all be settled soon. And in the name of heaven, I beg you, Don Julián . . ." said the Vicar.

As the leading citizens were leaving the Plaza, from the four *ayllus* the *wakawak'ras* sang out. In the dark Plaza, in the now-peaceful town, the *turupukllay* resounded; like a wind it blew through the streets. It was the *pukllay* of the twenty-eighth! In the depths of Don Demetrio's, of Don Antenor's, of Don Julián's con-

5. Yes.—Trans.

47

sciousness . . . a joyfulness welled up . . . and they walked more rapidly. The joy of seeing K'encho, Honrao taunting the bull, sticking out their chests.

From some of the shops on Girón Bolívar, the white lamplight shone out onto the street. Beneath the corner lamps there were round shadows; when the wind blew, the shadows circled round. The whitened walls by the lamps could be seen from afar, even with the crevices the rainstorms had made in them. But the *mistis'* street was silent.

In the K'ayau and Pichk'achuri square, the frogs were croaking. The whole *ayllu* was darker. And from there the *wakawak'ras* sang out: at times they sobbed loudly; it was as if the song were coming out of the heart of the square, from inside the chapel, and going as far as the big river.

"In Puquio they're working hard to get ready for the twenty-eighth," said the *mistis* who were sleeping on the haciendas.

"K'ayau, Pichk'achuri, they say, gonna fight on twenty-eighth," commented the hands on the haciendas by the big river.

"What an Indian town!"

The Provincial Chief of Police and the Judge of the Court of First Instance cursed Puquio.

6. The Authority

From his office balcony, the Subprefect watched the throng entering the Plaza from the Indian neighborhoods; arriving in crowds and all talking at once, they gathered below the Mayoralty. The Subprefect paced the balcony, thinking. From time to time the sound of the Indian mob rose up from the Plaza. The little corner lamps shed a dim light on the Indians who were coming in; they were like a dense drove, not even their heads could be seen; they moved across the open space as if they were sliding toward the Mayoralty.

"This is a theater! It's like a movie!"

He was not afraid. He neither saw the people nor understood what they were saying.

"They're nothing but cattle!"

On the lighted balcony outside the Mayoralty, also as if on a movie screen, the townsmen were talking. Under the lamp they gathered in threes and fours, waving their short arms; now and then the neckerchiefs many of them wore fluttered in the wind. When the Vicar arrived, his black cassock cast a shadow on the whitened wall. The town's citizens bowed to the Priest and entered the assembly hall after him. Then the wind carried the sound of the council meeting to the Subprefecture. Scattered words could be heard of what the Priest said, of what Don Antenor said, but Don Julián's raucous laughter filled the whole Plaza, and echoed back from the terrace before the church. The noise level in the Plaza increased when the *ayllus* heard Don Julián's guffaws.

The Subprefect went on watching the Plaza from the balconies of his office, as if in a dream. In the dark, silent sky a few little stars were sparkling; the sound of the barking of the four *ayllus'* dogs seemed to come down out of the deep, black sky. On the big square,

49

with its four kerosene street lamps, their little flames flickering in the darkness, the Indian throng waited by the jail wall. The Town Hall balcony, its limed wall illumined by the gasoline lamp, seemed to be suspended in air above the crowd of Indians.

"It's as if these towns were from another world. Only necessity, money, could make a man put up with this pigsty," exclaimed the Subprefect.

The Sergeant's voice interrupted his lamentations.

"Señor Subprefect! Can I talk to you?" he asked.

"Come on out, Sergeant. Here I am, watching the movie."

The Sergeant approached the Subprefect.

"You're a highlander, Sergeant."

"No, Señor Subprefect. I'm from Arequipa."

"You like this town."

"How the hell could I like it! What an ugly mob of Indians it's had. Over there I don't know what they're deciding to do. Wouldn't it be a good idea to get out the horses? These people'll have an uprising over any old thing. I've been close to the Indian mob; like water in the lakes they move—from one rim to another."

"Not now, Sergeant. The Priest is inside there, the Mayor, all the landowning exploiters, and Don Julián Aranguena. How could they have an uprising! More likely they'll beg to have the gutting on the twenty-eighth. What do you think of our country? It's a big mess. But anyway, how could this land produce anything else? Look how ugly the sky is, what a dismal town. Sometimes it puts me in a black mood, being up here in the midst of all these mountains. And it's nothing but a place for dogs to meet and howl in, and when it's not the dogs it's those bull-horns the Indians play on as if it were the Day of the Dead; or else it's the wind shrieking over the tin roofs. It's a mess. Or do you think it's all right?"

"Of course it isn't, sir! But the hypocrisy and hot air of these little exploitative landowners rubs me the wrong way, too."

"You're right. Sometimes I feel like cracking their heads with a whip. They steal, chew coca, get fat, and skin the Indians alive; and then they come into my office saying, 'Ai, Señor Subpre!' Looking so pitiful and sniveling. And if they could kill a person, how eagerly they'd do it! What a mess this is!"

"The only one who has any guts is Pancho Jiménez. And also that blockhead Aranguena."

"Oh sure! Pancho Jiménez! I don't know what to do with that dumb lout. Whenever I see him, it makes me feel like throwing him out like a mad dog, to sic him on Miranda, Fernández, and Cáceres . . . on all those scum who act as if they were decent people. But other times I'd like to smash him to a pulp."

As they were talking, the doorway of the Town Hall filled with the townsmen who were leaving.

"Get going, Sergeant. Watch 'em."

The Sergeant rushed down the stairs and ran out into the middle of the Plaza, where the policemen were.

But after the Mayor had explained things to the *ayllus* in Quechua, guaranteeing there would be a *turupukllay*, the Indian mob began to move toward the corners. In the Subprefecture, the Indians' voices sounded like a deep-pitched murmuring that seemed to be coming from inside the earth.

They left for their neighborhoods by all four corners of the Plaza. A man extinguished the Town Hall lamp, and the church roof, the stone tower, and the Town Hall balcony vanished. The Subprefect blinked to accustom his eyes to the darkness. And clearly, cleanly, the fountain water began to sing in the Plaza. The crickets that slept in the sorrel patches behind the Subprefecture made their chirping heard. The footfalls of the guardsmen rang on the ground as they neared the police headquarters.

"Nothing's happening now, Señor Subprefect. That's how these *cholos* are; they make their hullabaloo and then they disappear," said the Sergeant, once he was back on the balcony.

"Didn't I tell you? As if I didn't know my people!"

"But the Plaza's been left for dead."

"Everything's the same around here! Look at the Plaza now, look at the sky, look at this balcony. The stars are separating in the sky, league by league. This long balcony's like a dead man's coffin. The Plaza looks like a picture of the sky. And all the Indians have, within their bodies, the silence of these mountains, of the sky, of the Plaza, of all this mess! And when they shout, they shout horribly, and then, all of a sudden, they're quiet. Listen, Sergeant, go get Pancho Jiménez! Here have a little pisco. We'll make that *cholo* talk. See if we don't have a good time! What do you think?"

"Good idea, sir. To finish off this dreary day."

The Subprefect opened the door to his office and struck a match to light his way. Groping, match in hand, he went over to the table; when he came to the carpeting beneath the writing table, the match went out. He lit another and managed to reach the two-armed candelabra at one end of the table. The candles' light flickered a moment, as if the little flames were going to come loose from the wicks, and then took hold and began to grow. The white cloth ceiling, with its round stains where the rain had leaked in, showed quite clearly, as did the President's portrait and the high-backed chairs that were lined up almost to the end of the hall, where the candlelight did not then reach. Cursing, the Subprefect sat down in his big chair, behind the table.

"Puquio! What a trashy town!"

And while he was swearing, from the four *ayllus* the voices of the *wakawak'ras* rose up to the Plaza and came into the Subprefecture; more and more clearly, more strongly the *yawar fiesta* melody welled up in the town.

"Damnit! Those wretched Indians!"

He heard the Sergeant and Don Pancho's footsteps in the hall . . .

"Come in!"

With hat in hand and his hair down over his forehead, Don Pancho entered the large room.

"Good evening, Señor Subprefect!"

"Come over here. Come closer! You too, Sergeant."

Don Pancho shook the floor boards with his tread; he sat down in the first chair, by the Subprefect's table. With his hands on his knees, without leaning back against the chair, like everyone who is respectful of authority, he looked at the Subprefect mistrustfully.

"Here I am, at your command."

The Sergeant sat down beside Don Pancho.

"Why is your town so ugly, Don Pancho?" asked the Subprefect.

Don Pancho put his mind at rest. The Subprefect's voice was friendly, much more so than when he had been talking to Don Antenor.

"It all depends, Señor Subprefect. Well, why wouldn't it look ugly to you? You were born in a coastal town, just like the Sergeant, too, who's from Arequipa. For Don Demetrio, too, it's a dump. Now me, I'm from here; my body has grown up in this air; to me, to tell you the truth, Puquio isn't ugly. I've tried living in other towns, but it can't be done. Like you, I live sadly."

"What about Don Antenor?"

"What's that gentleman good for? He's not real; his soul's in Lima, but his belly's in Puquio. He's a damned scoundrel."

"What about you?"

"I'm a Puquian, a townsman born in Chaupi, at your command."

"Don't those Indian bugles bother you?"

"That's the *pukllay*, sir! Even if you buried the town under all the mountains you wouldn't silence the *wakawak'ras*. I'm not an ass-kisser like Don Demetrio and Don Antenor. You've done me the honor of having me brought to your office; I didn't come to bother you with my flattery and gossip, like the Lima-ized gentry of this town. Puquio is *turupukllay*. You think it's Girón Bolívar? My store is there; I'm a prominent citizen. Just imagine, sir."

"First you'll have a little drink. Get some glasses out of the cupboard, Sergeant, and the pisco, too."

It was hard for Don Pancho to believe that he could be so much in the Subprefect's confidence. He had thought he would spend the night walking around in the jail corral, along with the police horses. From the corral he had heard the noise the *ayllus* had made in the Plaza, the Indians' voices; he had also heard Don Julián's boisterous laughter. And just as he was stamping the ground with rage, when his heart felt faint from worrying about what might have happened in the town, the Sergeant had called him to take him to the Subprefect's office. Who, then would ever have thought it was to have a drink of pisco with the official, as if between trusty friends?

"I don't deserve the honor, Señor Subprefect. I'll do the same for you, always! Sometime it'll be. Lord!"

The Sergeant poured the pisco into glasses. He filled Don Pancho's glass more than half way.

"Finish it off, Don Pancho!"

"Why not, sir!"

Without even stopping for breath, Don Pancho tossed back this glassful; and, as if to put an end to the drink, he banged the bottom of his glass on the table. The Subprefect and the Sergeant celebrated the gesture by laughing loudly.

"Certainly, sir! I'll do the same for you."

"Now then, continue, Don Pancho."

"I tell you, Señor Subpre, the Indians are the town, the real Puquio. You think maybe it's Don Antenor, pussyfooting around, propping himself up with his cane, favoring his corns? How's the national government gonna do away with the Pichk'achuri bullfight? The cops would have to go from house to house, through all four *ayllus*, taking away the *wakawak'ras*; they'd have to climb these mountains, go into the stone huts, and take the *wakawak'ras* away from the highland Indians. Aren't you hearing them, sir? Let's see, stop a moment. . . . That bullfight music that sounds far off, like it was coming down from the evening stars, is from the *comuneros* up in the high country. They'd have to make the hearts of all the Puquians stop beating to keep the *wakawak'ras* from singing. Even Don Antenor's aching corns know that much. But he acts like a little saint, or, to put it a better way, and if you'll pardon the expression, he acts like a shithead. They're giving you bad advice, sir! Up here in the highlands, holidays of all kinds, whether they be saints' days or national ones, belong to the Indians. The townsmen might be loaded with money; they might tear the Indians' hearts out. But if there's a *fiesta* in the town, it's the *ayllus*'! They're the ones who make the litters for the saints; they set off the fireworks; they strew flowers on the streets so the Virgin or the town's patron saint can pass by. All we townsmen do is grow fat, that's all! That's how life is in the highlands, sir. That's the truth of the matter!"

"So far he's right. I've been in more than a hundred towns, from policeman up to Sergeant, and what Don Pancho says is the pure truth."

The Sergeant stood up.

"I told you so, sir. This Don Pancho is real."

The Subprefect arose also; then Don Pancho stood up, respectfully, clutching his hat in both hands.

"Before I say anything, let's have another drink."

The Subprefect poured them each half a glass.

"To each his own, and your health."

Once more they drained their glasses. Don Pancho banged the table with his glass again.

"'Sit ye down,' a phrase from Pliny," said the Subprefect.

The Sergeant and Don Pancho understood the invitation and sat down.

"I speak better when I'm walking. And now we're among men, aren't we?"

"Yes, sir!"

The Subprefect stepped out into the middle of the room. With his hands in his pockets he began to pace the whole length of the carpet.

"If it were up to me, I'd have this town buried! . . ."

A curse was searing Don Pancho's mouth, but with an effort he choked it down.

"You've spoken like a man, haven't you?"

"I, sir, have been a man ever since I was born."

"That's so! What use is your town? Don Antenor and his cronies are a pack of shameless hounds, ass-kissers, as you say; with their bellies here and their souls in Lima. And what about the Indians? A drove of mangy animals, filthy as pigs, drunks, and degenerates. All they're good for is to chew coca, sing, whimper, and fornicate. . . ."

His voice rose; he stopped every now and then before Don Pancho and moved his arms angrily, as if he were plucking the words out with his hand.

"I have seen the Indians putting lice in their babies' mouths! . . ."

"No, sir! Not in Puquio!"

Don Pancho arose from his chair and stood facing the Subprefect.

"Not in Puquio, sir!"

"Am I lying?"

The Subprefect stared at Don Pancho from the end of the carpet.

"Yes, Señor Subprefect. In Puquio no *ayllu* eats lice! I swear to God!"

The Sergeant also arose from his seat and, protecting Don Pancho with his body, spoke loudly to the Subprefect, face to face:

"I haven't seen that, either. Let's not fight, Señor Subprefect! We're among men."

He stepped aside. And the Subprefect once more gazed into Don Pancho's little eyes.

"But there won't be any bullfight in Pichk'achuri! You won't see anyone's guts ripped out this twenty-eighth! You might not be as dirty as Cáceres or Gutiérrez, but you're a savage, a degenerate, an eater of Indian blood!"

"Okay, sir! You may be right. Don't get mad, Subpre! We're different. And you, as an official, can make problems for this town with the Ministry's edict."

"Yes, Señor Subprefect! Don't take offense. You drink the last one!"

The Sergeant was about to pour it, but the Subprefect rushed over to Don Pancho. "Now he'll kick him," thought the policeman. But the Subprefect held out his hand to him.

"See you later, Don Pancho. Get going! But don't you take it upon yourself to herd the Indians against me. You're the only shrewd Puquian with a sharp tongue. But now you know! Be very careful! It could cost you your hide."

Don Pancho shook the Subprefect's hand.

"See you later, sir. I'll keep your words in mind."

And then he went over to the Sergeant.

"Thank you, Señor Sergeant."

In his little eyes, gratitude shone brightly and clearly.

Shaking the floorboards, Don Pancho walked to the door. In the shadow at the end of the large room, his body seemed to have grown; almost scraping the lintel, he went through the door. In the hall, the floor creaked from his tread, and there was the sound of his footfalls on the stone stairs, as he descended to the Plaza.

"Now he's in the Plaza, Sergeant!"

As if he were going to chase him, the Subprefect ran to the door.

"Come here, Sergeant! Hurry!"

The Sergeant went to the door.

"Look! He's in the darkest part of the Plaza, but you can see his white hat." He squeezed the Sergeant's arm angrily. "There's the rifle in the corner of the office! He's getting away! Do you understand me?

That shitty *cholo* is getting away. Shoot him! And you'll drop him like a dog." He spoke slowly, restraining his voice, which made his whole body tremble.

"Don't you understand? He must be killed! I have an order to kill these rebel leaders."

The Sergeant kept on looking out into the square; holding onto the lintel, his legs straddled the doorway as if he were blocking it.

"Calm down, sir! Take it easy!"

Don Pancho appeared, near the corner where the little light shone. There he began to whistle a mestizo *huayno*. When he came to the lamp, his whole body was visible; the light shone more brightly on his straw hat; the shadow of his whole body also appeared on the limed wall; and when he turned the corner, the light from the street lamp seemed to slide along the top of the wall. In the silence of the town, the *huayno* that Don Pancho whistled resounded as if it were filling the air, from one corner to another.

"You've been a coward, Sergeant."

The Subprefect spoke, raising his voice, as Don Pancho was leaving the Plaza.

"I don't kill treacherously like that, sir. Only bandits. Not *machos* like Señor Jiménez. Rest, and clear your head. Good night, Señor Subprefect!"

Clearing the doorway, he walked to the balcony and descended the stairs, at his usual pace.

The sky was not so dark now; the mountains surrounding the town appeared, like shadows; the white stone tower, the church, and the Town Hall were more clearly visible in the Plaza. But the sky seemed deeper, colder. The dogs went on barking from the four *ayllus*. The Subprefect felt as if his body were swelling, as if his chest wanted to grow until it filled the void of the sky and the silence of the town.

"Curse it! I'm getting out of here. These beastly highlanders, this wretched town. Maybe if he had dropped that *cholo* it would have calmed my spirits. But everything's mangy in this country!"

When he entered his office, the two tapers in the candelabra flickered humbly, fluttering in the air, at the other end of the hall. The picture of the President seemed to be trembling beyond that light.

"If you were here! You bastard!"

And the Subprefect strode to the front of the hall.

7. The Highlanders

Two thousand Lucaninos[1] lived in Lima. More than 500 of them were from Puquio, the provincial capital.

The Lucaninos arrived in Lima when eagerness to know the capital suddenly spread through all the provinces like a fever. To go to Lima, to see, if only for a day, the Palace, the shops, the cars hurtling through the streets, the trolleys making the ground tremble, and then to come back again! This was the greatest aspiration of all the Lucaninos from Larkay—which is inland, behind the high mountain ranges, between the great rivers that, from there, finally flow into the jungle—to Alaramante and Saisa—which border on the coastal region.

It was to Lima that the important people drove the hundreds of steers they had fattened in the valley's alfalfa fields; for Lima were the hundredweights of wool the townsmen collected on the punas, with whips and bullets; to Lima went the mule trains that come out of *Papacha* Don Christián's mines. From Lima came the hoops of fancy and ordinary cigarettes that hung from all the counters in the shops; from Lima came the cloth that filled the shopkeepers' cupboards; from Lima came the iron kettles, the sugar, the china pitchers and dishes, the bottles, the colored ribbons, the candy, the dynamite, the matches. . . .

One had to climb Kondorsenk'a[2] to go to Lima, crossing the mountain peak that rose up remotely at the head of the valley, up there where the yellow sun was darkened. And beyond Kondorsenk'a lay

---

1. People from the province of Lucanas in the department of Ayacucho. Lucana is also the name of an ethnic group and is sometimes written Rukana.—Trans.

2. Condor Beak Mountain.—Trans.

the great plain where the *comuneros* who had been "hooked" to work on the coast would die on their way home: Galeras Plain, where the rain fell blackly amid thunder claps, sounding like a flash flood on the mountaintops. And from there one still had to cross some dry hills, where those who had been "hooked" were worn out forever, by the thirst and the steep slope; and beyond that lay the sands, Tullutaka Plain, where the road is lined with crosses marking the bones of the malaria victims. . . .

"Where, wherever can it be?" the *comuneros* and mestizos would say, gazing at Kondorsenk'a Pass, which looked bluish when seen through the valley air.

Only the important people went to Lima frequently: the cattlemen, the merchants, the landholders, the mine owners, the authorities, the Judge, the District Attorney, the Priest. After two or three months they would return with new foreign clothing, bringing India-rubber balls, toy trains, bicycles, and little blue hats for their children, the *uña werak'ochas*.[3]

Sometimes the *"chalos"* went, as servants for the townspeople, and some of the mestizos and *comuneros* surrendered their children to the prominent citizens to take along as gifts for their *compadres*[4] and friends in Lima.

One or two of the *"chalos"* would stay there, with the townspeople's consent, or by running away from them. Others came home. On their return they seemed different; they'd walk briskly down the street, leaning backwards, and would speak nothing but Spanish, with strong Lima accents. And they astounded their friends by telling them they had seen houses that almost touched the sky, streets that were choked with people and cars that sounded louder than thunder in January and February. And that the girls were so pretty they left a person so he couldn't talk or move when they looked the highlanders straight in the eye. Others said, "just like Puquio it had been."

Those who stayed on in Lima earned a reputation with their employers for honesty, but also for being blockheads and hypocrites. They laughed seldom and obeyed on the run, in a flustered, simpleminded fashion. When they were beaten they would say nothing, but on any night they would leave, taking with them their little box of rags and papers. Almost all of them loved to read, and although it was hard for them to learn how, they did it. After a time they would

3. The *werak'ochas'* brood.—Trans.
4. Co-godparents to one another's children.—Trans.

buy themselves a guitar, and, quietly, when all their employers had gone out, they would play and sing the *huaynos* of their home towns, in a corner of their rooms, which were always up on the flat rooftop, or next to the garage. On their first days in the city, when they went out into the street on their Sundays off, they'd walk about almost without knowing where to go; they'd go to the parks, or to the Paseo Colón, and sit on a bench, sometimes hour after hour, watching the people and the cars go by.

"Look! A highlander."

The boys would discover them and toss banana skins at them; they'd snatch off their hats, insulting them. Sometimes they would escape, defending themselves by slapping those who taunted them, and they'd disappear around some corner while the gang of kids shrieked with laughter; at other times they'd get angry and fight until they frightened the kids away, or until some policeman would come and take them off to the station house.

But in those parks, sooner or later they'd encounter their fellow countrymen, or, more likely, another houseboy from Ayacucho, Coracora, or Huancavelica. . . . And they'd strike up a friendship then and there. One of them would invite the other to have a Coke or some ice cream, and they would talk a long time, and afterwards they'd go off for a walk any place. Some Sunday, one of them would invite the other to his room; they'd talk about their towns, about their *cholas*, about the big *fiestas*, about their favorite haunts; they would cheer up rapidly, drinking as much as a shot glass of pisco between the two of them. One would play the guitar and they would sing the most popular *huaynos* softly; later they would even weep, remembering their hometowns and saying that they were "orphans" in that great big town, where they walked out all alone. When they reckoned it was time for their employers to come home, they would say goodbye.

And thus, little by little, in a year or two, almost all of the houseboys from Puquio, from Coracora, from Chalhuanca would finally come to meet one another.

But in the month of January in 192— the news reached Puquio that in Coracora, the capital of Parinacochas, all the people had come together in a town meeting. That the Priest had spoken in Quechua and afterwards in Spanish, and that they had agreed to build a road to the port of Chala, to make it possible to travel to Lima in five days, to show that they were better men than the Puquians. The work would begin in March. Indians, "*chalos*," and townsmen were all in a commotion.

"When Coracora ever beating community of Puquio?" they said.

"*Jajayllas*! Puquios digging out street on big mountain, like it's nothing but lard!"

"Puquio community's in command!"

The members the four *ayllus* were swaggering around; staffbearers and elders spoke out against the Coracoras in the council meetings. In Pichk'achuri, the Chief Staffbearer pointed to the coastal range with his staff and said that if the poor little things from Coracora wanted to start competing with Puquio, the four *ayllus* would slice through the mountains and bring the sea right to the edge of town.

Every Sunday, in the *ayllu* council meetings, the rage against the Coracoras grew. Already, the year before, to frighten the Parinacocha *comuneros*, the Puquios had built the marketplace in two months. And now they wanted a duel?

"All right. Okay!" the *ayllu* bragged.

The last Sunday in April the big *ayllu*, Pichk'achuri, sent its staffbearers to talk to the Vicar. They wanted the Vicar to preach a sermon about the Coracoras, saying that the four *ayllus* wanted to build a road to Nazca, to be able to travel to the *mar k'ocha*[5] in one day, so that the machines from the "foreign land," the trucks, might roar through the streets of Puquio puffing out their little smoke. The Vicar accepted, because he knew his Puquio Indian parishioners well and he realized that if the *comuneros* wished, they'd make the road reach Puquio before the people of Coracora had built half a league of their road to Chala. Without consulting the authorities, the Vicar decided to speak about the *comuneros'* decision from the pulpit. It would be like setting off a bomb in the church!

The towns' citizens had never even dared to think about a highway from Nazca, in spite of the fact that they were the ones who would benefit the most from it. It was impossible. Three hundred kilometers, with the Coastal Range rising up like a barrier between Nazca and Puquio. It was not even to be imagined in a dream!

All of his sermon he gave in Quechua, the Vicar did. The Indians rose to their feet; even the women stood up. In Puquio, the staffbearers of the four *ayllus* are treated better in church than are the townspeople; they hear mass from the high altar railing. When the Vicar said that if the Puquio *comuneros* decided to do so, they could build a tunnel through the inside of the mountains to the sands of the coast, the sixteen staffbearers' joy was unrestrained.

"Of course, *tayta*! Of course!"

---

5. Ocean sea.—Trans.

They shouted from the main altar, raising their staffs; and they say the Pichk'achuris wept.

The authorities and the townspeople were in a commotion; like crazy people they stared at the Priest, at the staffbearers, at the Indian throng who stood listening, in silence, their eyes shining, filling the church and spilling over into the terrace and even out into the Plaza.

The townspeople and the authorities left the church and shouted in the Plaza, cheering Puquio and the four *ayllus*. The Indians remained in the Plaza for a time; they spread out all over the park, until they were pressed against the walls at the edges of it. The shouts of the prominent people could still be heard, but they were lost in the crowd of Indians. The sixteen staffbearers greeted the authorities; still talking, they entered Girón Bolívar; behind them, the Indians from the four communities left the Plaza little by little, with their women and all. When the last Indians had disappeared around the corner, the Plaza seemed deadened; and in the middle of it, yelling, like a little troop of beetles, were all the townspeople; their cheers and empty talk were still echoing in the church portico.

The Indian throng filled Girón Bolívar, the whole length of it, and they kept on walking behind the staffbearers as far as the *ayllu* of Chaupi. There, in the Chaupi square, the sixteen Indian leaders talked it over in a council meeting and decided, once and for all, to build the highway to Nazca.

At the Priest's request, the townsmen donated crowbars, pickaxes, shovels, drills, and sledge hammers, and bought dynamite, blasting powder, and fuses. Each citizen gave fifty to seventy-five gallons of cane liquor and one or two twenty-five pound sacks of coca leaves.

The staffbearers sent delegations to all the Indian communities in the province.

And on the last night of June, from all the ends of the town came the music of *bombos*,[6] of small drums, of flutes and *pinkuyllus*. In a little while tens of rockets rose up into the sky, and dynamite was set off at the entrances to the four *ayllus*.

Like a black troop of soldiers, the Andamarkas went to the head of the crowd; in the midst of the Andamarka staffbearers walked the Chief Staffbearer of Pichk'achuri, carrying a little Peruvian flag tied to a long *lambras*[7] pole. Lined up like conscripts, they entered Girón Bolívar; at the head went the *pinkuyllu* players and the drum band. By the light of the street lamps, practically in darkness, they marched

6. Bass drums.—Trans.
7. Trees with twisted, thorny branches.—Trans.

along solemnly, looking straight ahead. Behind the Andamarkas came the Chipaus, the Aukaras, the Sondondos, the Chakrallas, the Cabanas, the Larkays, the Warkwas. . . . And at the rear the Puquios, with fifteen staffbearers in command.

At the street corners the shovels, picks, and crowbars the majority of the *comuneros* carried over their shoulders glinted in the lamplight. Beneath the tools their *llikllas*,[8] containing provisions, hung from their shoulders.

Suddenly, from Chaupi, the Puquio staffbearers cheered:

"Long live Locanas!"

"Long may it live!"

"Long live highway!"

"Long may it live!"

"Long live Piruvian flag!"

"Long may it live!"

The 10,000 Lucana Indians cheered, from Chaupi to the Plaza. The robins and doves that slept in the pepper trees and in other trees in the neighborhoods were frightened by the Indians' shouting; they flew off in every direction in the darkness. The girls and *mistis* rubbed their eyes to see better; the glass shelves and windows in the shops were covered with dust from the Indians' passage.

Standing on the Town Hall balcony, beneath the gasoline lantern, the authorities and prominent citizens urged one another to hold their heads high before the Indian mob, which looked as if it were going to knock down all the houses on the Plaza if it kept on coming in.

"Stop! Stop! *Sayaychik!*"

From the Plaza, the Andamarkas issued this command. And the whole throng of Indians stopped where they were.

Pichk'achuri's Chief Staffbearer climbed up onto the concrete fountain, in front of the jail door, below the Town Hall. Everyone quieted down; the prominent citizens drew together on the balcony, sticking close to the railing. The lantern shed a dim light on the staffbearer's face, but the little flag, up above, caught the full force of the lantern, and seemed to be illumined before the gentlemen's eyes. The Chief Staffbearer spoke about ten words in Quechua:

"*Taytakuna, werak'ochakuna*: Yonder, all together, is Rukana Endians. We're going to build highway to Nazca for Joly twenty-eight. We're going to laugh at Coracoras. Puquio is in command. Rukana is in command. That's all, *taytakuna.*"

---

8. Rectangular cloths the Indians use for carrying food, babies, and other things.—Trans.

And before the Mayor could speak, the staffbearer jumped to the ground. The Andamarka band began to play the *pinkuyllus* and the *bombos*. And the Indians moved off toward the other corner, on the K'ayau side. Until almost midnight the Indians paraded. And until that time the town worthies could not go down into the Plaza.

The 10,000 *comuneros* were strung out all along the road to Nazca. The Vicar planned the highway's course, figuring out the valleys and skirting the stony ravines that crossed the bridle road. The staffbearers made the way straight as they thought best, when the Priest's way was not good; conferring amongst themselves they improved the route. The townsmen rode by the work places on horseback; as they passed they would shout:

"*Taytakuna*! That's the way!"

But they were observing carefully and with misgivings.

From the bottom of the valley, from the tilled fields and haciendas that lined the banks of the great river, one could see the dust the *comuneros* raised digging up the dirt on the mountains. From the little farms and roads on the high puna, from the crests of the high mountain range, the band of dust could be seen; it went down into the hollows, climbed the slopes, and disappeared into the deep ravines on the mountainsides. And from time to time, from the outskirts of town to the Kondorsenk'a Pass, they would use dynamite to blast away the rocks the road encountered. They worked from dawn until well into the night. And from the passes, from the valleys, from the little farms and villages that are in the mountains, people heard the songs of the Andamarkas, of the Aukaras, of the Chakrallas. . . . At night they played the flute and sang by *ayllus*, 100, 200, 500 at a time, depending on the towns. They lit fires of brushwood and dry grass by the roadside near the places where the tools were kept; they sang holiday, carnival, and *k'adihua* melodies. They drank the cane liquor the *mistis* had contributed, measuring it according to the staffbearer's orders. The little stars shone sadly in the sky; sometimes the clouds would slip all the way across the valley's horizon and playfully cover and uncover the evening stars. The moon would come out late, on the Kondorsenk'a side, and brighten the clouds and the valley. Little by little, as the moon was entering the sky, the *comuneros* would grow quiet; they'd lie down on the ground, by the bonfires, to sleep. When the *ayllus'* song had ended, the song of the *pukupuku* birds could be heard clearly, on all the mountains, and the sound of the river would rise up from the bottom of the valley.

On the twentieth day, the *comuneros* reached the "hills" along the coast. From the summit of Toromuerto they saw Cerroblanco, the *auki*[9] of the hills; they contemplated the Nazca valley. Like a broad, blackish serpent it left the base of the mountains, snaking across the sands, taking turns on the white earth of the coast, where the sun blazed down as if it were scorching the white dust, a thick dust that hid the horizon. There was the fever land! Below, in the thirsty stretch of sand.

From there the Sondondos, the Chakrallas, the Aukaras, the Andamarkas returned, on the brand new high road, improving it as they came and widening the way in the ravines, putting cobblestones in the mudholes. They were as fond of their high road as they were of the peach orchards that grew by the riversides in their home towns, and of the mourning doves that sang in the *lambras* that grew in the dooryards of their houses. The staffbearers from all the other towns remained in Puquio to await the entrance of the truck that was to arrive on the twenty-eighth, with the leaders from the four *ayllus*.

The Puquio staffbearers decided to go to the foot of the coastal mountains. One hundred Indians would carry water to those working on the road. From Nazca to the foothills, the coast-dwellers were working to meet the Puquians.

On July twenty-eighth, the first truck arrived in Puquio. It came in with the *ayllus'* sixteen staffbearers. All of the Indian women were running along behind the truck with the old people and the kids. In the Plaza, Puquio's 200 solid citizens and "*chalos*" cheered to see the sixteen staffbearers standing, gravely and calmly, in the back of the truck. Some of the townspeople could not hold back their tears when they saw the truck coming into Puquio.

"Long live the staffbearers! The masters of Lucanas!" they say Don Pancho cheered then, with hat in hand from the top of the big fountain.

"Long live the *papachas*!"

And his tears fell onto his chest.

All together the townspeople answered him:

"Long may they live!"

The truck went right up to the jail door, by the fountain. From above, Pichk'achuri's Chief Staffbearer spoke to the *mistis*, who surrounded the truck.

"Road's all ready, *taytakuna, werak'ochakuna*! Here's truck. *Ayllu* keeps word. *Comunero* is in command, always!"

And he got down carefully, slowly. First the Vicar and then all of

9. Mountain spirit, demigod.—Author

the most important people shook his hand. The staffbearers from Sondondo, Chakralla, Aukara, and Andamarka joined their ranks.

"We shall go to give thanks to God," said the Vicar. And they all went to the church, with the staffbearers in the lead and the citizens and mestizos following them. As they were about to enter the church, Pichk'achuri's Chief Staffbearer approached the Vicar.

"*Tayta*! You're gonna pray for five *comuneros*, dying on highway," he told him.

At midnight of that same day, the staffbearers from the other towns left Puquio. At the house of Pichk'achuri's head staffbearer they held a farewell party. The Llana harpists played *huaynos* from Sondondo, from Chakralla, from Andamarka, from Larkay. . . . They danced in the yard, by the pepper tree, with the women of the four *ayllus*. Not one *misti* or "*chalo*" came to the farewell party.

As they were singing, Pichk'achuri's Chief Staffbearer looked up at the sky; carefully he calculated the distance between the stars.

"*Taytakuna*! Time!" he said.

The singing ceased; the women put the *kipi*[10] bundles of all the staffbearers out in the yard. And they went out into the street, with the Llanas on ahead. The staffbearers from Chipau and Sondondo began to play their *charangos*, accompanying the Llanas. They went straight out on to the road to the towns. About five streets were filled with women. Just as they were leaving town, the women sang, in a high key, in their shrillest tone, the farewell *harahui*:[11]

Ay, kutimunki,	Ai, you shall return,
ayali ayali,	*ayali*[12] *ayali,*
ñanchallay allinlla,	my little road is just fine,
ayali ayali!	*ayali, ayali!*

In the silence, in the stillness of the sky, the singing made the staffbearers' hearts tremble. The women's high little voices went through the mountains like a needle. To end the song they raised the pitch higher, even higher, until it broke in their throats. And it was worse, even sadder, than if they had wept.

10. Load bundles.—Trans.

11. A short, mournful, commemorative folk song, usually sung by a women's chorus.—Trans.

12. My little dead one.—Trans.

Amas para	No, rain
amas para chayankichu	you shan't fall, rain
ayali ayali!	*ayali ayali!*
Amas rinkichu	You shan't go
amas wayra rinkichu	you shan't go, wind
ayali ayali!	*ayali ayali!*

By the creek, by the Yallpu, the women stayed behind with the harpists. All of the staffbearers began climbing the mountain. From the stream, by the sad light of the stars, the staffbearers were seen slowly moving up the road, as if in a dream. From time to time the women sang.

They were singing until daybreak, along with the town's roosters. As the Indian leaders neared the pass, the women's voices came up to them even more sorrowfully from the edge of town; it was almost as if all of the *ayllu* women had gotten lost in the darkness and were calling. With the dawnlight they fell silent.

On the mountaintop, the staffbearers were chewing their coca leaves at that hour; after each had baptized the ground with his provisions of cane liquor, they offered one another drinks for the last time on that communal work project.

Little by little, the new road showed forth on Sillanayok' mountainside, as well as the town with the *ayllus* of Pichk'achuri, Chaupi, and K'ollana; K'ayau was behind Tok'to Hill, and all of it was not in sight. In the middle, broader and straighter, cutting the town in two, was Girón Bolívar with its tin-roofed houses; and at the end of the *misti* street, large and silent, empty like a clearing in the town, was the Plaza de Armas.

All of the staffbearers stood up and said goodbye. The leaders from the other towns sprinkled a bit of *aguardiente* over the air of the big town, the capital of the Rucanas, and went through the pass.

The Lima newspapers mentioned the Nazca-Puquio highway. One hundred and eighty miles in twenty-eight days! By popular initiative, without government support.

And that's when all the other towns began. In the north, middle, and in the south of the country, even in the jungle, people held large town meetings in the squares; they sent telegrams to the national government and began work on their own. Anyone at all would trace out the highway's course to the coast, figuring out how to cross the mountains and the valleys. Finally, the national government remembered some of the towns, sending engineers, money, and tools. Then the hacienda owners fought amongst themselves to have the roads pass through their farms. And the highways that the engineers planned would almost always curve around and go down into the valleys, breaking through the crags and rocky places for months on end, sometimes for years, so that the road might enter the important people's haciendas. The people in the towns began to lose their confidence in, their enthusiasm for the highways. From then on, road building was a business. And the people from the towns worked as day laborers, or because they were forced to do so. The Lieutenant Governors, the Subprefects, the police—all of the authorities—began to drive the Indians with whips and bullets to make them work on the highways.

Meanwhile, the trucks were coming into Puquio, one after another, on the *ayllus'* road. When they'd enter the town, the schoolchildren and the older kids would follow the truck in a crowd; people would come to the doorways of their houses; in the Plaza citizens and *"chalos"* would gather to ask the drivers about the road.

"It's a road for goats!" they'd say. Nevertheless, they kept on coming in on that same highway.

The trucks suffered on the steep grades of Tambora and Toromuerto; they went up bellowing, water spouting from their radiators; the motors would roar and it seemed that the machines were going to split apart. But they'd conquer the slopes. And when they reached the high, bleak tableland, they'd speed up. Vicuñas and llamas would run to hide in the draws: from afar the puna farmers would stare at them fearfully. 'Neath the rainstorms, while the hail rattled on the mountain peaks and lightning rays flashed by the roadside, the trucks would be traveling across the puna.

The Coracora people abandoned their road to Chala and began to build their highway to Puquio.

"It's all done! Now to really forgive, *perduncha!*" said the *comuneros* from the four *ayllus* of Puquio.

And it was by this same highway that the 2,000 Lucaninos and the people from Coracora got to Lima. At the same time, on all the new roads, highlanders from the north, south, and middle of the country went down to the capital.

The University, schools of every description, ministries, business concerns, factories, and all the companies filled up with highlanders.

Once again, after 600 years, perhaps after 1,000 years, Andean people were going down to the coast in multitudes. While various governments were building four-lane asphalt avenues and having "American" buildings constructed, while the newspapers and magazines were publishing pretty European-style poems, and gentlemen

67

in derby hats and frock-coats were responding to invitations from the national government, embassies, and clubs, the highlanders— Indians, half-*mistis*, and "*chalos*"—were coming down from the uplands with their *charangos*, their *bandurrias*, their *kirkinchos*,[13] and their Indian Spanish. They'd buy or appropriate some land near the city. There they'd remain, living in roofless enclosures, brush arbors, and mud brick houses, without façades or running water. As in the highland towns, they carried their water from a distance, from two or three stone troughs or water taps they would have installed in each neighborhood. And in their houses, in their brush arbors protected with adobe walls, illumined by little kerosene lanterns as in Puquio, Aukará, Chalhuanca, or in Masma and Huancavelica, the highlanders would hold their *fiestas*, with *huayno* and *bandurrias*, with harps and *quenas*. On the big holidays—July twenty-eighth, the Carnivals, and New Year—they would rent the private gardens available in the new districts. They'd hire jazz orchestras, and one or two hundred of them would fill the dance floors in those gardens; like clodhoppers they would dance to jazz, tango, and rumba rhythms. Finally, they would silence the orchestra, and with their harp, guitars, *bandurrias*, and songs the party would catch fire. Out onto the avenues, where luxury automobiles were passing, would go the *huayno*, the voices of the *charangos* and the *quenas*: the song of the highlands, in Quechua or in Spanish, the soul of the valleys, of the puna and of the rivers, of the gorse, the *kiswar*,[14] and the *k'eñwa* woods.

The gentlemen, too, followed the "*chalos*" and the half-*mistis*. They dug their money out of the hills or house foundations where it had been buried, or they took it out of the banks. They selected lots on the avenues and opposite the rich people's palatial homes; alongside of the embassies and residences of the coastal landholders they would build their houses: just like the others had, with garden, garage, and elegant bathrooms. They even bought foreign dogs to exhibit in their gardens.

And Lima grew; in ten, twenty years it spread out onto the large farms roundabout. The plots that had grown onions, lettuce, cotton, and grapes were urbanized into slum neighborhoods that were dark and dirty, full of people, babies, street vendors, and Japanese and Chinese shops, or else into districts that were elegant, quiet, clean, and peaceful, where, at a distance from one another, the big tile-roofed

13. These are all stringed instruments; see glossary.—Trans.
14. *Beauleia incana globosa*—a leafy bush growing in lower areas of the highlands, with leaves like an olive tree's—Trans.

and vine-covered residences, surrounded by wide parks where nobody was to be seen, displayed their European façades—districts with wide, tree-shaded streets.

The *cholos* and the few Lucana Indians who had come down first (the ones the prominent people had brought as gifts for their friends in Lima) welcomed those who came down later by the highway. They took them to the poorer neighborhoods, to Ascona, Chacra Colorada, and La Victoria. They showed them the factories, business firms, and new construction projects, so they could go there and ask for work. And without anyone's organizing it, the entrance of the Puquios, like that of all the highlanders, took place in an orderly way: the *"chalos"* helped the *"chalos,"* first taking them to their houses while they were hunting work; the half-*mistis* helped those of their own class, the *mistis* the *mistis*, showing them the avenues where they should build their houses, presenting them to their friends, connecting them with "society." The students also helped one another in an equally orderly fashion, in accordance with how much money their parents had: the poor ones looked for small rooms near the University or the Engineering School: they made do with servants' rooms on the rooftops, below stairs, or in the ancient seigneurial mansions, which are now about to fall down—those are the houses that rent rooms to workers and poor people.

But it was to the Ascona district that the majority of the poor Puquians went to live, those who were the sons of the half-*mistis*, of the impoverished gentry, of the legitimate *"chalos"* who went to try their luck in the capital. Some students from Puquio and its outlying districts also reached there. It was there, in Ascona, that the "Lucanas Union Center" started. At first it was a sports club; they named it "Lucanas," but the captain of the soccer team was a Lima black. By then, with all of Lima's districts and schools full of highlanders, contempt for the *"chalos"* had died down amongst the common people. The invasion of people who had come down from all the Andean provinces was gradually imposing respect for the highlanders. The Lima black, captain of the Lucanas team, was proud and happy to present himself on the soccer field at the head of his *cholo* and half-*misti* players. And the Lucanas Club had won the neighborhood championship many times.

When the Lucanas Club fans wanted to convert their club into a Cultural Sports Center, to be the organization for all the sons of the province residing in Lima, there were already more than 200 provincial organizations of people from the highlands in the capital. The Center held its last session in the place where they had always met, the room of Gutiérrez the tailor, with Escobar the student presiding.

As in Puquio, two penny candles lighted the room from a little cow-hide shelf. That night more than forty members attended, and they barely fit into the premises.

"Fellow countrymen," said the President. "The sons of Chal-huanca, like those from Caraz, those from Jauja, those from Huama-chuco . . . already have their Cultural Sports Centers. There are hundreds of Andean provincial organizations in Lima. These centers look after the interests of their own provinces; they defend their communities from abuses by landowners, authorities, and priests. And they are raising the cultural level of their members by organizing public lectures, evening receptions, libraries, and even by publishing magazines. These centers also keep the memory of our own part of the country alive; they have their typical orchestras, and hold their festivals in their hometown ways. There are now more than 2,000 of us Lucaninos in Lima, and we're all asleep. Meanwhile, the big landholders and the petty politicians keep on exploiting the *comuneros*, just as they did 200 years ago, by putting them in the stocks and by flogging them. We who have already had our eyes opened and our consciousness freed should not let them get away with skinning our brothers alive. I put the organization of a Lucanas Union Center to a vote!"

Way out in the street, the applause with which the Lucaninos approved the Center's creation was heard. After the President, about ten more people spoke. Rodríguez the bus driver, and ex-*comunero* from Chakralla, began talking in Spanish, but as he was unable to continue, he went on in Quechua:

"Brothers! We Indians know how to protect ourselves from the wind, from the rain, from the lightning ray, from the storms that sometimes arise on the earth; but the littlest snot-nosed brat from a prominent family can spit in our faces. Just last year Don Jovenal Arenas fenced in the spring that supplies the town with drinking water. How long will these abuses go on? Who does the water belong to? Every year, in December, the Priest, with the whole town in procession, used to bless that Chakralla water. And, 'It's mine' saying, the landowning exploiter has fenced it in. It shall not be! That's what the Chakralla people are here in Lima for. That's the way it is. We will be the respect."

Ten days after this session, the Lucanas Union Center held its first public meeting, with 200 members. Escobar the student was elected President; Tincopa the student, Secretary; Martínez the chauffeur, Comptroller; and Gutiérrez the tailor, Treasurer. Rodríguez the bus driver, Vargas and Córdova, laborers, as well as the clerical workers

Guzmán, Valle, Altamirano, and Gallegos were elected to be members of the governing board.

Some of the Lima newspapers, in their Education sections, printed the news that the sons of the province of Lucanas residing in Lima had organized a Cultural Sports Center.

The prominent citizens of Puquio who had taken up residence in Lima read the news items, with their lists of officers, contemptuously.

"Even here those *cholos* have to make a noise."

"That Escobarcha! Pretty soon he'll be thinking about running for Congress!"

"And that Indian Martínez! What a disgrace!"

"They're a bunch of starvelings who've come down here to make us feel sorry for them."

And while the leading citizens and their families were insulting the Center, the other townspeople who read the news went to sign up and pay their membership fees: butlers, house servants, carpenters, bus drivers, gardeners, chauffeurs, laborers, and even some white-collar workers and students from other provincial clubs.

At the beginning of July, 193—, the day after the *mistis* had held their big council meeting to discuss the Minister of the Interior's edict, the President of the Lucanas Union Center received a telegram from the Mayor of Puquio.

"Request you hire professional bullfighter for twenty-eighth bullfight at expense of this council stop Details letter stop."

At the same time the Minister of the Interior received the telegram from the town notables thanking him for suppressing bullbaiting throughout the Republic.

Escobar the student could not understand how Puquio's leading citizens could do without the Indian bullfight. All year long they awaited the twenty-eighth of July, to go up onto the Cabreras' balconies with bated breath to watch K'encho and Honrao Rojas dragging in the drunken Indians against the wild bulls from the great puna. Don Antenor, Don Lucio, Don Pancho, Don Jesús, Don Julián . . . they'd grown up having the right to do that. How could they be requesting a professional bullfighter now?

The Ministry?

In the Ministry of the Interior, he was informed that fights without trained bullfighters had been prohibited, because in all of the highland towns the twenty-eighth of July bullfights were real massacres of Indians. They told him that the distinguished citizens of Puquio had sent a telegram expressing their congratulations and gratitude for the prohibitory decree.

Escobar the student was then completely certain.

"The Center will support the Minister of the Interior's edict. The Center will go to Puquio! Never again shall the Indians die in the Pichk'achuri square to give those pigs pleasure! This telegram from the Mayor is nothing but boot-licking. But this time they're in trouble: we've got the Ministry on our side. It had to happen some day!"

He called a meeting of the Lucanas Center's governing board for that night in his room on Loreto Street, across from the district market's garbage dump.

Tincopa the student, Martínez the chauffeur, Guzmán the clerical worker, Rodríguez the bus driver, and Vargas and Córdova, laborers, attended. Three of them sat on the student's little wooden cot, and the rest on boxes. A photograph of Mariátegui,[15] nailed to the wall at the head of the bed, dominated the room. From a peg beneath the portrait hung a guitar, with a rosette of ribbons in the Peruvian national colors adorning its pegs.

Escobar gave a detailed report of the steps he had taken and of the news he had been able to gather on the prohibition of bullfights without trained fighters.

"They're in trouble!" said Martínez. "There's no way out, now. And these imbeciles have given us the job of hiring the bullfighter. We'll all go in my *carcocha*,[16] including the bullfighter."

"It'll be a triumph for the Center!" exclaimed "Bishop" Guzmán, who jumped up and landed in the middle of the room. His rotund body was interposed between the men sitting on the bed and the others.

"But leave us some room, Monsignor. We have to see each others' faces to talk."

Guzmán drew back beneath Mariátegui's portrait. The light from the electric bulb shone full on his face. His enormous stoutness had almost made his smallpox scars disappear; a short growth of unshaven beard shadowed his face, and Guzmán, "the Bishop," looked like a Morochuco bandit.

"This time we'll make ourselves respected! They've put the knife in our hands themselves. It's a miracle, comrades. I'm going to make trouble. Even if I have to dress up like a civil guard and take up a rifle

---

15. A prominent Peruvian writer on social and literary matters in the early twentieth century.—Trans.

16. Jalopy.—Trans.

against some old landowning exploiter. At this moment we are the forces of order."

"You said it, Monsignor! I'm going to let my beard grow and I'll look like an Antichrist."

"What do you mean, Monsignor?"

They resolved to talk to the Minister of the Interior, hire the bull-fighter, and all travel to Puquio.

When the meeting was over, Escobar arose from his seat and, turning to Mariátegui's portrait, began to speak directly to him, as if the picture were one more member of the Lucanas Union Center.

"You'd like what we're going to do, *werak'ocha*. You haven't just spoken to us for the pleasure of it—we're going to put into practice what you have preached. Don't worry, *tayta*: we're not going to die before seeing the justice you have called for. Here's Rodríguez, a *comunero* from Chakralla; here we *cholos* are—Córdova, Vargas, Martínez, Escobarcha; we're in Lima; we've come to find out where the exploitative landowners' support comes from; we've come to test their strength. On the road the *ayllus* built we have come. If only you could have seen that community work project, *tayta*! Your legs and your blood might have gotten the better of you. If you could have known Puquio! But our Bishop is going to play you a Lucana *huayno* and we're going to sing for you, like swearing an oath. Ready, Monsignor!"

The Bishop took down the guitar; the seven of them gathered beneath the portrait, and sang in Quechua:

Tullutakapis[17]	On Tullutaka Plain
inti rupachkan	the sun is blazing.
Tullutakapis	On Tullutaka Plain
runa wañuchkan	people are dying.
Ama wak'aychu hermano,	Don't you weep, brother,
ama llakiychu!	don't you mourn!
Galeras pampapis	On Galeras Plain
chikchi chayachkan,	the sleet is falling.
Galeras pampapis	On Galeras Plain
runa saykuchkan,	people grow weary.
Ama wak'aychu hermano,	Don't you weep, brother,
ama llakiychu!	don't you mourn!

17. Tullutakapis means "Place Where Bones Rattle" in Quechua.—Trans.

Llapa runas	All the people,
mancharillachkan,	are frightened, they say,
wañu wañuy	for dying, death
chayaykamuptin,	is on its way.
Ama wak'aychu hermano,	Don't you weep, brother,
ama llakiychu!	don't you mourn!

And while the mestizos were singing in Lima, in the community of K'ayau the staffbearers were encouraging the Indians to go up onto the puna to get Misitu. On all the streets in the neighborhood the leaders were talking, threatening the Pichk'achuris, threatening Misitu, having forebodings about and preparing for the *yawar fiesta*.

"K'ayau'll be first! How many'll be left widow on twenty-eighth!"

8. Misitu

Misitu lived in the *k'eñwa* woods, high up on the great K'oñani punas. The K'oñanis said that he had come out of Torkok'ocha,[1] that he had neither father nor mother. That one night, when all of the old people on the puna were still babies, a storm had fallen upon the lake; that all of the lightning rays had struck the water, that even from a distance the lightning was running, flashing in the air, and striking the islands in Torkok'ocha; that the lake water had boiled up so high it had made the islands vanish, and that the sound of the rain had come up to all the little farms of K'oñani. And that at daybreak, with the dawn light, when the storm was dying down, when the clouds were leaving the sky over Torkok'ocha and were turning white in the early morning light, at that time, they say, a whirlpool formed in the middle of the lake by the big island, and in the middle of the whirlpool Misitu appeared, bellowing and tossing his head. That all of the ducks flew away from the islands in a flock, their wings whirring, and went far away, beyond the snow-clad mountains. Moving all the water, Misitu swam to shore. And when the sun came out, they said, he was running across the puna, seeking out the *k'eñwales* along the Negromayo River, which he made his favorite haunts.

All of the puna-dwellers told this story, from Puquio to Larkay, from Larkay to Querobamba, all over the province of Lucanas. And as far as Pampa Cangallo, to Coracora, to Andahuaylas, as far as Chalhuanca, Misitu's fame spread.

The K'oñanis said he gored his own shadow, that he broke down the *k'eñwales*, that he plowed the earth with his horns, and that the

1. Muddy Lake.—Trans.

Negromayo ran muddy whenever Misitu came down to drink water. That by day he grew furious looking at the sun, and by night he'd run leagues and leagues chasing the moon; that he'd scale the highest peaks, and that they'd found his trail on the slopes of K'arwarasu, in the place where he'd been seen pawing the snow all night to reach the summit.

Who, then, would ever dare to enter the *k'eñwales* along the Negromayo? The *comuneros* crossed themselves whenever they went near them, and they stopped from time to time to hear whether Misitu were bellowing.

The K'oñani *comuneros* would frighten travelers who were crossing the farms.

"You gonna watch out, *tayta*. Misitu like a tiger is. Quiet you'll walk."

And when Don Julián Arangüera sent his men to get Misitu, the *punarunas* gathered to talk to the foremen.

"Master *taytallaya*! You gonna die!" they told them. "Not going in boss. You're sure to stay in there. Little dog'll eat your guts."

But some "*chalos*" screwed up their courage, readied their horses, and emptied half a bottle of cane liquor apiece; they hurriedly mounted their horses and ran off down the road to the *k'eñwales*. Then the puna people all trooped out onto the road; they played the *wakawak'ras*, small drums, and flutes loudly; the women wept as they sang the *ayataki*,[2] as if the men who had been sent were going to their death, as if they had gone crazy and were running blindly to hurl themselves into the gorge.

"*Ay taytallaya*! *Ay taytallaya*!"

Out in the open, on the great puna, the singing and the voices of the *wakawak'ras* carried a long way. And as they were going down into the Negromayo Canyon the hirelings began to despair; they suddenly turned around, spurred their horses savagely and went galloping back.

"A curse!" they exclaimed. "Beastly Indians! That music—the heart can't take it! This shitty valley, these *k'eñwales* must be under a curse!" And they retraced their steps, swearing; they gulped down the cane liquor.

Just as they were about to go back down to the town, they thought better of it.

"What'll we tell Don Julián now? That we're a bunch of queers? That the women's singing scared us so much we pissed?"

2. Song of the dead.—Trans.

"It's a problem, brother! But that canyon where the bull lives is scary. I don't know why, but he bellows and a man loses his courage."

"Yeah, man, that's the honest truth. I think Don Julián would get scared too."

But Don Julián decided to head the cavalcade.

"You're like women, *wak'ates*.[3] You cry over the stories the Indians make up to scare little kids. It's nothing but nonsense. Now with me you'll see how it is! And if the little bull doesn't want to come out of the woods, I'll sink a bullet into his body. This year the people in Lima will dine on steak from Misitu's flesh."

Twelve horsemen rode up to K'oñani. Don Julián was on his black and white pinto, the bravest horse in the valley.

When the K'oñani Indians saw Don Julián approaching, with twelve horsemen coming on behind, they had a premonition that he'd come for Misitu. This time it would happen! They just might drive him in! Don Julián was determined; he was angrier than all the "*chalos*" and overseers who rode herd on the little farms. His hands and the Puquio *comuneros* used to say that he wasn't even scared of Taytacha up in heaven; that he had even scolded the Priest in a loud voice; and that once, on a holiday, when he was drunk, he had heard mass on horseback, from the main church doorway.

The K'oñanis sent out a herdsman. And as Don Julián was coming onto his ranch, the herdsman left for the Negromayo with his *wakawak'ra* and with his provisions of coca leaves and cane liquor.

It was almost nightfall when Don Julián reached K'oñani, and he decided to get up early in the morning to go after Misitu. But that night, from the time it was really dark until close to daybreak, a mournful cry was heard, which seemed to be coming down out of the center of the sky. It was not clearly audible; one could not make any sense out of it. But it was a strange song, sometimes like a man's, deep and slow, sometimes on a much higher pitch and sadder, like an infant's. The twelve peons had slept on the ranch house porch. And as they listened in silence, one of Don Julián's herdsmen came dragging in.

"*Taytakuna*," he addressed them. "Are you hearing? Misitu's soul's walking the mountains. It's crying for the blood of the hirelings he's gonna kill. Well, who'll it be, *tayta*? How many'll it be?"

And he went running off, as if the fear of dying had gotten into him.

Don Julián could not hear anything from his room, as he was

3. Weeping women.—Trans.

tightly shut up in there, and he fell asleep quickly. But the overseers were quietly deliberating. Every hour, as if marking the time, the cry came down.

It was the herdsman who had gone up to forewarn Misitu. Seated on a rock, he was singing loudly, almost without speaking.

"*Aaaai! Waaai! Ripuuy!*"[4]

He'd move a long way, to the other end of the grassland; from there he'd sing in another key. And he'd purposefully play the *wakawak'ra* in a deep quavering tone, for a long time; without variations he'd hold a single note as loudly as his strength permitted. On the wild puna the wind carried the *wakawak'ra*'s voice across summit after summit, amplifying it or muting it, according to the range and strength of the wind.

At daybreak, when Don Julián opened the door of the stone house, the twelve overseers were sleeping.

"Okay, okay, goddamnit! Get up, you slugs! These sloths sleep like hogs! Let's go, let's go get the horses!"

They started up fearfully and ran to get the beasts. The K'oñanis had already gathered in the corral.[5] Don Julián harangued them in Quechua.

"Goddamnit, Indians! With me there's no screwin' around. Right here you're gonna wait till I bring Misitu in all tied up. And none of those *wakawak'ras*, or *tinya* drums or whimpering. I'm not any queer little '*chalo*' overseer. I'm the boss, damnit; and you don't scare me with your crappy little tunes! Like cattle, damnit, you're gonna wait here till I come back! And the first one who leaves, I'll split his skull open. Like this, damnit."

He pulled out his revolver and hammered a shot into the wall of the corral. The bullet lit up the yard and struck sparks from the stones in the wall.

"Right here, and no farther, guanacos!"

He mounted his pinto horse and, followed by his foremen, dwindled away on the plain; meanwhile, the sky was brightening with the early morning light.

He went galloping down into the bottom of the Negromayo Canyon. The *k'eñwa* trees grew blacker along the river banks; the tall evergreen *waylla* grass reached up into the *k'eñwa* branches; the horses jumped over the *waylla* plants and went along rapidly, nearing the river.

4. Go away!—Trans.
5. A big, bare yard in back of the ranch house, enclosed with a stone wall.—Trans.

The black-and-white horse went splashing through the water and crossed the river with leaps and bounds; he ran through the *k'eñwales*, appearing and disappearing behind each tree. In a clearing in the woods, Don Julián stopped his horse; he put two fingers of his left hand into his mouth and whistled loudly. His overseers surrounded him. The whistle reechoed from the crags and mountains for a long while. The *"chalos"* kept quiet and watched the boss. The wind was shaking the branches of the *k'eñwales* and making the tall *waylla* plants bow down; it was whistling frightfully through the woods and ruffling the dry grass on the mountainsides.

"Let's wait a while. If he's as wild as they say he'll come here: either we'll throw a lasso over him or I'll sink a bullet into him."

They were listening for a good while. Whenever the *k'eñwal* moved, or some little bird came flying out of the woods or made a sound, the twelve *"chalos"* would rein their horses in as if to be ready to run away.

From afar, as if from the head of the canyon, a deep-toned song came to them through the woods, lasted a while and, little by little, faded away, as if it were withdrawing into the midst of the *k'eñwa* boughs. The *"chalos"* did not want to look at one another, and waited.

"Don Jolián, maybe the bull's gone off to another *k'eñwa* thicket; through all these grassy places he walks at night," said Fermín.

"What a bunch of sissies you are! The Indian in you guys comes out ten times a day. At bottom you're pure Indian, and your blood turns to water every time you have to put your bodies in danger. Where is Misitu? Not a soul has entered this little canyon in years, for fear of that bull. . . ."

As he was speaking, the bushes near the river swayed; the water splashed; and as if someone were pulling on the tops of the *k'eñwales*, the tree branches were heard to break. From above, the herdsman shouted like a devil:

"Get going, Christians! Run!"

Misitu's head appeared; the bull stared out at the horsemen, and bounded into the clearing in the woods. The twelve *"chalos"* dug in their spurs, flapped their reins, and took off up the slope like madmen. Don Julián pulled his horse up short.

"You shits! You'll soon see, you *k'anras!*" he shouted.

He got his lasso ready and moved his horse aside, to wait in a good place. Misitu ran straight for him, lashing his tail, with his head held high and his broad hump rising higher than his horns. The pinto stood there trembling, wiggling his ears, pawing the ground with his hind hooves.

Just as Misitu was upon him and about to thrust a horn into the horse's chest, Don Julián threw the lasso and made the pinto jump. On the run, he tied the lasso to his saddlehorn and dug his spurs in furiously. The lasso held for a moment, and then slipped free.

"I'm more than an idiot. Hell!"

He was about to turn around again to face Misitu, but he saw his men already reaching the crest; he drew out his revolver and fired at the mass, at the *"chalos."* Driving his spurs in deeper, he leapt across the river and came out of the brush as if he were going over the air. He looked back to see Misitu right behind him, in hot pursuit. His hump seemed to heave; the bull looked as tall as a church because he soared through the air, leaping over the *waylla* plants.

"He's my bull, goddamnit! He's mine!"

And it made him proud. He had intended to kill him, but he went on shooting at the sky, from joy as much as from anger.

And he began to coil up the lasso.

"Those *k'anra* overseers. I'm going to kill them, instead!"

Misitu stopped almost at the rim of the canyon, and looked out over the plain, across which the pinto was still running; he stood still a while, as if he were getting set to turn around. And breathlessly, foaming at the mouth, he went trotting back to his haunts.

Don Julián pursued the *"chalos"* over the plain.

"Stop, damnit! Stop, *k'anras!*"

He was yelling, with revolver in hand.

When he neared the ranch the head overseer, Fermín, pulled his horse up short, but the others kept right on, turning onto the road to Puquio.

Once he was quite close to it, with his last bullet, Don Julián felled Fermín's horse.

"I'm not killing you, *k'anra*, because I'm a Christian," he told the man.

But it was because that was no longer so easy to do in those days.

"Excuse me, *papay!* You can't get anywhere with the devil. Instead I've prayed to God for you, Don Jolián. Lord, he might have killed you! That's enough rage, now. Poor little horse! My poor little thing! Little horse!"

He left him whimpering beside the dead horse. And he went on to the ranch. He let his Indians go and then had the pinto rest for a while. And afterwards he set off at a walk on the road to Puquio.

Night was falling as he rode into town.

In the pool hall, to the silence of the other important people, he recounted what had happened to him with Misitu.

"To tell the truth, I think I threw the lasso with my eyes shut. The bull can't be that big, but when he runs he looks like a temple. What a smashing bull!"

And he got as drunk as if it were a holiday.

"Misitu! No man's as brave as Misitu! Even the stones tremble before him. He's my bull."

He was shouting, sticking out his chest, as if he were defying him.

But Misitu was not from K'oñani; he was not, therefore, from Don Julián's herd. He had come to the K'oñani punas when he was already a grown bull, escaping from another ranch—who knows whether it was from Wanakupampa, Oskonta, or farther away? He suddenly appeared in the *k'eñwales* along the Negromayo River. And from that time on the *punarunas* would not go near the little Negromayo Canyon on the K'oñani side. Misitu would not let any animal into his favorite haunts.

And all the while, year after year, in the woodsy solitude, he kept getting wilder. Sometimes he would come out, in October and November, looking for better grazing; he'd go all along the Negromayo, and in the evening he'd seek out the *k'eñwales*.

The puna people carried his fame to all the towns. And even far away in the interior towns, around Sondondo, Chakralla, Andamarka, they spoke of Misitu as if he were an *auki*, a demigod. The K'oñanis feared him. They convinced all the *comuneros* in the uplands that he had come out of Torkok'ocha, that at night his tongue blazed like fire; only a few of the herdsmen would go near the edge of the canyon to see him.

But when Don Julián came up to the ranch to drive Misitu to Puquio, the K'oñanis despaired. They sent Kokchi the herdsman to warn Misitu, because they said Kokchi was a *layk'a*[6] and could make the animals understand him. And early in the morning, while the boss was still sleeping, they gathered to beg him to sell Misitu to the K'oñanis. But Don Julián had waked up angry and harangued the *comuneros* in the ranch house corral; he had fired his revolver to silence them. And the K'oñanis lost their courage.

When he set out to hunt for Misitu with his twelve "*chalos,*" the K'oñanis sat down on the ground. The old men looked up at the sky to figure out what time it was. They all hid their anxiety and glanced at one another from time to time. They wanted to go out and run across the plain to stop the *misti*, to all jump down into the canyon together. Because they knew that Don Julián would just go ahead

6. Sorcerer.—Author

81

and shoot his bullet. And he was sure to fell Misitu. But they did not move. They all opened their little woven bags of coca leaves and calmly chewed away.

When they heard the shot Don Julián had fired at Fermín's horse, they all jumped up. They heard the pinto gallop across the plain. Bathed in sweat, trembling with fury, the pinto entered the yard.

Don Julián's eyes were still gleaming with rage, but he sat tall in the saddle, with his head erect, just as he did when he pulled the pinto up short at the corner of the Plaza in Puquio, to look down upon the other *mistis* scornfully from on high.

"Misitu had words with boss. Up yonder he's gonna stay, on Negromayo. K'oñanis gonna take care of him, always," he said.

"Thanks, *werak'ocha!*"

"Thanks, *papituy!*"

The old men went up to the pinto and kissed Don Julián's stirrup.

Don Julián carefully got down from his piebald horse; he hung up the reins and sat down for a while on the stone bench in front of the ranch house. The K'oñanis were not brave enough to speak loudly; they looked at one another happily, all of them by the wall, praying the boss would get on his pinto and leave the ranch.

Don Julián tightened the horse's cinch himself, mounted suddenly, and turned the pinto around.

"So long, *taytakuna!*"

"*Allinlla werak'ocha!*" [7]

The pinto left the yard, his feet striking the ground just as they did when he ran along the *mistis'* street. Behind the horse, the K'oñanis entered the passageway, as Don Julián was crossing the field of tall grass. They watched him leave, all of them, without moving. When he descended into the ravine, on the way to Puquio, they ran like madmen to catch up with Fermín.

Kokchi came into the ranch yard to find the K'oñanis hugging one another, already drunk, weeping on the ground. By that time they no longer knew how to play the *pinkuyllo* nor raise the *wakawak'ras*. Now and again they would speak in hoarse, choked tones.

"Misitu, damnit! Brave men! There aren't any, damnit!"

"Don Julián's a dawg, damnit! To die, damnit, for Misitu."

"Ai Misitu, my Misitu. *Jatun*[8] master!"

Fermín was stretched out in the middle of the yard; on his hands he still had the horse's blood. Meanwhile, the ranch dogs were in a frenzy to devour the overseer's horse; the biggest ones had already

---

7. "Just fine, sir."—Trans.
8. Great, big.—Trans.

started in and were licking the blood from the wound.

The snow on the mountain peaks was sparkling in the sun; the noonday light shone down on the lakes, on the smooth stones in the rocky places, on the flowers and on the thorns of the *sok'ompuros* that grow amid the fields of tall grass.

The K'oñanis laughed when they got the news that the boss had presented Misitu to the *ayllu* of K'ayau. They had always used Misitu to frighten the Indians from Puquio; the members of the four *ayllus* spent their time crossing themselves whenever they came close to the Negromayo. You think they'd go into the *k'eñwales* now? Who'd go in?

"*Jajayllas!* Go right on in!"

Not even Don Julián had been able to do it; the pinto horse, too, had been terrified to face Misitu; when he got back to the ranch his legs were still trembling. How could K'ayau community want to do it? The K'oñanis felt sorry for the *comuneros*. And when the K'oñanis who went down to town came back frightened, the others laughed.

"*Atatau!* Not fooling us!" they'd say.

But those who went down to Puquio were more doubtful. They'd enter K'ayau *ayllu* and hear the *comuneros* talking, even the women and the children. In the tilled fields, on the road, on the street, inside of the houses, the K'ayaus would be threatening Misitu. As night fell they would play the *wakawak'ras* furiously. And hearing them frightened the K'oñanis.

They went down to the town, group after group of them. And finally, one moonlit night, they all met in the corral behind Don Julián's ranch house. From there they set out with good provisions of coca leaves and cane liquor. Following Kokchi, on that frosty night, they walked hour after hour until they reached the foot of *tayta* Ak'chi.[9] The vicuñas were also crying out with cold, from their fields, hidden in the hollows in the stony ground. *Tayta* Ak'chi's snowy peak shone, augmenting the light of the moon, but the black rock of the snowless slopes, in the great silence, was awesome; and the K'oñanis went straight into the shadow of the *auki*, the guardian father of the K'oñani farms.

An icy wind was blowing down off the summit. Up there at the foot of the Ak'chi Mountain there is nothing; no *ischu*, nor herbs; not even the mournful *pukupuku*[10] bird goes there. Not even the

9. Ak'chi Mountain is the guardian spirit of the K'oñanis. The *ak'chi* is a hawklike bird of prey.—Trans.

10. Small nocturnal songbird.—Author

vicuña climbs that high; he stays down below in the fields of tall grass, looking up at the rocks. The human voice sounds differently at the foot of the Ak'chi; when people speak, their voices grow louder in the crags; they seem to strike the rock as if it were tempered steel.

"Now, *tayta*! Here's your little children!"

The voice of Kokchi the sorcerer went on for a long while, as if it were going up over the crags to reach the summit.

He put down his provisions, heaped up some dry grass on the ground, and lit it with a match. The *ischu* caught, flaring up. The K'oñanis gathered round the fire; the blaze did not let them see very far. Kokchi scraped a hole in the ground with his knife and prepared the offering: on a sheet of red paper, he mixed long-grained wheat from the valley, white corn from Utek' plain, many-hued ribbons, gold paper and silver paper, and a nice new real coin, and on the mixture he stood a little earthenware bull with a wide neck and its horns almost coming together.

"*K'oñanikuna!*" he said.

The *punarunas* gathered around the sorcerer. Kneeling, raising his hands, Kokchi prayed to the *auki* in Quechua:

"*Taytay, jatun Auki, taytay Ak'chi*:[11] Your little children, here they are, together, every one of them, on your side, where you start up from the earth. They're crying for you, *jatun tayta*, with weeping they're asking you to look after Misitu, to leave him in peace, in his *k'eñwal* on the Negromayo. K'ayau, they say, is raging in the valley; gonna come, they say, to take your Misitu away from your domain, from your puna. You're not gonna want it, *tayta*. From your summit you're watching Torkok'ocha, your lake; from there comes Misitu, from inside of it; from its water your animal has awakened. Here's your K'oñanis, come in the night, walking a long way in the frost, in the cold, in the wind, to let you know: 'K'ayau's raging for Misitu,' saying! You're not gonna let them take him, *auki!*"

He buried his offering in the hole, tossing dirt on it with his hands. And they turned back, walking rapidly. Now the dawn was coming, and the frost growing. From time to time they'd drink cane liquor. Their consciences were clear. *Tayta* Ak'chi was the greatest *auki* on all those barren uplands. Who was greater in Puquio? *Tayta* Pedrork'o, Sillanayok', even Chitulla[12] were like the sons of *Tayta* Ak'chi. They were like babies to the *auki* of the K'oñanis. They'd never drag Misitu away!

11. "Our Lord, great Prince, our Lord Ak'chi."—Trans.
12. These are all high mountains.—Trans.

"*Jajayllas!*" the K'oñanis shouted loudly, and drank their cane liquor.

But K'ayau's Chief Staffbearer was thinking of asking K'arwarasu, father of all the lands of Lucanas, to protect the K'ayaus. He himself would go out that week, bearing an offering for the great mountain spirit.

Meanwhile, Misitu was calmly grazing along the Negromayo, keeping watch over his favorite haunts, sleeping in the woods, in the shade of the *k'eñwales* that sheltered him from the frosts.

9. The Day Before

The town notables presented the Subprefect with a purebred horse, "to ride whenever you go out to inspect the districts, and as a token of the affection of your Puquian friends," as the letter drafted by Don Demetrio stated. The Subprefect accepted the gift because, by his best reckoning, the horse was worth at least 500 soles.

The next day, the Subprefect received a petition signed by forty citizens requesting that the Minister of the Interior's edict not be posted on the street corners. "The Indian mob, Señor Subprefect, is liable to run riot if they find out they positively will not be allowed to hold the bullfight in the customary way. For among the citizenry there are people who are scheming to prevent the edict's enforcement, so that K'ayau can hold its duel with Pichk'achuri. We, the most responsible and prominent large taxpayers, on the other hand, will hold ourselves personally accountable for seeing that the supreme mandate is complied with. And, to that end, we enclose a copy of the telegram from the honorable President of the Lucanas Union Center, in which telegram he congratulates us for the order said Center was given to hire a professional bullfighter, and promises us that it will be carried out immediately."

The Subprefect granted their request and immediately sent for Don Demetrio Cáceres, Mayor Antenor, Don Jesús Gutiérrez, and Don Julián Arangüena.

He received them sternly, as if he were displeased. No sooner had he shaken their hands than he asked them to be seated. When everyone was there he had his office door closed and sat down in his big chair, with a gesture of annoyance. The leading citizens looked at him mistrustfully; only Don Julián put his hands on his knees and calmly gave the Subprefect a quizzical look.

"Gentlemen: I have granted your request. But I want to know how you can guarantee that edict will be complied with, and who are the people who are disobeying the national government's order. And I also want to know now what Señor Arangüena hoped to gain by donating his bull to the *ayllu* of K'ayau. . . ."

Don Julián stirred as if he were about to speak.

"Wait a minute! I'm first!" the Subprefect said, in a louder tone. "I want all of you to know, in the first place, that the edict will be respected, above all else, no matter what the cost. And that it doesn't frighten me that some savages may be scheming and inciting the Indian mob to disobey the Supreme Government's edict! For those people I have the jail, and even the lash."

He suddenly fell silent. And he looked at Don Julián, glaring at him to let the others know to whom the threat applied.

"That *cholo* Jiménez—I've already fixed him. He's slept on the horse manure, and after that he knows very well what's waiting for him if he lifts a finger against the authorities."

As he was speaking, he did not take his eyes off Don Julián, but the *misti* remained calm, moving his leg and glancing first at the Subprefect and then at the ceiling or the other *mistis*.

"I know which ones are laughing at the orders the authorities hand down. And I know what I'm going to do to make those wretches repent. Don Julián Arangüena, you may speak!"

Don Julián arose. Don Julián had a big, jet black birthmark by his right eye; when he was furious, that birthmark and his curly, golden-brown eyebrows gave him the look of a wild beast. That's why the Puquians thought Don Julián was conjuring up the devil whenever he scolded them loudly and that the devil would enter his body through the black birthmark on his face. Don Julián stood up; and even though they were enjoying the Subprefect's insults, the other *mistis* were frightened.

"Your Honor . . ."

His voice would come out deep and strong like that when he used to mount his horse and ride into the arena at Pichk'achuri, yelling to taunt the bulls that made the other townsmen tremble. Don Antenor and Don Demetrio remembered that very well . . . even though by that time it had been several years since the leading citizens had fought the bulls from horseback with lances.

"Your Honor . . . since you're new here you don't really know Don Julián Arangüena. You know Don Antenor better, because he's a bit of a windbag, and Don Demetrio, because he's been squandering his inheritance treating people to drinks and cleaning out all the expensive liquor in the pool hall. Don't take offense, sir, I know my duty!

I'm going to talk fast. I don't mind if the Ministry orders the Indians not to take it upon themselves to fight the bulls with their ponchos. The President we have now must be good-hearted. But it's ugly for the townsmen to be sending little telegrams with lies in them. Now Don Antenor, here, he always buys two or three kegs of rotgut rum to get the Pichk'achuris drunk and make them go into the ring so the bulls can do their slaughtering. And when he's in the presence of an official, he washes his hands like a saint!"

"I protest!" Don Antenor stood up, raising his arms.

"Just take it easy, Don Ante. We're all friends here."

"But mind your tongue! Or it'll go badly for you!" said the Subprefect, stepping out into the middle of the office and stopping before Don Julián. The latter kept right on talking.

"That's how our Mayor is, sir. What I'm really doing is helping you to know who your friends are. Now, I'm going to tell you about Misitu. I've presented him to K'ayau for reasons that Mayor Antenor knows better than I. Because Misitu—no one can get him out of K'oñani. Not even I can do it, sir! As for having a laugh—just thinking that in Puquio there's going to be a bullfight with a Lima bullfighter makes me laugh. Is the toreador coming from Lima just so Don Antenor and his little kids can watch him? As you must have noticed, I didn't sign that petition. I don't get involved in womanish matters, sir. Now tell me, Your Honor, is there any other way I can be of service to you in your office?"

"No way! You can get out of here!"

"Then so long, Señor Subpre, fellow citizens. . . ."

He turned around and made for the door, shaking hands with no one; lifting the latch, he went out, closing the door behind him.

"Idiots!" he said in a near shout. And he went down the steps into the Plaza, without first looking to see if there was anyone on the balcony. The important people and the mestizos, who were awaiting the Subprefect there, watched him leave.

"Bad! Don Julián comes out furious. What's going on in there?"

In the office, the three townsmen and the Subprefect remained silent for a while. To himself the official said, "That Arangüena doesn't have a stupid hair on his head; he's slyer than Judas."

Don Demetrio arose and went over to the Subprefect:

"He's a real exploiter, Señor Subprefect! He eats up the Indian's blood!"

Don Antenor and Don Jesús also approached the Subprefect.

"But he's not really on the side of the Indian mob, if the truth be told. We don't know how much money he might have stashed away. All he does is pile it up. Nothing else matters to him. Like a beast, he is; life doesn't matter to him. And when he chews coca, he gets as fuddled as an animal. It's better not to pay any attention to him."

"He sure has killed lots of Indians. But that was up in the high country, when he was rounding up cattle and collecting wool."

"But they can't put him in jail!"

The Subprefect hardly heard them; he was trying to think of a way to bring Don Julián to submission.

"Could you help me put that savage down?" he asked suddenly, glaring at them. The three townsmen blinked.

"You better not tangle with him, sir," said Don Demetrio. "What do you care about that crud? First comes your peace of mind. Isn't that right, Mayor?"

"Yes, Señor Subprefect. Your peace of mind, above all else! You're not from around here. And Arangüena makes a beastly enemy. As for yourself, sir, it's to your interest to assure your future in Ica. And we, here, are your sincere friends."

"Now, for example, see that the edict is enforced! And you'll be a great Subprefect."

"That's the crux of the matter."

"Your job is to civilize this backward little town!"

"Well, you see how it is, Señor Subprefect."

They wanted to make him forget Don Julián, to have the idea of harassing Don Julián vanish from his mind. Even if it took thousands, they would give it to him! Who had advised him to threaten Don Julián? Now Pancho Jiménez was a different matter. A *"chalo"* who was loaded with money, that's all! But Arangüena made them tremble, more than anyone else in the world!

"Señor Subprefect, we, here, are your friends!"

They did not need to come to an agreement; they could guess what was in each other's hearts; their eyes glowed with fear, as if Don Julián's birthmark were before them, all swelled up, like a poisonous spider.

"The professional bullfighter must come, Señor Subprefect. Our plan is the following."

The Subprefect divined their thoughts; the notables were impatiently waving their hands in his face, as if they wanted to erase Arangüena's name from the air, the three townsmen surrounding him, breathlessly, interrupting one another. "Hogwash! These bastards!" The Subprefect felt disgusted. And instinctively he sniffed out where his interest lay: "Now's the time! Afterwards—to hell with them. I won't miss this chance!" And suddenly his rage against Don Julián was extinguished. Another more urgent matter came into his mind.

"All right, all right! My dear friends!"

The three of them felt like laughing.

"Indeed! I'm in a tight spot. Could you lend me about 1,500 soles? In return I will help you out. . . ."

The eyes of the three *mistis* grew murky, as if a great remorse had arisen from the bottom of their consciences. Their eyes grew round, as if they were hardening. But Don Demetrio replied rapidly, in a firm, dreamlike tone of voice:

"Not another word, sir! It's all settled."

And he asked the two worthies:

"What do you say, Antenor? What do you say, Don Jesús?"

"At three in the afternoon," Don Antenor answered forcefully.

"That's a good time," said Don Jesús.

"The hour that Christ died," the Subprefect said to himself. He took Don Antenor and Don Demetrio by the arm and, beckoning to Don Jesús, led them over to his table.

"Now let's sit down, gentlemen. We'll discuss the bullfight."

Although the voice of the man from Ica was kindly, he could not help sounding as if he were making fun of them, softly but unmistakably, wounding the hearts of the three leading citizens.

"I've granted your petition. It can all be done according to your plan, with the sole condition that the edict be complied with. Now it's time for us to come to an agreement."

By then, the four of them were at one end of the office, sitting around the table. The Subprefect's eyes danced with joy, and the three notables looked at him rather shamefacedly. Don Demetrio had lost the loud voice of the quite civilized prominent citizen; he was speaking softly; Don Antenor seemed calmer, and Don Jesús Gutiérrez was neither speaking nor hearing anything. He wanted to leave.

"All right, sir,"—Don Demetrio felt obliged to talk about "the plan." "The Lucanas Union Center is going to rush to hire the professional bullfighter because its ringleaders are refined *"chalos"* who speak out against the exploitative landowners and in favor of the Indians. The *ayllus* must not be told the toreador is going to fight the bull all by himself. Like every other year, let them bring in the bulls; if they can, let them bring Misitu; let them get everything ready for the bullfight. But on the twenty-eighth, we'll put the toreador in the ring, and the policemen will keep the Indians from going in to fight the bull. What do you think of that?"

"That's fine! I'm in complete agreement."

"There's only one hitch. Maybe you will give us some advice."

"About what?"

"The toreador—will he want to fight the bull with his cape in the Pichk'achuri square?"

"That's it. You're right. That square is a great big field. Without any peons to assist him, bullfighting all alone, I don't believe any professional would agree to perform there. And what do you think you'll do?"

"The Reverend Vicar has an idea. But we don't know if you'll agree to it."

"Of course I'll agree to it. I've promised to help you. And I'm going to do even more now that I'm going to be owing you an important favor."

The three of them remained silent; by now they had gained a bit of confidence and were brave enough to keep quiet for a while intentionally. The Subprefect understood, and took the initiative:

"Of course I shall always retain the right to reject any measure if I don't think it's a good idea. . . ."

Don Antenor spoke loudly. All four of them were startled. They had all been whispering; and the three townsmen were out of breath. But when the Subprefect began blustering again, Mayor Antenor replied loudly; his voice filled the whole office, and the townsmen rejoiced to hear him.

"The Vicar has thought up this measure, sir, to help the authorities and the town."

"Tell me what it is!" said the Subprefect, also in a loud voice.

"We'll have a little bullring built of eucalyptus logs in the square at Pichk'achuri. The *ayllus* will do it—K'ayau and Pichk'achuri. The Vicar will tell them that for the contest to be legal and easier to see, there must be a little ring, with good seats, where everybody would be accommodated to watch from up close. And so that they won't make excuses, he'll tell them there's nothing graceful about going in against the bull with dynamite. That the only manly way to fight the bull is one-to-one, with a cape."

"If the Priest can manage to arrange that farce, I have no reason to oppose it. Only the Priest can make the Indians swallow that pill. And I have no objection to that trick."

"Trick or no trick, sir, it'll give you a chance to enforce your superior's orders."

"Because otherwise you might have to lay hands on some rifles to stop the *turupukllay*."

"So what? It's not my responsibility. And isn't it all the same whether the Indians die from having their guts ripped out or from bullets?"

"You'd have had to kill several dozens."

"But it would have served as a deterrent. And the disemboweling would never be repeated. German style, once and for all. Only we're talking too much. I accept your plan, in every particular, for your peace of mind and for my own. Or did you have something else to bring up?"

"Nothing else, sir."

"Then it's all agreed. We'll let the Vicar know about it."

"There's only one thing that's a bit ticklish," replied Don Demetrio, making a move to rise.

The Subprefect immediately suspected what Don Demetrio would request.

"It's about Pancho Jiménez, isn't it?"

"Yes, sir. You've let him go free, and that man is dangerous, because he's in touch with the *ayllus*. And that's not an unfounded accusation. Don Jesús, here, can tell you so."

"Yes, Señor Subprefect. Don Pancho has a following amongst the Indian mob, and if he wants to he can obstruct our efforts. And they say he's threatened to kill Don Demetrio."

"All right, gentlemen. After three this afternoon I'll have him called in to my office. As a precaution he will sleep in the police headquarters and during the day a policeman will watch his store. I'll have him picked up and put into the barracks by six in the afternoon. How do you like that, Don Demetrio?"

"Very well!"

The three leading citizens stood up to take their leave.

"So long, Señor Subprefect. Many thanks."

"Until three o'clock, gentlemen. And I thank you, too."

"So be it."

The Subprefect accompanied them to the stairs.

The three went walking across the Plaza at a slight distance from one another, as if they were resentful. As they neared the big fountain, Don Jesús motioned to Don Demetrio with his arms.

Watching the three prominent citizens, the Subprefect said, "I've got a good hold on them," and went back to his office.

"Secretary! Show the people in, sir."

From the office the Subprefect's loud and infectious laughter reached the balcony.

No sooner had they turned the corner of the Plaza than Don Jesús came to a dead halt in the street.

"I've got nothing to do with this deal. Why should I give my money to that hustler? You guys will lose out. . . ."

"You have to help us, Don Jesús. But don't make a scene in the street. We'll go into my house and argue."

Don Demetrio's house was on the second block of Girón Bolívar. Don Jesús did not want to go up to Don Demetrio's study.

"We'll settle this quickly, Don Demetrio, right here in the yard. I'm not giving a cent. Why should I be giving?"

"Then why'd you agree to it in the office? Why didn't you stand up like a man and refuse? Well, speak up, speak up!"

Don Antenor made him back away, pushing his face into the other man's as he was speaking.

"How was I going to refuse? Instead, I was helping you. How was I going to refuse, knowing that the Subprefect was so hungry for it?"

"Well, that's what you're going to pay for now! For being chicken."

"And for you guys being the same."

"No, we're going to scare Pancho stiff. We're going to guarantee the bullfight."

"Let's settle this once and for all! The council will give 500 soles: let Don Demetrio give 500, me, 300 and you, 200. Is that all right?"

Don Jesús was staring at the door as if he wanted to make a getaway.

"Don't be such a tightwad. Your Tile-pata Indians alone give you 1,000 a year. And for nothing at all!"

"Ok, ok! But goddamnit, we're being fleeced. Without even telling us why or what for, this Subprefect takes our cash. You guys encourage him—being the most important people in town—instead of putting a stop to his abuses."

"You know, Don Jesús. The authorities are the authorities. They take the leather for our leashes out of our hides."

"Right. So long! I'll send the money after lunch. And for the record, all three of us turn chicken when Don Julián speaks!"

Don Jesús rushed out into the street.

"How in hell did I ever get involved with those *k'anras*?"

His insults and regrets did not cease until he got home. At lunch he threw a dishful of hominy in his wife's face, for no reason at all, because he was still furious at the Subprefect.

"That bitch of a woman!"

He went running to his bedroom. From underneath his bed he pulled out a big bag, full of money. Hurriedly he counted out 200 soles, knotted them into a kerchief, and ran out. He went to Don Demetrio's house. The latter was not there.

"Here's the money. And tell your husband that he's a hustler."

As Don Jesús was putting the money on the dining room table, Don Demetrio's family watched his angry face and hard eyes with astonishment.

Don Jesús went home in a calmer mood. He quietly sat down at the dining room table. And he ate his peppery potato stew, hominy, and boiled broad beans in silence, without looking at his wife. Afterwards, he mounted his horse and rode out to see to his cattle and wheat fields.

At three in the afternoon, Don Demetrio and Don Antenor handed over the 1,500 soles to the Subprefect. The three of them embraced each other several times and talked animatedly. And they made a date to meet in the billiard parlor that night.

"We'll celebrate arranging the bullfight."

"We'll toast Puquio, gentlemen."

Don Antenor and Don Demetrio crossed the Plaza on their way home, walking rapidly.

"Are we in command, or aren't we, Don Antenor?"

"We're in command, Don Demetrio. We've got the town in our pocket."

But before their eyes, as if in a dream, appeared Don Julián's head, his commanding eyes, and his murderous look.

The President of the Lucanas Union Center contracted the Spanish bullfighter Ibarito II. For 500 soles, his round-trip fare and lodging, he would fight six bulls on the afternoon of July twenty-eighth.

Ibarito was a *banderillero*[1] from the Acho bullring. He had come from Spain almost ten years before, with a famous bullfighter, and had stayed on in Lima because he was no longer good enough for the Spanish arenas. When the season of the matador who had brought him in his team had ended, Ibarito signed a contract to fight in Ica, Chincha, and Pisco. While he was in Ica he heard people talking about the twenty-eight-day communal work project in which the Indians of Lucanas Province had built the Nazca-Puquio highway.

"I don't like to fight bulls in the highland towns because the bulls they toss in at you already owe at least three or four lives. They're all reruns. I won't go to Puquio for less than 500 and expenses," he said, stating his conditions.

Escobar the student knew the Spaniard was right, that in Puquio, and all over the province, the bulls that had not been dynamited always came back to fight again the following year, that those bulls sought out the body behind the poncho or the cape, and that they

---

1. Bullfighter under the orders of the matador who helps run the bull with the cape and place *banderillas* in pairs in the bull's withers in the second act of the bullfight.—Trans.

charged with every guarantee of success. They were experienced and knew how to kill.

"That's all right, sir. I'll ask for instructions so we can sign the contract. As you say, bullfighting in the highlands is hard work."

The Mayor accepted the conditions of the contract. And the professional bullfighter, Ibarito II, was engaged to go and initiate Spanish-style bullfighting in Puquio.

More than twenty Puquians had decided to go to the bullfight on the twenty-eighth, in representation of the Lucanas Union Center. Escobar the student informed a meeting called expressly for the purpose that he knew Puquio's leading citizens were divided into two factions, that Don Julián Aranguena was the ringleader of the most backward landowning exploiters, and was scheming to prevent the enforcement of the edict. He said Don Demetrio Cáceres, the Priest, and the Mayor had resolved to support the Subprefect, but that none of them could be trusted because they always did whatever they thought would keep them on good terms with the national government. "Who doesn't know Don Demetrio, Don Antenor, and the Vicar? If they've come to an agreement on something, we have to be suspicious of it. When that kind of people get together, no good can come of it." He also told them Don Pancho Jiménez had been jailed on the Subprefect's orders and at the request of Don Demetrio and the Mayor. "Don Pancho may be a lout," he said, "but he's a friend of the Indian communities. If he sticks up for the *turupukllay* it's because he doesn't realize that it's bad for the *comuneros*. We've got to go!"

"The Bishop" asked for the floor and spoke in a near shout. They were meeting in the United Societies Hall, across from the former Palace of Justice, and the Bishop's voice could be heard on both street corners. The policemen came to listen in the doorway.

"The Ministry is now with us," said the Bishop, when he saw the police. "We'll have the law on our side when we go to defend a national government edict. With their scheming, Don Julián and Don Pancho have set the most important *ayllus* in town, Pichk'achuri and K'ayau, in opposition to each other; as if they were at war, the two *ayllus* are now hating each other. And, as if that weren't enough, Don Julián has given his bull, Misitu, to K'ayau. You all know what people say about that bull; not even the exploiter himself, together with all his overseers, riding the best horses in the province, have been able to get that wild beast out of his K'oñani haunts. What'll the K'ayaus do? They'll let themselves be used for bait. How much longer are we going to stand for these abuses? Let's go to Puquio! Are we sons of Lucanas or aren't we? We have a sacred duty. . . ."

The Center would send a deputation to Puquio; those who could not go would each give five reales for the traveling expenses of the delegation.

In Puquio the Vicar called in the town's sixteen staffbearing leaders. According to the agreement, he was to convince the *ayllus* to build a bullring in Pichk'achuri, a small ring, beside the cattlepen where they kept the wild bulls.

When the sixteen staffbearers reached the parish house, the Vicar had them sit on the stone benches on the porch. He held a black book in his hand and spoke to them in Quechua:

"I, like a Puquio Indian, am Indian. That is why I have supported the *comuneros*, always. In sickness or in health, in rain or in good weather, I have gone to give final consolation to the Indians; to their communities I have walked to hear confession and to administer last rites, when typhus was raging in their neighborhoods, when the infants, the old, and the young were dying of the fever. . . ."

"*Arí, tayta, papay.*" The four Chief Staffbearers went up to the Vicar and kissed his hands. "Always have, *taytay!*"

"On the highway project, too, at the head of the line I've gone. I have marked out the road, through a good place, climbing up over the rocky crags like a cat; shivering with cold on Kondorsenk'a, on Galeras Plain, sleeping out in the open, with the Indians from all over Lucanas. Like a little brother I have been to the *ayllus* of Puquio."

"Always, *taytay! Ayllus* love you!"

"That's why at bullfights on twenty-eighth I have wept for Endians. Like devil the bull chases the Christians! Like enemy he rips the *comuneros'* flesh to shreds; their blood waters the ground at Pichk'achuri. Could that blood be yours? *Tayta* God has put the heart into the Christian's chest that he might live contentedly, praying, respecting the Christian's blood. What right do the Pichk'achuris, the K'ayaus have to turn their heart over to the bull? All their blood, still nice and warm, they pour out onto the ground to delight and entertain the devil who looks out through the eyes of the wild bull."

The staffbearers were saddened; they stared fearfully at the Vicar.

"Now, on twenty-eighth, K'ayau gonna fight Pichk'achuri. Into big square they're gonna go in drove, to give up their life to Misitu! Misitu is devil!"

"Nu *taytay!* Big *sallk'a*, that's all!" exclaimed K'ayau's Chief Staffbearer.

"Misitu is devil. That's why he lives all alone in the woods; with his shadow, too, he's angry. Killing's all he lives for; against the little birds in the woods he rages too; the water he dirties with his tongue."

"By his tail gonna drag Misitu, K'ayau Endian, *tayta*!" said the Chief Staffbearer of Pichk'achuri. "Like dog gonna come into Pichk'achuri; with dynamite we'll blow out his chest, then, in big square," replied the K'ayau's Chief Staffbearer.

"Don't you see? I believe the devil's already in your soul, *taytay* Chief. Like a brother you're defending Misitu."

"We're gonna kill Misitu, *tayta*," said Pichk'achuri's Chief Staffbearer, standing up before the Priest.

"His chest we'll blow out with dynamite!"

"All right, all right! Honrao Rojas, K'encho, Raura, Tobias, Wallpa . . . let them go in! That's all right; they have the skill. . . . Innocent *comuneros* will watch from a distance. What do you say, *taytas*?"

The sixteen staffbearers looked at one another, conferring.

"Innocent *comunero*'ll just watch; like sheep he'd probably go to Misitu's horn. Chief Staffbearer will be responsible. K'ayau *capeador*, Pichk'achuri *capeador*, like man let them fight K'oñani bulls. . . . What do you say?"

"That's all right, *tayta*."

"But in big square's no good. Little bullring we'll make in Pichk'achuri, next to cattlepen. Out of eucalyptus, out of weeping willow logs. We'll make bleachers so Indians from K'ayau, from Chaupi, from Pichk'achuri, from K'ollana, important *werak'ochas*, *tayta* Judge, *tayta* Mayor can sit down. From close up they'll see bullfighters' great rage. We'll see who's first on twenty-eighth— K'encho from Pichk'achuri or Raura from K'ayau. Well-known Indian bullfighter, good young men will fight bull; innocent Indian men, children, women, *werak'ochas* will watch from close by. There'll be hole in the ground, too."

"That's it, *tayta*," exclaimed the Pichk'achuri leader.

"But *auki* Pedrork'o, *auki* Sillanayok' likely to take offense; bleachers liable to block off their summit," replied the one from K'ayau.

"We'll just make the fence low; all the mountain peaks will look on happily from on high."

"That's it! We'll put up a bullring, with bleachers."

"That's how staffbearers is, with knowing has to be command, agreeing with Vicar, in friendship with *Taytacha* God."

The staffbearers went off to the *ayllus* to order the construction of the bullring.

Everything had been consented to.

"These fairies are ruining the Indians' courage; they're watering down the people's blood. Before long there won't be any men left in Puquio," Don Julián cried angrily.

"What do they expect? K'encho, Honrao, Raura will always be the *papacitos* on the twenty-eighth," Don Pancho would say, every evening, as he was going to sleep in the policemen's dormitory.

10. The Auki

The Chief Staffbearer of K'ayau commended his community to the mountain spirit K'arwarasu. The *auki* K'arwarasu has three snowy peaks; he is the father of all the mountains of Lucanas. From the Ayacucho road, from the top of Wachwak'asa, just as one is starting to go down to Huamanga, K'arwarasu can be seen. Through the cold air of the great puna, forty leagues away, summit after summit come into view in the blue distance, as if at the end of the world, the three snow peaks glowing in the sunlight amid lightning flashes and the darkness of the storms.

"*Ay tayta*! K'arwarasu *tayta*!"

The Indian travelers sprinkle cane liquor, regarding him respectfully; their eyes strain to distinguish him well, beyond all the mountaintops.

"*Papay! Jatun auki!*"[1]

The Lucanas mule drivers speak of him affectionately, greeting him by sprinkling cane liquor into the air. Their eyes sparkle with adoration of the *auki*, keeping watch over and taking care of all the Lucana land.

For K'arwarasu is the sign of the province of Lucanas. When the travelers climb up Wachwak'asa to go to Huamanga; while they are climbing Soraya, on their way to Chalhuanca; as they pass through Tambora, going down to the coast; as they go up along Sarasara on their way to Arequipa, they see the three snow peaks shining, high and bright.

"There's K'arwarasu!" they say. "How grand he had been. How imposing!" Then, pointing it out, the mule driver or the guide says,

---

1. "My father! Great spirit!"—Trans.

"Yes, boss. Right there before you, in one of those valleys is Puquio; on the other side, in the background, are Aukara, Cabana, Sondondo, Chakralla, Waykawachu; over there, through where the middle peak appears, are Querobamba, Andamarka, Larkay . . . ; and right at the foot of the middle peak, almost where the snow begins, is Chipau. . . ."

And he goes on pointing out and naming almost all of the districts of Lucanas, all of its towns, its rivers, its plains, its lakes. And up above, looking out over all the lands of the Lucanas, keeping watch over them is K'arwarasu, tranquil. And through the whitest and coldest of snows black crags jut out and cast shadows on the snow.

The Chief Staffbearer of K'ayau had the right to commend himself to *tayta* K'arwarasu, because K'arwarasu is the mountain deity of all the Lucanas, even though the members of Chipau community deny it. The K'ayau headman knew he had the right, because Puquio is the Lucanas' biggest town; it is their capital, and the staffbearers from Puquio can make all of the towns in *tayta* K'arwarasu's care get up and go.

On three white llamas, K'ayau's Chief Staffbearer carried his community's offering; a staffbearing councilman and a young man from the *ayllu* accompanied him. After three days, he returned with a sorcerer from Chipau. The sorcerer wanted to go after Misitu alone; he said *tayta* K'arwarasu had given him power over all the bulls on all the punas belonging to the *auki*. But the Chief Staffbearer did not agree to this; he said the mountain spirit had ordered him to go with the whole community. That when he was scraping away the snow to find the ground and bury the offering, the *tayta* had told him so, speaking right to his heart.

"My sorcerer is going to guide you, but you're going to go up to K'oñani with the K'ayaus; you're going to take Misitu out so he can fight in the Pichk'achuri bullring. I'm going to watch the *yawar fiesta* from my summit. I'm for K'ayau, *tayta*; K'ayau will take the saddlecloth; first it'll be on twenty-eighth."

And hearing the voice of the great mountain spirit, he had wept, and his warm tears, too, as an offering he had buried.

"All set! All set!"

"Not long now!"

"Not long now!"

"Poor little thing! Misitu!"

"Ay Misituy Misitu! Weeping you'll come down!"

"All set, *taytakuna*! Not long now!"

"*Tayta K'arwarasu! Jatun tayta!*"

"You just for K'ayau *ayllu*!"

"Ha! Damnit! Just with farts, we'll drive Misitu!"

"There isn't any sorcerer! Just by pissing a long ways we'll drive Misitu."

"*Yauuú taytakuna! Tauuuuú!*"

K'ayau *ayllu* was seething. The staffbearers were shouting from the open places in the neighborhood; the *comuneros* were yelling in the doorways of their houses.

From the chapel tower, Raura played the *wakawak'ra*. Scornfully he pointed to the tower's little bell:

"*Atatau!* Like little child it cries! It's no good!"

He held out his big *wakawak'ra*, with its three coils and steel mouthpiece, and said:

"There it is for *mak'ta*![2] This one K'ayau *mak'ta* hears a long ways off, too!"

And he'd blow it furiously. His face would even swell up; but like a bull's voice the *wakawak'ra* sobbed; quaveringly the sobbing came out of its round mouth; it shook the K'ayaus' souls deep down inside of them. Coming out of the little tower, the *wakawak'ra's* voice entered the K'ayaus' hearts; then their eyes burned, their hearts despaired.

"*Maypim chay Misitu carago!* (Where's that Misitu, damnit!)" they shouted.

The K'ayaus shook all over with rage. They set out for the little neighborhood square, striding along with firm tread. When they reached the corner of the square, they threw the ends of their ponchos over their shoulders, and pushed back the front brims of their hats defiantly:

"*Maypim chay Misitu, carago!*"

And standing with legs apart, their bodies erect, they looked at Raura rather questioningly.

Behind the Indian men ran the women and little children, watching the youths and *comuneros* swaggering around angrily in the square, calling upon one another to go up to K'oñani once and for all, arguing loudly and beating their fists against the wall. The children, large and small, ran as if they were being chased. Hearing the *wakawak'ras* and their parents' angry shouting, fear grew in their souls, like a black shadow, like the sound of the rainstorm.

"*Ay taytaya! Taytallaya!*"

In the square they encountered the uproar, the fury of the K'ayaus, who were threatening Misitu, ripping open their shirts and baring

2. Young man.—Author

101

their chests. And they trembled and cried loudly, their eyes searching the Indian throng.

"Hey, goddamnit!"

Some of the *comuneros* nudged the little children with their feet and kicked the women to make them take the babies away.

"Damn *k'anra*! Take little kid away quick. Nothing but men in square!"

Then the Chief Staffbearer gave the order. It was the twenty-fifth of July. K'ayau was ablaze. Not a man would stay behind. Well, who was going to stay behind in the Indian quarter as a babysitter for the women and little children?

"Now it'll be! There's corral, little corral, so Endian body'll be easy for wild bull to find," and they pointed it out, gesturing toward the new bullring that had been built of eucalyptus poles in Pichk'achuri.

"Even if it's in church, K'ayau'll fight bull. On high altar, too, just fighting bull," they bragged.

They were to leave at midnight, each one carrying his lasso and provisions. On the edge of town they'd meet. The sorcerer would go first, and after him the staffbearers, Raura, and Tobias. . . .

"All set! *Tayta* K'arwarasu will watch over us and take care of us, of his *ayllu*, K'ayau!"

Some *mistis* had been waiting since an early hour on the Yallpa Creek bank to see the K'ayaus go by. Two pairs of civil guards had also gone there to oversee their departure.

Don Julián waited on the other side of the stream, mounted on his horse, alone. Fermín and Don Julián's other overseers mingled with the mestizos who were on the other side; they fearfully looked for the boss, in the shade, on the other side of the creek.

Don Pancho knew the K'ayaus would leave that night.

"Sergeant, Sergeant! Let them take me—even if it's in handcuffs— just to the edge of town. Don't be like that, so stubborn. From just a little ways off I'm going to watch the K'ayaus passing by."

"I'm not going either, Don Pancho. So I can keep you company. The Subprefect's got his eye on you. Don Demetrio and Don Antenor are watching you like devils. We could both get into trouble. Until sunup we'll talk, if you want to."

Don Pancho wanted to go on pleading with him. He was a man, as good as the best of them. But he knew that by that time, all of the K'ayaus were on the move, that the *comuneros* were going to leave, filling the road; that Raura, Tobias, Wallpa, and Paukar were to take the lead, making the valley thunder with their *wakawak'ras*.

He paced back and forth in the police station, with long strides. A small gasoline lantern illumined the sleeping quarters. The broad shadow of his body crossed the wall, swelling and shrinking according to his distance from the lantern. He was speaking.

"I think I'm going to take revenge on those ass-kissers pretty soon. Nobody's worse! And the national government, too—how come it's meddling in town affairs? Who's doing anything to the government around here? And then there's that little saint, the Vicar. Why'd he build that little corral out of eucalyptus poles in Pichk'achuri? Between him and the ass-kissers there's an understanding. Like a fish in a soup plate, Misitu'll be waggling his tail in that corral. Right away he'll catch the Indian bullfighters. There's no room, goddamnit, not even for Misitu to take a shit. And just one good blast of Honrao's dynamite will blow the rear ends off the people sitting in the box. Best thing that could happen! Right, Señor Sergeant? Whoever is a man will be a man there. And starting with the little bullfighter, all those flunkeys, are going to leave their snot in that corral. I'm going to see that! I'll split my mouth, yet, laughing to see the girls and Lima-ites so scared they'll piss when Misitu sticks his tongue into the eucalyptus boxes. *Ja caraya!*"

Now and again he would stop beside the Sergeant.

"Let me go, *werak'ocha*! We'll watch the K'ayaus leave and we'll come back, nice and calm, like men of our word."

The Sergeant looked at him gravely. He went up to him and made him sit down under the lantern at the table.

"Let's play casino, Don Pancho."

"I'm ready! I'll play you for my going out. If I win, we'll go to watch the K'ayaus."

He sat down hurriedly.

"Get out the cards, *werak'ocha*. Not long now!"

His eyes were gleaming, as if the door had already been opened for him.

"Don Pancho! You're like a little kid! Stop fooling around! We'll have a shot of pisco, if you like. And cheer up. To see the Indians you'll have lots of chances yet. The rest is women's stuff."

Don Pancho shrugged, raised his head, and looked straight at the Sergeant.

"Then it's a pound note a game."

"Make it a half."

"Good, good. Deal the cards."

As they played, the sobbing of the *wakawak'ras* came in, from a distance, but quite clearly. To Don Pancho it seemed as if the lantern light flickered and grew a bit dimmer when the *wakawak'ras'* singing entered the policemen's sleeping quarters. It came in like a sudden gust of air; he felt it on his eyes, and his heart suddenly contracted; he felt a kind of hot flash in his blood, as if the lantern were burning inside of his chest.

"Sergeant! I'm getting womanish," he said. "Shut me up in a dark room! Inside, in the courtyard there's a room where you keep the tools, buckets, and brooms. . . ."

"All right."

They went to the courtyard. There, in the darkness, muting the high little voices of the crickets who were calling from the weeds in the corral, the *wakawak'ras'* voices were heard more clearly; it seemed as if the stars were trembling in the sad depths of the sky because they were shaken by the *wakawak'ras'* singing. Don Pancho entered the dark little room, almost grazing the ceiling with his straw hat. The Sergeant locked him in, without saying anything. And then he went back to the sleeping quarters.

"That Don Pancho is a pesky *cholo*. If they don't rein him in he'll pull more than one of them up short."

In a dense drove, the K'ayaus reached the creek. About a hundred *comuneros* were playing *wakawak'ras*; Raura was in command of the trumpeters. They splashed through the shallow stream water like horses galloping through large puddles left by a downpour.

"You can't see their faces," said the *mistis* from the roadside. "But it's sure to be Raura who's livening up the horn players. The little troop at the head are the staffbearers and the sorcerer."

"Good luck, *taytas*," some of them shouted.

They struck matches, but the little flames would flare up for a moment, lighting the faces of the notables who had lit them, and then go out, as if they had been cut with a knife.

"How could we have come without lanterns; how dumb of us!"

One of the civil guards shone his flashlight on the faces of the Indians who were going by. They carried their lassos looped over their shoulders, with their ponchos draped over the same shoulder, as well as their little woven pouches of coca leaves.

"Give a good light, officer!" they shouted from all sides.

The K'ayaus passed by silently. But the *wakawak'ras* resounded throughout the canyon. Up above, in the narrow part of the stream bed, grew a eucalyptus wood; in that wood the *wakawak'ras'* song seemed to throb more loudly; from there the bullfight melody re-echoed as if it were coming from inside of the mountains.

When the troop of staffbearers had crossed the creek, Don Julián called out,

"Chief! *Sáyay!* (Stop!)"

The Indian leader peered into the darkness and made out Don Julián's black and white horse.

"At the pass my foreman, Ciprián, is going to give you a couple of bushels of wheat. For rations," said the boss.

The Chief Staffbearer was about to go up to Don Julián. He doffed his hat to climb up from the road.

"Pass on by! *Pasaychik!*" commanded Don Julián, in his imperious tone of voice.

"*Papay!* Thank you, *papay!*"

And they went on climbing the mountain. The sound of their footfalls could be heard from the creekside.

The leading citizens and the "*chalos*" stayed behind on the creek bank for a long while, until the *wakawak'ras* sounded from high up on the mountain.

"Those Indians! How many of them can be going?"

"At least 600."

Talking, they went back to town.

In the K'ayau quarter, the women and little children were weeping. Empty and quiet was the *ayllu*.

Don Julián passed through the group of citizens who were returning to town. When they heard the ring of the pinto's horseshoes, they made way for him. The pinto galloped by, his shoes striking sparks on the stony roadway.

"Don Julián!"

"It's Don Julián! Misitu's owner!"

In a moment the sound of the galloping was silenced at the entrance to the town.

The K'oñanis were frightened; they sounded *wakawak'ras* when they saw the K'ayaus coming up out of the ravine on the road from Puquio. Like black ants, they came up onto the pampa; in herds, in herds they appeared endlessly on the plain. They spread out over the grassland and advanced in a horde on Don Julián's large ranch. None of them walked on the road; like a drove of loose horses, they came over the field of tall grass. The four staffbearers and the sorcerer went on ahead, leading them.

The K'oñanis ran out of all the fields, little farms, and stone huts that are up on the hillsides by Ak'chi Mountain; they rushed down the hill on the big ranch road. Meanwhile, Don Julián's herdsmen dolefully played the *wakawak'ras*.

By then the sun was high, glistening gaily on *tayta* Ak'chi's snow, and the mountain's shadow extended far out over the plain. The air was calm; white gulls and lake birds called out as they circled in the sky.

When they neared the entrance to the big ranch, the Puquios also answered the K'oñanis. Suddenly the trumpeters began to play; the *wakawak'ras* thundered over the pampa, raising a wind, and the *ischu* grass began to sway on the plain. The gulls took fright in the sky and flew off toward Torkok'ocha.

The K'oñanis herded together in front of the ranch; leaning against the wall of the yard they watched the K'ayaus fearfully. They were trembling when the Chief Staffbearer reached the settlement.

The *wakawak'ras* stopped sounding and the K'ayaus felt as if their chests breathed more freely. They straightened up a bit and raised their heads to receive the staffbearers, who spoke with them in Quechua.

"*Taytakuna*, we're gonna take Misitucha for twenty-eighth. Don Jolián's orders."

The herdsman who was the overseer of K'oñani pointed his finger at *Tayta* Ak'chi, sparkling in the sunlight, close by there at the edge of the plain.

"*Jatun auki* Ak'chi will take offense, *tayta* Chief. Won't he? Misitu is his little child, his animal."

"No *taytitu*! *Auki* K'arwarasu commanding. There is sorcerer from Chipau. *Tayta* K'arwarasu in command."

The K'oñanis blinked.

"There is sorcerer."

The sorcerer went over to the herdsman.

"That's right, *tayta*," he said. "Great *auki* K'arwarasu commands; Misitu is for K'ayau, he says. From his summit, he says, he's gonna watch Pichk'achuri *yawar fiesta*; for him Misitu gonna fight. From Torkok'ocha he's gonna raise up another *sallk'a* bull, bigger, wilder, smoky, for his K'oñani people, in place of Misitu. To Negromayo Canyon he himself, K'arwarasu, is gonna drive him with golden sling. Gonna visit his K'oñani people."

The herdsman was reassured. Perhaps it was true. Perhaps the great *auki* K'arwarasu would come to K'oñani.

"But careful they'll go," he warned. "Misitu smells people's blood and fights for it."

While the Chief Staffbearer was talking to the K'oñanis, the K'ayau *comuneros* surrounded the settlement. The small group of houses was encircled by a thick wall of K'ayaus, just in case. The staffbearers knew that the K'oñanis would fight for Misitu if they didn't believe the Chipau sorcerer was a peon of the *auki* K'arwarasu.

But the Chief Staffbearer and the sorcerer spoke carefully to the ranch overseer; they explained to him at length how the K'ayau *ayllu* had taken an offering to the great *auki*, that the sorcerer had come under orders from the Apu[3] K'arwarasu. That it was the *auki*'s will that Misitu should fight in Pichk'achuri. That a smoky bull was going to come out of Torkok'ocha to replace Misitu for the K'oñanis.

Then the foreman ordered Misitu's farewell. The women who were in the ranch house began to wail; they entered the corral and from there called to the women in all the fields:

Ay Misitu,	Ai Misitu,
ripunkichu;	you're going to leave;
ay warmikuna,	ai womenfolk,
wak'aykusan!	we're going to weep!
Ay Yanamayu,	Ai Yanamayu,
sapachallayki	alone
quidark'okunki!	you'll be left!
Ay K'oñani pampa,	Ai K'oñani plain,
sapachallayki,	alone,
sapachallaykis	all alone
quidark'okunki!	you'll be left!

Hearing the singing, the women left the other farms; already crying on their way down the mountain, they came running, as if they were asking for help, as they do on the nights of an eclipse, when the moon dies and they run to the hillsides to set fire to the *ischu* grass and cry out to the heavens, weeping as the moon darkens.

With all the shouting, as the women's song grew louder, the Chief Staffbearer began to offer Don Julián's cane liquor to the K'oñanis. Full mugs he gave them. The K'oñanis drained them, closing their eyes. The women's singing welled up in their consciousness, rose up to their eyes, flaming.

"Courage, *taytakuna*," the Puquios told them.

Shutting their eyes tightly, they swallowed the cane liquor, the drink burning their chests a bit. And they went on drinking. The four staffbearers served them hurriedly.

This was really it! Nothing could be done about it now! There the women were, already singing the farewell song! Misitu would go down to the valley; they'd get him out of his *k'eñwa* thicket; with lassos they'd drag him along the rocky road, like any dirty *sallk'a* bull. In the Pichk'achuri ring they'd set off dynamite under his

3. Great lord, ruler; Apu K'arwarasu is the regional god of Puquio.—Trans.

chest. All worn out he'd come into town, perhaps even bleeding at the hoof.

Hearing the women singing intensified the suffering in the K'oñanis' hearts; it increased as the rivers grow, roaring, when the rain falls in February. They sat down carefully, quietly, by the ranch house wall.

Ay K'oñani pampa,	Ai K'oñani plain,
sapachallayki,	alone,
sapachallayki	in silence
quidark'okunki!	you'll be left!
Ay Yanamayu	Ai Yanamayu
sapachallaykis,	all alone
quidark'okunki!	you'll be left!

The K'ayaus, the *comuneros* from the big town of Lucanas, were hearing the song, were watching the K'oñanis' faces. It might have been better if they had run for home, disappearing into the ravine. But the Chief Staffbearer regarded the K'ayaus calmly and went on offering the *punarunas* and their women his drink.

By nightfall, the K'oñanis and their women were out of breath; snoring and purple to their foreheads from drunkenness, they slept, stretched out along the walls like dead dogs.

When it was near dawn, when the little puna birds were hopping about, exploring in the tall grass, and the stars were fading from the still twilit sky, the K'ayaus silently went down into the bottom of the Negromayo Canyon. They sort of slid down, bent over, carefully treading on the lush green grass. The blue ponchos of the K'ayaus and the dark homespun flannel of their tight, short pants looked black in the tall grass of the little valley. Over almost half a league of grassland they spread out and quietly neared the *k'eñwales*, as if they were growing toward them.

They reached the *k'eñwa* trees and jumped over them. The *k'eñwa* tree is low, but its trunk, covered with red scales, is hard and many-branched. They clambered up onto the boughs, unwound their lassos, and got ready to throw them from a distance. The grass that grows along the river in the shade of the trees is dark green and tender; they walked there and jumped over the trees.

The Chief Staffbearer, the sorcerer, Tobias, and Raura, with a troop of about a hundred men, came to the biggest clearing in the *k'eñwales*. The other leaders were distributed the length of the Indian throng, commanding, and on every side of the crowd there was a staffbearer.

In the clearings in the *k'eñwales* the *ischu* grass is yellow, tall, and tough. It seems as if the daylight reaches there first; no sooner does the dawn light shine forth than the yellow grass is illumined, while the *k'eñwal* stays dark until the sun really rises in the sky.

The sorcerer stopped at a distance from the trees, in the clearing in the *k'eñwa* thicket. He was carrying a lasso made of llama hair; he had no poncho and was all alone. He was the sorcerer from Chipau, the son of K'arwarasu; Misitu had to know his voice; he'd stand right up to him. He had wanted to enter the Negromayo Canyon all alone.

When the last K'ayau reached the *k'eñwal*, everyone shouted, all together, shaking the tree branches. The sorcerer went on standing in the tall grass. They yelled two or three times, together, beginning with the Chief Staffbearer's troop.

From down below, almost from the bend, way down where the Negromayo enters the valley of the big river, the *comuneros* shouted,

"Bull, bull! Misitu! He's running!"

"*Yauuú!*"

"He's coming!"

The sorcerer swung round to that side; he raised his arm as if he were asking for silence. And as they watched that place on the river, while they all waited, with hearts that now seemed about to burst, Misitu appeared, with his hump raised high, tossing his head. The light was strong now, and they saw him run leaping to catch the sorcerer; he ran like a veritable puma.

"Whoa, *sallk'a*! Whoa, damnit!" screamed the sorcerer. *Sáyay!*[4]
And he stretched out his arm to Misitu.

"*Sáyay!*"

Right below his chest the horn hooked him; the bull had impaled him easily and began to shake him; he turned him round and round.

"*Yau, yau!*" the Indians screamed, seeing how the sorcerer's blood ran down the bull's chest and dripped onto the grass.

Misitu trampled the sorcerer's body; he came straight for the trees; he trod upon the llama hair lasso that was tied to the sorcerer's waist; he trampled and at one go opened up the sorcerer's body, which fell onto the *ischu*, ripped open from belly to groin.

"Goddamn *k'anra*! Shit!"

Deeply, like the voice of a big *wakawak'ra*, Raura shouted. Rage

4. "Whoa!"—Trans.

was seething in his chest, and his voice was amplified by it, as though it were coming out of a mine shaft. He threw his lasso well, judging the distance without exposing himself, and looped it over both horns, right over Misitu's face. When the K'ayaus had their eyes wide open, Misitu was bucking, leaping high, and Raura was pulling on the lasso, which was belayed around a *k'eñwa* limb.

"Because, damnit, I *k'ari*! I K'ayau!" proclaimed Raura.

"That's it!" shouted the Chief Staffbearer, jumping down onto the tall grass. "That's it, damnit!"

He too, aiming calmly, lassoed the bull by the horns, while Misitu was jumping around like crazy, while he was getting closer to the *k'eñwal*, without realizing that there's where it would end. Feeling the other lasso, Misitu bellowed; he let out an ugly-sounding roar.

"Now he's crying! Goddamn it!"

The Chief Staffbearer ran to the woods to tie the rope securely to a *k'eñwa* trunk. Misitu looked at him, and tried to run in that direction, but Raura's lasso held his head tight. The whites of his eyes were already bloodshot.

Then all of the K'ayaus came down into the clearing. They hastily picked up the sorcerer's body, carried it into the shade of the *k'eñwal*, and covered it with ponchos. Tobias played the *wakawak'ra*. Even the lowliest of the *comuneros*, even the most effeminate one, looped his lasso over Misitu's head. The bull began to defecate, with his head tied to the *k'eñwa* trunk, trembling like any ordinary little bull that is ready for the bullfighter to bring him down.

The Indian leader, Raura, Tobias, and Wallpa got him ready. They fastened the biggest lassos tightly over both horns and released those that were useless.

Meanwhile, from the upper and lower ends of the canyon, the K'ayaus were coming in; they crossed the clearing and ran over to Misitu.

"No, *tayta*!" they said.

"*Mánan!*"

They didn't want to believe it.

"There's Misitu!" Raura pointed to him, calmly. "Misitucha!"

Raura seemed disheartened.

The K'ayaus went up to get a good look at Misitu. He was streaked, dark brown with streaks of yellow. He was not large; he was like any ordinary puna bull, but his hump was quite big and round and his horns thick and pointed, like a weaver's shuttle. On his chest and on his face he had blood, and it had dripped down onto his hoofs.

"Who, *tayta*?" they asked.

"Sorcerer. With his life he's paid the Negromayo for Misitu."

"But he's going to die in Pichk'achuri, with dynamite."

They went to look at the sorcerer's body. He was slashed from top to bottom; his entrails were deposited beside the body.

The whole clearing in the *k'eñwales* filled up with Indians. In a little corner, Misitu was trembling. The K'ayaus stared at him sadly. He was nothing but a puna animal. There he was! Tied good and tight to the *k'eñwa* tree by Raura! Now there was no anger; everyone was quiet.

At that moment, the sun shone forth from the head of the valley, shining over the crest of the mountains that lined the Negromayo. It came out big, illumining the *ischu* plants that grew on the edge of the canyon; it brightened the dark green of the *keñwa* trees and shone directly into the eyes of the Indians who were looking at Misitu.

"Ready!" ordered Raura.

A little troop of K'ayaus, the toughest, chosen by the Chief Staffbearer, went up to Misitu. Five of them grasped each lasso. There were six ropes, three to drag him and three to hold him back.

"Move 'im!" ordered the headman, when the draggers were ready.

Misitu wanted to leap forward, but those restraining him held him back.

"Now, damnit!"

"Pull!"

"Get 'im up!"

In their midst they dragged him. It was no use for him to buck, no use to try to pull back or turn around. His hooves scored the sod as they dragged him along.

And close behind, they dolefully played the *wakawak'ras* for him. The troop of K'ayaus followed the horn players. In a peaceful mood, rather quietly, as if they were returning from an ordinary day's work.

They took shortcuts, climbing the mountain slopes, going through the tall grass, the sooner to reach the road that ran along the canyon.

A short distance behind them came four Indians bearing the sorcerer's body on a litter of *k'eñwa* boughs.

In a while they reached the summit. The Chief Staffbearer made an offering of cane liquor to the Negromayo *k'eñwa* woods in Misitu's name. After all, it was the wild bull's favorite territory. Never more would there be a Misitu in the *k'eñwal*. The woods would be left in peace. The little lambs, too, would go down to drink from the river. K'oñani would be left in peace. K'oñani, Osk'onta, Tak'ra, Tinkok' . . . all, all of them. Tranquilly they'd walk the puna up there, by night and by day. The K'ayaus were removing the great fear; there he was, tied up, being dragged down into the valley at a walk. Now he would never come back out again. On the puna there would be silence. Misitu's name had gone out unto Chalhuanca, unto Coracora, unto Pampachiri; all over the high country in the outermost towns of Lucanas, people had been frightened by Misitu's reputation.

"They say all tied up, like a dog, the K'ayaus had dragged him," people were saying on all the little farms and in the towns.

Even the little children would go right down into the Negromayo now. Before, they had cried whenever dusk caught them as much as two leagues away from the *k'eñwal*.

How much, how much the K'ayaus would talk in the high country. Year after year, year after year, they might never get done telling about the K'ayaus coming; their entrance into the *k'eñwa* wood would be recounted by the old people until the end of the world.

"All tied up they took him off. In peace the *k'eñwal* was left."

The Chief Staffbearer knew. He poured almost half a bottle of *aguardiente* over the edge of the canyon as an offering. In his heart, in his mind, and speaking respectfully, he asked the Negromayo and *tayta* Ak'chi to forgive him: "*Taytay*, your animal I am taking away! Your Misitu! In Pichk'achuri he's gonna play for the big *ayllu*, for K'ayau, for your little children!"

The K'ayaus knew, they were divining the Chief Staffbearer's prayer, and they, too, looked to the great snow-clad mountain. They bowed their heads and asked his permission.

Meanwhile, Misitu was waiting. From in front and from behind, they pulled the ropes taut to detain him for a while at the summit.

They took him, leaping, down to the ravine; they got him to the road. League after league, the men dragging him were replaced.

As night was falling, they came to the Pedrork'o Pass. In the shadow Puquio looked big. The *ayllu* of K'ayau faces Pichk'achuri, and in the Pichk'achuri square, by the cattlepen wall, was the Vicar's little bullring, like some kind of corral to keep calves in; seeing it, the K'ayaus laughed. The pen was already full of cattle; the other *ayllus* had already sent their wild bulls. In the community of Chaupi, near the big fountain, at the foot of Makulirumi Rock, the field was full of Indians. The ground was black with them.

"The Tankayllu must be dancing!" said Raura.

It was already the evening of the twenty-eighth. It was the Tankayllu, for sure. In his new clothing, he'd be coming out onto Girón Bolívar.

Raura blew his *wakawak'ra*. All of the trumpeters played on the mountaintop. Misitu was waiting, all worn out and weak by now, tightly bound by the thirty rope pullers.

Clearly and sharply, they saw the Indians in the Chaupi square turning round to look at the mountain, and running back and forth. The little square was emptied. But the Tankayllu—it was him for sure—entered Girón Bolívar with a little troop of Chaupis.

"Tankayllu! When he ever getting scared?"

The Chief Staffbearer saluted the town by pouring out half a bottle of cane liquor at the pass. Afterwards he looked off toward Chipau, where the *jatun auki*, the glorious K'arwarasu lives. All of the K'ayaus doffed their hats.

"*Tayta! Jatun tayta!*" he said. "Here's your *ayllu*, intact. By your will. There's Misitu, your animal. For you we're going to fight the bulls in Pichk'achuri, with great rage, so you'll be K'ayau's guardian, always. Thank you, *jatun auki!*"

And they crossed over the pass. Before midnight they would arrive.

While the Chief Staffbearer was speaking to the *auki*, Kokchi the herdsman reached Don Julián's house. He ran in. Don Julián was pacing back and forth on the courtyard porch.

"*Taytay!* Misitu! He's already coming down the hill. All tied up, like thievin' bull."

Don Julián stopped dead.

"Did you say Misitu?"

"Yeah, boss. They've caught him. He's already coming down the hill. With six lassos they're dragging."

"And how many Indians has he killed?"

"Not a one, I think, boss. Just one stretcher is coming."

Don Julián became thoughtful. The K'ayaus had gone into the *k'eñwal*. The Indians had dared to do it.

"They broke your Misitu, boss. Like common thief they've dragged him. Like dog. Shall I saddle up pinto, boss? Shall I saddle up?"

It was true, then. Kokchi's eyes were brimming with tears.

"Let's go, *papay.*"

The herdsman was becoming frantic. He was scratching the white stone of the pillar with his fingernails.

"Shall I saddle up the pinto, boss?"

He knew that on the pinto Don Julián could climb the slope in an hour, that when he met the K'ayaus he could give the Chief Staffbearer a furious look and, with a single shot, make them unfasten the lassos. Misitu would go back. Maybe he wouldn't even think of running the K'ayaus off; he'd go straight through the mountains to his haunts.

But Don Julián could not make up his mind. The ranch hands and overseers gathered round the herdsman in the courtyard.

"Sure, they're already bringing him down from Pedrork'o."

113

"Sure, boss."

"I've lost ten dozen beers," said Don Julián.

"Are you gonna let him go, boss?" asked Fermín.

"You think Misitu's mine now? He belongs to K'ayau. If they've brought him down, they've brought him down. Tomorrow he'll rip the guts out of the K'ayaus; he'll rip the guts out of the little bullfighter. He'll get his revenge in the ring, Kokchi! Your Misitu's worthless; the K'ayaus have him tied up. Go to the kitchen and cry."

"You gonna let him go, boss?" Kokchi asked again.

Don Julián stepped down into the courtyard, and calmly went over to Fermín.

"And you're asking me, you shitty fag?"

With a single punch he knocked him to the ground.

"Have you already forgotten how you turned chicken and ran out of the *k'eñwales*?"

And he kicked him over and over, all around the courtyard.

"No, *patroncito*," pleaded the foreman.

But the boss wouldn't let him get up. Every time he tried to stand he'd kick him until he fell flat on the ground.

He left him as good as dead, lying near the door in the entryway. And he went into the street.

The lady had Fermín carried onto the porch. But whenever Don Julián was kicking his foremen, the whole household would keep quiet.

Don Julián went straight to police headquarters. He wanted to announce to Don Pancho that the K'ayaus were already dragging Misitu down the mountain.

Girón Bolívar was quiet, the stores closed. On the narrow side streets, the streetlamps burned humbly in the darkening dusk. Don Julián hurried to the Plaza. Around the big fountain there was a ring of Indians; the Subprefect's balcony was full of prominent citizens. The sight of Don Julián's arrival caused quite a stir among the townsmen and Indians.

Out of the Indian throng, the Tankayllu appeared. He clicked his steel scissors loudly; dancing skillfully, he moved toward the corner, as if to catch up with Don Julián. A hawk's skin swayed on the dancer's head; on the green velveteen of his pants mirrors glittered; on his jacket multicolored streamers and big pieces of lantern glass glistened.

Before the *danzak'* could speak to him, Don Julián tossed him a pound note.

"Misitu is coming," he told him. "Get ready to receive him."

And he quickly passed him by.

On the balcony of the Subprefecture, the *mistis* drew closer together; they seemed to be conferring as Don Julián approached. When he had almost reached the door of the police headquarters, they all stood still in their places, as if waiting. Don Julián did not even glance at the important people; he went straight into the headquarters. The Corporal was seated at the little table in the police station.

"I want to see Señor Jiménez."

"It can't be done, sir. You have to get the Subprefect's permission. Go up to the office; that's where he is."

"I'll go up."

The *mistis* watched Don Julián walk along rapidly, close to the wall of the Subprefecture. He was heading for the stairs, to go up to the balcony.

"This is the only really dangerous time. Here's your chance. If you don't stick him in jail now, afterwards it might be too late."

Escobar the student was speaking softly, almost in the Subprefect's ear.

"You have to take a firm hand with him. Once he's inside, all of his enemies, all of Puquio, will take courage; they'll back you up. Be bold, sir!"

They heard his footfalls on the stairs, and Don Julián's head appeared on the balcony; he kept on coming up. And he greeted them from the stairway.

"Good evening, gentlemen."

They answered him. Among the citizens Don Julián saw Escobar the student, Guzmán, Martínez the chauffeur, Tincopa, Vargas . . . all of "the renegade half-breeds," as he called them; the ringleaders of the Lucanas Union Center. It angered him. "Those *k'anras!* What did they come here for?" he asked, without their hearing him. And he calmly walked forward. The leading citizens and the mestizos were crowded together along the balcony. The Subprefect, Escobar the student, Don Demetrio, Don Antenor, and a slovenly blond stranger were in front.

"Señor Subprefect, I've come to ask your permission to have an interview with Señor Jiménez."

Don Julián spoke from a distance of about three meters. The twilight was still strong enough to cast Aranguena's shadow on the balcony floor.

"Can you tell me what is the urgent matter you must speak to Señor Jiménez about?"

"Of course, sir. It's not about anything dangerous. I'm just going to tell him that he's won our bet and I'm going to give him a hug. At

115

this very moment the K'ayaus are dragging Misitu down Pedrork'o slope."

"And that circumstance has made it impossible to carry out the numbers planned for this evening; the schoolchildren's torchlight procession, for example."

"Why, sir? No, siree! There's nothing for you to be afraid of; Misitu's coming in all tied up."

"You think the schoolchildren are as dumb as you, Don Julián, and won't be scared by the arrival of a wild bull?" Escobar said loudly, before the Subprefect could reply, and as if he meant to give everyone courage.

"Don't you be thinking of how it was in your day, Escobarcha," answered Don Julián. "You'd have been scared shitless, but the boys of today have their little pants on. This gentleman must be the bullfighter. He's the one who really ought to be scared."

"Don Julián, you're nothing but a trashy little landowning exploiter. And that's all!"

Talking, talking, Martínez the chauffeur pushed his way through and came up from behind to stand by the Subprefect.

"A thief who's walking around free in the streets."

Don Julián blinked. Who in hell could have said that to him in Puquio? His birthmark swelled; his heart felt heavy as lead, it was burning him.

"You filthy Indian! You must not be afraid of hell if you talk to your *werak'ocha* like that!" he yelled.

And in his mind, in his burning heart, he had decided the driver's fate.

"Silence!" The Subprefect stepped forward to face Don Julián. "Nobody threatens anyone else around here. You are in the presence of authority. Don Julián, you have five minutes to talk to Señor Jiménez! Go!"

Don Julián spun around, crossed the balcony with long strides, and descended the stairs. The Subprefect watched him from the railing; Don Julián walked over to the police headquarters and went in. Then the official also ran down the stairs at full speed. By the time he reached the police station, the Corporal had already had Don Julián go into the jailyard and was opening the room in which Don Pancho was held. The Subprefect waited long enough for Arangüena to enter the room, and then went into the jailyard and called out to the Corporal.

"Lock them both up! Right away!" he ordered.

He went with two policemen. And as the Corporal was pointing his pistol into the room, the policemen closed the door.

"I bet my neck the Subprefect is going to order them to jail Aran-güenita," said the Bishop when the Subprefect ran down the stairs.

"Some day!" said Martínez the chauffeur. "The problem will be when he gets out."

Don Antenor, Don Demetrio, Don Gregorio, and Don Felix were not talking; they were rather subdued; they looked at Escobar the student, at the Bishop, at Martínez, and at the bullfighter; they glanced at one another and seemed surprised. These "*chalos*" had just arrived, and nevertheless they were moving up close to the Subprefect, just as the most important people did; they were looking at the prominent citizens as if they were their equals. Martínez, Vargas, Escobarcha . . . weren't their parents still living, walking around in the Indian quarters and on Girón Bolívar in tatters? Where had they gotten that air of pride, that determination, which gave them the courage to confront Don Julián, to stare at the leading citizens of the town with such self-possession? The *mistis* were half-stunned; they watched the delegates of the Lucanas Union Center with a sort of concealed envy. But the half-*mistis* who were at the end of the balcony craned their necks to see Martínez, Guzmán, and the student. To have brought Don Julián up short like that? To have called him "thief" so cold-bloodedly and in front of the official? They would have liked to move forward and embrace him, to have joined that Indian who had learned Spanish in order to tell the biggest exploitative landowner in Puquio the truth. And they saw clearly the confusion in the minds of the other notables; they saw how Don Antenor turned around, without knowing what to do, and looked at the ground.

"This is starting out with an altercation," said the Spanish bull-fighter. "Bad sign!"

They heard the footfalls of the Subprefect, who was coming up the stairs. Escobar the student went over to the stairway to greet him.

"Señor Subprefect, my congratulations. For once I see an official who's a stickler for justice."

The student shook the Subprefect's hand. In whose name, as what personage did he congratulate the Subprefect like that, with such flowery words? The leading citizens felt offended. All the Lucanas Union Center members surrounded the Subprefect, speaking to him in loud tones.

"The man to tighten the screws on that bandit has finally arrived."

"Señor Subprefect, you have set the town a good example."

The Subprefect went over to the *mistis*.

"So . . . how does this strike you? The devil's bottled up now."

But the townsmen were not quick to reply.

117

"Wouldn't you say, Don Antenor, that Señor Arangüena was a saint?" asked the Bishop.

"It's all right, Señor Subprefect. Just so long as this step you've taken doesn't do you any harm. . . ."

It was hard work for Don Antenor to speak.

"Does this make it any easier to enforce the edict, or doesn't it?" inquired Escobar in a loud voice.

"Yeah, sure, maybe Don Julián might have raised a ruckus about this bull. But . . . who doesn't know how Don Julián is?"

"It's all right, Señor Subprefect!"

"It's quite all right! We'll back you up!"

The least of the *mistis*, the ones who were against the wall at the end of the balcony, spoke loudly.

"Yes, gentlemen. And the national government is not afraid of anybody. That you must remember. The government commands. Whoever opposes the government ordinances is crushed. Tomorrow the professional bullfighter will perform in peace. And now, let's make sure that the bull's entrance does not cause any trouble."

"We'll go see about that, Señor Subprefect. With your permission."

Escobar the student and the other delegates of the Lucanas Union Center took leave of the Subprefect.

"Good night, gentlemen. And come along with us, Ibarito. You're going to make the acquaintance of your bravest enemy."

They left. By now the Plaza was in darkness; in the little streetlamp on the corner the wick was sputtering; through the lamp's glasses shone a dim, yellowish light, and it was flickering on the white wall at the corner.

Escobar and his group entered the Plaza and approached the fountain in the middle of it.

"We're leaving too, Señor Subprefect," said Don Antenor.

"Run along and don't worry; I've detailed the Sergeant and two pairs of policemen to oversee the bull's arrival."

The *mistis* said goodbye. Out in the Plaza, they separated into groups. Don Antenor went off with the most notable citizens. They were talking.

"That Escobar looks suspicious. Mightn't he be thinking of stirring up the Indian mob? He was pretty hard on Don Julián!"

"These lettered *cholos* are dangerous."

"The government shouldn't let them into the University."

"This way the country is walking on hot coals."

"We'll have to find a way to crush him."

"And that Escobar is sharp! He's got the Subprefect in his pocket."

"But fortunately we know the weakness of the man from Ica. A

118

little cash is all it takes."

"As for Martínez, sooner or later Don Julián will have him skinned alive."

"That's as good as done."

They went off, whispering.

Ibarito did not want to go, in the darkness, to watch the bull's arrival.

"I know how these famous highland bulls are. Either they're reruns, and plant themselves in the middle of the ring and wait for a man to put his body up to their muzzles so they can charge, or they're some poor fraidy-cats who dash all around the the arena and flee the cape as if it were the devil. It's better I stay in the little hotel, resting. Tomorrow I'll see about the bullring. And I'll figure out a way to finish off that 'Mesito,' or whatever they call him."

They let him go.

All of the Lucanas Union Center delegates set out for Yallpu. They had to go down Girón Bolívar, enter Chaupi *ayllu*, and go out through that side of town to the K'oñani road. When people heard the K'ayaus sounding the *wakawak'ras* on Pedrork'o summit, and when the Indians ran to the *ayllus* announcing that the K'ayaus were calling down from the road, they shut the doors of the houses and stores on Girón Bolívar. The ladies and girls would have liked to go to meet the bullfighter. The news of his arrival had spread to all the townspeople since Martínez' car had entered the plaza with the Lucanas Union Center delegates. But while the Spanish bullfighter and the men from the Lucanas Center were going to the Subprefecture to greet the official, the *wakawak'ras'* song had come down from the mountaintop and the citizens had also run to the Subprefecture to reach an agreement on what to do. It was certain that the K'ayaus were bringing Misitu down, that's why the Chief Staffbearer had announced the *ayllu*'s arrival, from the top of the mountain. They were proclaiming from the pass that they were coming down, bringing the bull.

And the town was left in a fearful silence. The Pichk'achuris were scurrying around their neighborhood; the staffbearers were bustling about, talking, as if someone had rung out the alarm signal on the *ayllu*'s little bells. And the shadow was advancing across the sky, extinguishing the yellow twilight clouds. In the neighborhood lanes, in the open fields, in the *ayllu* squares, people were running. The K'ayau women came out of the houses and looked to the mountain; they called to one another.

"Misitu's all set! From Pedrork'o he's coming down."

"All tied up he must be coming down."

And when it grew dark and the night began, even the Pichk'achuris went into their houses.

"In nighttime his tongue blazes, they say," is how they spoke of Misitu when they thought of him.

Only the Tankayllu went on dancing from corner to corner. A group of Chaupis accompanied him; apprehensively they managed to lead him away from K'ollana, far from the Yallpu road. As never before, the Tankayllu was dancing in silence, almost for nothing. The sound of his steel shears carried a long way in the dark neighborhood; the harp and the violin that were playing the *danza* also cried loudly in the stillness. When had the great *danzak'* ever danced like this in the open?

"He and the devil are pals, that's why he's not scared," they said, when the clicking of his scissors rang through the lanes and the empty fields of the neighborhoods.

Not even at the Chaupi fountain did the Lucanas Center delegates encounter any people. There the little streetlamps came to an end. On Calle Derecha Chaupi *ayllu* begins, and from there on they do not put up any more streetlamps; everything is dark on moonless nights. Only in the chapel doorway, hanging from the lintel, a little parchment lantern was glowing; it was not there to shed light, but rather as a sign of the chapel. In the darkness the leather lantern looked dreamlike, suspended in the air.

"It would take us a thousand years to save the Indians from superstition," said Guzmán, seeing the square of Chaupi, the happiest *ayllu*, so black and gloomy on the eve of the twenty-eighth.

"It depends, brother. A friendly national government, one of our very own, for example, would uproot sooner, much sooner, that awe the Indian has of the earth, of the sky, even of the valleys and the rivers. We know their soul; we would enlighten them from close by. But what do you expect, brother, with governments that support all the beastly, hardhearted, landowning exploiters like Don Julián Arangüena? Those guys are pushing harder and harder all the time, and with hellishly deliberate calculation they force the Indian to become rooted in that dark, fearful, and primitive life, because it's to their advantage; that's why they command and rule. And they're powerful people, brothers, because they, too, know the Indians' soul, perhaps just as well as we do. They drive the Indians headlong into darkness, into what we call 'the mythical fear' at the University. The Indian sees K'arwarasu; the clouds that surround his summit are always dark and imposing; and up there it always looks like a storm is about to begin. Contemplating him, what does the Indian

120

say? He kneels, his heart trembles with fear. And the landowners, the priests themselves, all the people who exploit them, who make money at the expense of their ignorance, try to confirm the belief that the Indians' fear of the great forces of the earth is good, is sacred. But if we were the national government, brothers! What would happen? We'd smash the causes that have made primitivism and serfdom survive for so many centuries."

On Calle Derecha, in the dark, silent *ayllu*, the student's voice resounded. The mestizos, the Lima *"chalukuna"*[5] who walked with him, listened to him quietly. Escobarcha felt free to talk that way in the calm darkness of the *ayllu*; his heart became more and more inflamed with passion as he went on speaking; and he felt as if a great tenderness were warming his eyes.

"When I learned that K'ayau was going after Misitu, I was angry and sad. It would be a slaughter of Indians. But now that we're going out to meet the *ayllu*, I'd like to shout with joy. Do you know what this means, brothers—that the K'ayaus have dared to go into the Negromayo Canyon? That they've roped Misitu and dragged him all the way across the puna to the Pichk'achuri bullring? They've done it out of pride, to show the whole world how strong they are, how strong the *ayllu* can be when it wants to. That's how they built the road to Nazca; that's why: a hundred miles in twenty-eight days! Like in the time of the Inca Empire! Some students in Lima said, 'Stupid Indians, they work for the benefit of their exploiters.' It's a lie! Which way did we go to Lima? Which way did we come back this time? Why can I speak with this consciousness that I have? I found the way to illumine my spirit to serve their cause, the *ayllus*' cause, by going to Lima on the road they built. All of us did, brothers. Martínez, the chauffeur from K'ollana *ayllu*, Martínez the Indian, has just castigated, once and for all, the most terrible exploitative landowner in Lucanas. How? The *mistis* blinked with fear when the K'ollana Indian called the most powerful of the leading citizens a thief. If it hadn't been for that road. . . . What does it matter if Misitu may have ripped the guts out of ten or twenty K'ayaus, if in the end they've lassoed his horns and are dragging him along like any old wild highland bull? They've killed an *auki*! And the day they kill all the *aukis* who are tormenting their minds, the day they become what we are now—'renegade *"chalos,"'* as Don Julián says—we shall lead this country to a glory no one can imagine."

5. Lima *cholos*, a derogatory term for mestizos who go to live in Lima and adopt the speech, dress, and manners of non-Indians.—Trans.

By then they were at the edge of town. The student's words fell like fire on the spirits of the Lucanas Union Center mestizos. At that moment, and all alone, they would have fought the whole world to defend the *ayllus'* cause.

They crossed the creek, figuring how to jump from stone to stone. Almost all of them splashed into the water. The Bishop slid way down a rock and sat down in the middle of the stream.

"You might have put your belly within reach, Monsignor, and I'd have crossed over on top of you," Vargas yelled at him.

"Lucky there's a good breeze blowing; it'll dry your seat in a little while."

"Did our Bishop fall in? Might be a bad sign."

The Bishop had just finished crossing the water with two good leaps, and went to the head of the line to go up the hill.

"You guys are all mouth. We'll see who's the first to sweat going up the slope." And with long strides he started up the mountain road.

The wind shook the branches of the bushes and the blades of grass; it rustled along the ground, dragging weeds and leaves with it, carrying off dust from the road and the parched mountainsides. In the clean, deep black sky the stars were shining freely; they seemed to hear the crickets' song. The high-pitched barking of the mongrel dogs came up clearly from the *ayllus*. The lamps on Girón Bolívar were visible from the mountain, in the hard black of the night, motionless, tiny, and spaced out like beads on a string. And there was the sound of the stream that came rushing down the mountain, sobbing in the silence.

"Our land, Bishop! You hear? The water, the crickets, and the dogs, lifting up their song unto all the mountains. Doesn't your affection for our land grow when you walk these mountains by night?"

"Yes, brother. And I was just recalling the stories of I don't know how many things that have happened to me."

"I was remembering the nights I've slept on the wheat-threshing floors of K'ollana."

"You remember everything when you walk these mountains by night."

"And look at Puquio. Its little streetlights look like playthings."

"Beautiful, our town!"

"At least the little streetlights serve to let us see our town from the heights, even if it's a dark night."

All of a sudden they heard the noise the K'ayaus were making dragging Misitu.

"They're coming!"

"They're already close-by!"

"You hear?"

Not only did they hear the sound of sandals slipping on the stones in the road, the K'ayaus' words were coming down to them now, loud and clear, and more far-reaching than the hubbub of the council meetings. And over the voices, which sounded like the mountain talking, the shouted orders of those doing the dragging came down more loudly.

"Get him up!"

"Pull!"

"Stop!"

"Hold 'im tight!"

The mestizos left the road and stood up on top of the pasture wall that bordered it the whole way to the top of the mountain.

"We'll wait here. Farther up the road narrows," advised Martínez.

The noise the K'ayaus were making on the mountain was slowly drawing closer. It seemed that they were already nearby, but it was taking them a long while. The mestizos from the Lucanas Center no longer spoke; they watched the road, which the starlight barely marked out among the bushes and the dry grass.

"They're right close now!"

"Yeah! They really are!"

And the men doing the dragging emerged, one after another, like little shadows.

"Pull, damnit!"

"Pull, K'ayaucha!"

The wall was about thirty feet from the road. Neither the men dragging nor Misitu saw the mestizos. Misitu went along with his face to the road, and those dragging were pulling carefully.

"There's Misitu!"

"The captive *auki*, brothers!"

When the draggers and the bull had gone by, the great troop of K'ayaus appeared, filling the road. All the *"chalos"* jumped down into the roadway.

"*Taytay* Chief! It's all right!"

"Long live K'ayau *ayllu*, brothers!"

"Long may it live!"

They ran. The K'ayaus stopped short.

"Escobarcha's who I am, Chief!"

"Martinizcha, K'ollana."

"Guzmán, Chaupi."

"Vargas, Pichk'achuri."

"Rodríguez, Chakralla. . . ."

The student hugged the Chief Staffbearer.

"It's all right, *tayta*! K'ayau's a great community, always."

The other mestizos hugged the *comuneros*, indiscriminately. Martínez got Raura. They recognized each other.

"*Mak'ta* Raura!"

"*Taytay* Martínez!"

And they held each other in a long embrace.

"*Jatun* Raura! Like dog, by God, Misitu is going! Man, K'ayau community, by God!"

"Let's go, let's go!" yelled Escobar.

"Long live K'ayau!"

"Long may it live!" all of the *comuneros* then replied.

"Puquio is looking like graveyard. K'ayau *ayllu* scaring Puquio, important people. Everyone, everyone!"

The Chief Staffbearer and the *comuneros* laughed contentedly. From behind, people were jostling each other, trying to see who had entered at the head. The mestizos divided up and entered the crowd at intervals. Rodríguez fell in with the last of them, beside the sorcerer's stretcher bearers. All of them told the K'ayaus that the town was silent; that there had been no torchlight procession or fireworks castles in the Plaza; that the *danzak'*, Tankayllu, had been dancing all alone, through all the neighborhoods; that he was clicking his scissors in the silence, as if in a dead town. The K'ayaus laughed. That was what they had wanted. To scare Puquio. To be in command—even if only for a day—of the whole town.

"*Jajayllas*, damnit!"

Some of them had skinned their hands. All those who came on behind had taken their turn, and many of them had had the palms of their hands cut by the lassoes.

They raised a dust on the road. Everyone was talking. The Lucanas Center men had to use their wiles to keep the *comuneros* from asking them about Don Julián. The whole time the mestizos kept inquiring about the lassoing of Misitu, about the entry into the Negromayo Canyon, about the K'oñanis. The K'ayaus kept saying that the demigod, K'arwarasu, had favored their *ayllu*. That all of a sudden Raura had put the first lasso on Misitu. But that, surely, out of friendship and respect for *tayta* Ak'chi, the *auki* K'arwarasu had paid for Misitu with the blood of his sorcerer. The K'ayaus questioned them about the highway, about the coastal towns; some of them wanted to know about Lima. And on that subject the mestizos spoke at length. Afterwards, they also talked about the *aukis* for a while. They wanted to make the K'ayaus understand that Misitu had fallen because the *comuneros* were resolute, because Raura was courageous, because man could always overcome the *sallk'a* bulls. The

K'ayaus seemed to believe them. But the mestizos realized that it was not easy, that the *comuneros* were certain the great K'arwarasu had protected the community, and that all of them would die adoring the *auki*, as the father of the *ayllu*.

From the head of the troop, the Chief Staffbearer shouted.

"Shift! Change!"

Martínez was next to Raura.

Thirty Indians stepped forward.

"Stop, stop!"

Those doing the dragging restrained the bull, pulling on him fore and aft.

Suddenly Martínez jumped forward and lined up with those who were taking their turn.

"Listen, Escobar, I'm going to drag in the name of the Center."

"Me, too!"

"No, brother, you'll wreck your hands. Tomorrow you have to stand up for us. I'm the one who's more Indian, and I have a right."

"*Taytay, Alcalde!*"

The two asked if Martínez could take a *comunero*'s place. The Chief Staffbearer hesitated for a moment.

"Grab arm, *tayta*. For K'ollana I'm going to drag!"

The headman tested the driver's muscles.

"All right," he said.

In the Staffbearer's voice, the two could sense the Indian's joy that a mestizo friend, a Lima "*chalo*," would enter the town with the *ayllu*. The driver hugged the Indian leader and lined up with those who were taking a turn. A *comunero* stepped out of line.

The Chief Staffbearer put Martínez in with those doing the dragging. They went around behind the wall to change over.

The creek was close-by now. It was the last shift. The town's little streetlamps could be seen more clearly.

Martínez was on the shift that was to make the bull go into the Pichk'achuri cattlepen. Sometimes the bull pulled hard and the lasso burned. But there, shoulder to shoulder with the K'ayaus, he felt prouder than ever before; his arm bore up well and he was dragging furiously.

"Good, *tayta* Martineza!"

"Now you got it! That's the way!"

"Pull!"

"Get 'im up!"

The *comuneros* who were pulling with him realized how strongly the "*chalo*" was dragging.

"Now you got it!" they shouted at him.

"K'ayau first, always!"

The others also pulled furiously. And Misitu slid through the stones, plowing the ground with his hooves.

When they reached Yallpu, Raura gave the signal with his *wakawak'ra*. All at once, all of the trumpeters began to play. Misitu tried to buck, but they made him jump the creek and dragged him on the run down the street leading into town.

Through the wide street, they came into the *ayllu* of Chaupi. Whitened walls lined the straight street. As they entered the town, those who were dragging shouted:

"Get 'im up!"

"Pull, goddamnit!"

"Hold 'im tight!"

The deep-voiced *wakawak'ras* thundered against the street walls; the dogs came out, barking furiously. The K'ayaus ran behind the draggers, pressing against the doors with their bodies.

"*Yauúú,*" cried the Chief Staffbearer.

They came out into the Chaupi square and passed the chapel door, doffing their hats. The little lamp still burned.

"Long live K'ayau!" yelled Escobar in Spanish, as loudly as he could.

"Long may it live!" answered the K'ayaus.

The civil guards who had been waiting at the entrance to the town came running along behind them; they ran with their rifles over their shoulders, swallowing the dust the K'ayaus raised from the ground.

The Chaupis came out into the street resolutely when they heard the K'ayaus running by. They ran too, following the guards. The police went along, choking, in the midst of the Indian mob; before and behind them ran a black troop of *comuneros*, filling all the streets from wall to wall.

"What a mess! We're in trouble!" They were raging and cursing.

And behind them, the Indian mob kept growing. Out of all the streets they came, first the Chaupis, and after them the K'ollanas; they were running to get ahead of one another, passing the policemen in herds.

And the sky remained dark; beyond the Sillanayok' Pass, it was barely growing light with the glow that announces the moonrise; and the stars kept vanishing in the reflection the moon radiated from inside the sky, over the edge of the pass.

They entered the big square at Pichk'achuri. The Chief Staffbearer, Escobar, and the other Indian leaders ran to the gate of the cattlepen. They opened it, and the other bulls milled around against the back wall. When Misitu entered the corral, the draggers ran to the other gate, the one that opened onto the Vicar's arena. Martínez opened it, and then went into the ring; they closed the gate and tied the lassoes to one of the eucalyptus logs that held up the stands. They left Misitu with his muzzle to the eucalyptus gate, ready to tear out into the bullring.

The square was filling up with Indians. With a little lantern made of a sheep's bladder, Pichk'achuri's Chief Staffbearer came in from the chapel corner, walking slowly toward the gate of the cattlepen. They made way for him.

"*Taytay Alcalde!*"

"*Taytay Alcalde!*"

The two staffbearers greeted one another. The glow of the street-lamp barely reached the ground.

"There's Misitu, *tayta*," said the one from K'ayau, opening the gate of the cattlepen.

"Let's see."

Pichk'achuri's Chief Staffbearer entered the pen, followed by K'ayau's Chief Staffbearer and councilmen, Escobar, Guzmán, Martínez and Raura. . . . They walked over to the *sallk'a*. Pichk'achuri's Chief Staffbearer raised his little lantern high. Misitu's streaks were visible, his broad hump, his mucked rump, his dirty tail, his big horns grazing the entry gate to the ring.

"It's all right, *tayta*! It's all right, K'ayaus!" And Pichk'achuri's Chief Staffbearer turned around to go back to the square. Everyone followed him. The little lantern slowly crossed the cattlepen and came out into the big square. By then it was full of all the Indians of Puquio. They were jostling one another and talking. K'ayau's Chief Staffbearer stayed behind, tending the cattlepen gate.

"Way! Make way!" they yelled from the opposite corner, by the K'ayau entrance.

Above all the noise in the square, loudly and clearly, the Tankayllu's steel scissors could be heard.

"Way! Young Tankayllu is coming in!"

They quieted down a bit, and the clicking of the dancer's scissors rang through the square, as if steel were raining down out of the sky. He advanced to the center of the square. There they made a place for him. And he began to dance for all the Indians from the *ayllus*, for the *comuneros* from all over Puquio.

In a little while, the edge of the moon shone out from the Sillanayok' Pass; its light reached the mountaintops; it traveled a long way to the ends of the valley, illuminating the mountains of San Pedro, Chillk'es, and Casa Blanca.

11. Yawar Fiesta

From San Pedro, from Chillk'es, from San Andrés, from Utek', from San Juan, from Ak'ola, from all of the neighboring districts, people set out in the early dawn, on foot and on horseback, for Puquio, to see the great bullfight, with K'ayau challenging Pichk'achuri. Indians and townsmen came by paved roads and by footpaths, reckoning the time so they could arrive early and find a place in the arena. From the morning on, *comuneros* and leading citizens from the towns were coming into Puquio. One could identify the *comuneros* by their clothing, by the color of their ponchos and the shape of their hats, by the form of their sandals and the way they were sewn, by the color and cloth of their homespun pants and jackets, by the designs on their vests. One could tell them apart a long way off: "Chillk'es," "San Pedro," "Utek'" . . . and the prominent citizens could also be recognized.

"Good heavens! This year all the towns have been emptied into Puquio; almost all the Ak'olas, the San Juanes, the Utek' . . . have come! Where will they all fit in?"

"It's gonna make work for the police. That little bullring the Vicar had them build—I don't think it'll even hold the people from the *ayllus*."

Indians or townspeople, the first thing they did when they got to Puquio was run to the cattlepen to see Misitu. The Pichk'achuri square and the cattlepen walls were full of people. Like thorns set into the tops of walls to make them more secure, that's how the people from Puquio and the other towns were sticking onto the tops of the walls. Standing, seated, or astride, watching Misitu, waiting there for the bells to ring out, calling people to high mass.

In the place where the eucalyptus arena began, seated by the palisade, Kokchi had awakened, in the best place, near the bull. It was barely daybreak, when the first dawnlight shone into the town, that Kokchi spoke to Misitu. Weeping, he had been waiting for the first streaks of day. When he saw Misitu's head, with his muzzle tied to the eucalyptus logs by the gate, when he saw his hind legs, soiled with all they had made him shit, Kokchi cried like a baby, hugging the eucalyptus log where the bullring began:

"*Papay! Papacito!* How can it be! How they've brought you in, *mak'ta!* You might have run away, child; running, you might have left your *k'eñwa* thicket; straight across the plain you might have gone to your lake; calmly you might have entered the water of your lake, of your *mamay.* Ay, Misitu, *papay!* Right in you might have gone, to the deep part, to the depths; how much you could have slept, too; and later, once it was February, in January, when there's nice green grass in your *k'eñwal,* you might have gone back to your Negromayo."

He wept as he spoke to the bull. The K'ollanas, the Pichk'achuris, the K'ayaus, the Chaupis who were in the square were listening to him. They were silently chewing coca leaves, concealing their sorrow with difficulty.

"*Ai, papacito!* Now you'll never go back, never again! They'll blast away your chest with dynamite; your blood will stay in Pichk'achuri. And up in the high country, on K'oñani plain, they're weeping, all of them, all of them; *tayta* Ak'chi too, the brush too, the grass too, the river, the Negromayo too; all the bushes, all are weeping for their *mak'ta,* just for you, *papay.* Into Torkok'ocha not even the ducks go any more; its water is a whirlpool, weeping. *Ay papacito!* Misitu!"

For a long time the herdsman was talking. And when the people climbed up onto the walls to see the bull, when the town notables and the police arrived, he fell silent, watching the *sallk'a.* The Spanish bullfighter came too, with about twenty *mistis;* he entered the cattlepen and went right up to Misitu, almost close enough to touch him.

"He's a good bull," he said. "I hope he's clean. But according to what they tell me, he's already killed one, and that means trouble. It only takes one lesson for these beasts to learn."

They left. The *comuneros* did not know who that blond *misti* was. But several of the delegates from the Lucanas Center remained in the Pichk'achuri square.

"For the *mistis* he's gonna fight bulls; he's come from foreign land for that," Martínez the chauffeur explained to the staffbearers. "They say he does beautiful capework; with *danzak'* clothing he's gonna go into the arena, competing with Pichk'achuri and K'ayau. But at the

129

head, first of all he's gonna go in, when Misitu is mad all over."

The *comuneros* were gathering around the driver. Then the others also spoke, each one to a large group of Indians. They were talking loudly, explaining that the blond *misti* had come at the townsmen's expense, to fight bulls in Pichk'achuri in the important people's behalf; that he would perform first, because he was a master at capework, so they could watch his bullfighting, Indians and *mistis* alike.

"Let the *werak'ochas* go in themselves if there's courage!" Pichk'achuri's Chief Staffbearer answered loudly. "How come bringing in hireling from foreign land to bullfight for *misti*? No, *tayta*! Before Judge, with court clerk, a little substitute'll be sworn in to go into bullring? None of that! You think K'ayau sends in substitute? Raura'll go in, Tobias, Wallpa;[1] for Pichk'achuri community K'encho will stand up, Honrao Rojas. . . ."

All of the *comuneros* spoke at once.

"Of course, *tayta*!"

"Sure, *tayta*!"

"Nothing, nothing, foreigner!"

"Misitu is for Endian."

The Lucanas Center delegates looked at one another apprehensively. Their plan had turned out backwards. The Indians threw their ponchos over their shoulders; they pushed back their hats.

"Let important people go in. When little substitute?"

"Misitucha!"

They were all bragging. They were going to the cattlepen gate, pointing to the corral, and saying,

"I *k'ari*, I *papacito*!"

By now they were really lit up. All night long they had been drinking cane liquor in the square.

The Lucanas Center delegates met by the chapel.

"They want to die, brothers. What'll we do?"

"The bull will catch them easy in that little ring."

They were watching the Indians swaggering around the square. They did not understand, did not even want to.

"They went about this in the wrong way, in bad faith. They should prohibit the bullfight. We've just brought the bullfighter up here for nothing."

"Why'd that two-faced Vicar have them build this bullring?"

By all four corners people were coming in; Indians from all the towns were running to the cattlepen, asking questions; they ran to find a free place on the walls of the corral where they could climb up

---

1. The name "Wallpa" means "Hen" in Quechua.—Trans.

and look at Misitu. And the more the people kept coming in, the more the K'ayau Indians shouted their defiance of Pichk'achuri.

The sun was blazing down out of the clear sky; climbing rapidly, it was leaving Sillanayok's summit far behind and entering the depths of the sky, over the town. The tin on the rooftops was burning and shining with a bright glare.

"Let's go tell Escobar. Let's go to the Subprefect's office. There's still time."

"It can't go on like this. They won't see a drop of blood in the bullring this year," said Martínez, leading the way. "Or else we'll never return to Lima, and we'll stay here working as overseers for Don Julián. And if any blood is shed, it won't be the *ayllus'*, goddamnit! It'll be another kind."

The streets, too, were teeming with people. On Girón Bolívar, *mistis* and girls, in holiday garb, were standing on the corners and in the shop doorways, talking.

Peruvian flags were fluttering by the doors of all the houses on Girón Bolívar; crowds of *comuneros* were walking down the middle of the streets; and since the sun was kindling the whitened walls the street was really in a festive mood.

Just as they reached the Plaza, the bells began to peal in the big tower. It was the first call to the solemn mass of the twenty-eighth.

In the Plaza, before the main church door, the Tankayllu was dancing. Through the temple's open doorway the entire main altar was visible. The Indians had cleared a path from the church entrance to the place where the *danzak'* was dancing. The Tankayllu was doing *atipanakuy*[2] figures, and as soon as he finished one he'd stand erect and click his scissors, pointing them toward the rear of the church.

When they heard the first call, the Indians headed for the Plaza de Armas; behind the Lucanas Center delegates, they began to come in through every corner of the Plaza.

Martínez and the group with him encountered the lieutenants of the four Indian communities in the Subprefecture.[3] The Police Sergeant and Escobar, with the other mestizos from the Lucanas Center, were also in the office.

"The situation is bad, Señor Subprefect," said Martínez, as he walked up to the official's desk.

"What's happening?" asked the student.

"The *comuneros* are furious about the bullfighter. They say

2. Competition figures.—Trans.
3. These lieutenants are mestizos appointed by the subprefects to enforce the law in the Indian communities.—Trans.

they're the only ones who have a right to fight Misitu; that's why they brought him down here. The situation is serious. It's hard to make them understand, sir."

"We'll make them understand! That's what the lieutenants are here for."

"We're in trouble," Martínez whispered to the student. "They want to go in to fight Misitu all by themselves. They're making threats in the Plaza."

The Subprefect arose from his chair and stepped out onto the rug.

"Nothing else works! We'll have to use force on the blockheads! Listen here, you lieutenants: notify all of the staffbearers that we'll put a bullet into the first Indian who jumps into the ring. And that they're to fill in that hole they dug in the ring. Señor Sergeant: notify them also that the saddlecloths are canceled. You Sergeant, with your civil guards, are now the ones who are responsible for carrying out higher orders. You must proceed like men; there's no other road at this moment."

The four lieutenants were half-breeds. They gave the Subprefect and the Lucanas Center delegates frightened looks.

"Do you think the threat will have a good effect?" asked Escobar.

"The Indians are scared of the bullet, and they just might quiet down."

"Yes, sir. The Indians tremble at the sight of a rifle. They're sure to calm down."

"You're from K'ayau, and you're from Pichk'achuri, aren't you?" asked Escobar, pointing to those who had spoken.

"Yes, sir."

"Scare the hell out of them, then. Tell them the cops are hankering to kill Indians, that if they make a move to jump down into the ring you're going to shoot at them, right at their chests."

"Yes!" The Subprefect confirmed Escobar's words, raising his voice. "Tell them it's serious. That we'll teach them a horrible lesson."

"Your orders will be carried out, Señor Subprefect. By your leave, sir."

The Pichk'achuri Lieutenant left, with the other three following. From behind they all looked alike, with their suits of webbed wool and their collars black with grime. Their shoes, made by Chaupi cobblers, struck the office floor-boards like stones. From the doorway they made their final gesture of respect, bowing from the waist as they did when they passed before church altars.

"By your leave, sir."

"And you, what do you think?" the Subprefect asked the student, once the lieutenants had gone.

"It's all right, Señor Subprefect. And since you have to go to mass, we're leaving too."

They said goodbye and went out onto the balcony. By all four corners, the Indian throng kept coming into the Plaza. Entering the church, they filled the doorway, the women with their shawls or *llikllas* spread over head and shoulders, and the Indian men with hats in hand. The *danzak'* had already left; he was probably dancing in the Pichk'achuri square and would come with the largest crowd of Indians, at the third call to mass. On the Plaza ground, the shadow of the police headquarters flag was playing and moving about, fluttering.

"The bullfighter! He's the only one who can save us," said the student.

And they rushed down the steps of the Subprefecture.

"If Ibarito starts out fighting well, if he stands right up to the bull and does his capework with a will, the Indians will keep watching him from the stands. He'll hypnotize them, you understand?"

"Of course."

"Let's go and encourage him."

The sexton began to ring the last call. The K'ayaus and the Pichk'achuris were now coming up Girón Bolívar. The Tankayllu came on ahead. Behind the dancer were the staffbearers and the well-known Indian bullfighters: K'encho, Honrao, Raura, Wallpa, Tobias. . . . From the balconies the *mistis* and girls were looking on.

"K'encho! There goes K'encho!"

"Honrao! He's a real Indian . . . the most *macho* of all."

"Raura! The first to put a lasso on Misitu."

"There's Tobias!"

"But now they're not going to fight the bulls."

"Who says so?"

"But it's really been forbidden now! That's why they brought the Spanish bullfighter."

"That's the truth!"

"But if they enter the bullring, you'll see that they'll really fight, that they'll go in like men."

"I hope so! I'd like to see them with that bull of Don Julián's."

The Indians filled more than a block; they walked along slowly, following the *danzak'*.

When the dynamite blast set off in the middle of the mass shook the walls of the police headquarters, Don Pancho crossed himself, doffing his hat.

"They're elevating the Host, Don Julián."

"Sure. The dynamite just now exploded."

There Don Julián was, peaceful as could be. At no time had he become really angry. When the guards had pointed the gun at him and shut the door of the lockup, Don Pancho had thought that with one good kick Don Julián would knock the door boards loose. He thought his eyes would blaze with fire and that he'd rock the police station with his shouting.

Lock up Don Julián? Even Don Pancho himself was frightened. He watched him expectantly, his heart pounding in his chest. But Don Julián had calmly held out his hand to him.

"I came to see you, Don Pancho. But in our old age, I think, we usually make fools of ourselves. What nerve! Who would ever have believed it? The two of us in jail, like Indians."

"And it's an abuse."

"It's not an abuse. I just made a nuisance of myself. But those renegade 'chalos'—I sure am going to do something awful to them. But now we can still talk about our little bet. The K'ayaus are coming down with Misitu now. Did you hear the wakawak'ras announcing it?"

"Yes, I heard them. What did I tell you? The K'ayaus are really tough. I might as well speak plainly; the Indians, if they got together and agreed to it, could even put a lid on the inferno, like a pot. Lord, if they knew we were here, they just might get us out, out of pure cussedness they'd knock down the door and crash right through the cops and take us out to see Misitu."

"You they might take. As for me, many's the time I've beat them up. Down inside they must surely be cursing me. Well, that's understandable. Me, I drive 'em just like dogs. Now you know, Don Pancho, there's plenty of Indians that I've made trouble for. Well, that's the way it is. God's put me in Puquio so I can put up with them. Lord! And up on the puna I've really made them yell, from Coracora to Chalhuanca, from Pampachiri to Chipau. I've tamed them as I would a mean stallion, like that, just by knocking them around till they fell to their knees on the ground. You, now, are something else; another kind of heart's what you've got. And that's reasonable. You've made money just by selling them drink and provisions; nice and quiet and of their own free will they've brought the profits right to your own house. Anybody could do it that way! That's why you stand up for the ayllus; you're friendly with K'ayau, with Pichk'achuri, and defend them as if they were your own children. 'Goddamnit, the comuneros are papachas!' you say. And you stick up for that mob of Indians every chance you get. You sure do! That's the way it has to be. But I have to run the puna well armed, and I have to sink the spurs into them hard. But, to tell the truth, you and I have never fought. The other townspeople bite me harder than the Indians do."

"Don Julián, you're like a sire bull in Lucanas; you go from one end of it to the other, shoving people around and taking advantage of them. But the truth is we haven't fought one another. And now we're in jail together, like brothers. And when we get out they're likely to put us back in, and the next time it won't just be for laughs."

Don Julián was looking up at the smoke hole in the roof, cupping his jaw in his right hand, pensively, as if he were watching the night swiftly coming through the window and growing in the room.

"Do you remember Martínez, the Indian from K'ollana? The one who's a chauffeur in Lima now?"

"Yes, yes, I remember him, Don Julián."

"Now he's wearing serge already. Now he's come up here bringing the bullfighter; with the 'chalos' from the Lucanas Center he's come. What do you suppose he's thinking by now? People who are going to die suddenly, they say, have premonitions about it and feel sad, even if they're terribly tough. . . ."

His face was no longer visible; the room was dark, and only on the ground beneath the window, in one small part of the room, was there any brightness—the twilight that was still coming in. Through the middle of the room, that little bit of light shone on Don Julián's body, and made it possible to see him sitting on the pepperwood bench that the police had left in the room. Don Pancho heard the menace in Don Julián's voice quite clearly; the misti's words were smoldering with suppressed rage. Don Pancho could not see his face, but he sensed that the black birthmark on his right cheek was growing larger and putting itself on guard, as the big spiders, the apasankas, do when they become angry and stand up high on their legs.

"That's the way it is, Don Julián."

He didn't want to inquire; he waited for Don Julián to speak of his own accord, to tell him about why he had been jailed and about the sentence he had passed on Martínez.

They conversed far into the night. A guard came to offer them a candle, but Don Julián sent him away; then they hung a lantern in the jailyard, at the entrance to the room, on the corner of the wall. The yellow lantern light shone in through the cracks in the door, crossing the yard and tracing on the ground and on the walls of the room little rays of light that barely brightened the ground and the whitewashed walls of the lockup.

When the police headquarters had quieted down, they heard the sound of the Tankayllu's scissors in the distance; the harp music and the clicking were nearing the Plaza; they passed close behind the headquarters, as if they were going to K'ollana, and faded out, gradually, in the direction of that *ayllu*, going into the heart of the neighborhood.

Don Pancho was figuring it out in his mind: "By now they must be almost to Yallpu; pretty soon the *wakawak'ras* are going to call." Don Julián was also waiting. And while they were quietly listening, the *wakawak'ras'* song came tumultuously in through the air, from Yallpu.

"Now, Don Julián! Now they're coming in! Misitu! Your bull!"

Don Pancho ran to the door, as if to leave; he pressed his forehead to the boards, trying to look through the cracks.

"What do you say, Don Julián?"

"The poor thing must be old by now. His balls must be weighing him down. When I saw him up the Negromayo Canyon, he was a tiger; he was leaping around like a puma. His hour has come, Don Pancho. And he's going to die his way. Damn! Who would have believed it?"

"Pretty soon the town will wake up! You'll see. . . ."

"Of course! When they figure he's already in the cattlepen. These Indians are all different. Look here: K'ayau brings Misitu in, dragging him, and the other *ayllus* crawl into their houses like *viscachas*."

"But pretty soon they'll be coming in. I'd like to be in Pichk'achuri! To see the entrance. Wouldn't you? Damn my luck!"

"I just might have got so mad I'd have plugged that *sallk'a*. I might have knocked him down right in the middle of the Indian mob, the way it should be done. Or I might not have gone, not even to the bullfight."

"Well, now, Don Julián. You're really mad!"

And later they heard the K'ollana Indians running, behind the police headquarters and in front of it. They heard the Tankayllu going by, almost running, because the sound of his scissors passed the headquarters rapidly.

"Now the Tankaylla's going by!"

The rockets burst in the sky, in threes and fours.

"Don Julián! What a dog's luck I have! I'd like to be out there by the cattlepen. I'd pour firewater on the K'ayaus' feet.[4] I'd play the *wakawak'ra* with Raura, with Tobias. The least I can do is to give this door a punch! Hell! The goddamn bastards!"

And he almost knocked loose the board near the latch.

"Open up, goddamnit! Or I'll do something horrible!"

---

4. Before any risky undertaking, a little strong spirits or *aguardiente* is poured out; before traveling, people sprinkle it on the horses.—Trans.

Don Julián did not budge from his place.

"Another one, Don Pancho, so you can really let off steam."

But the cops arrived, and from the courtyard the Corporal shouted.

"Do you want me to hang you from the bar, like an Indian?"

Don Pancho retreated to a corner of the room where the light that shone through the cracks did not reach.

"What must you be saying, Don Julián? But sometimes my anger makes me turn chicken."

For that reason, when he heard the dynamite blast in the middle of the mass, he crossed himself with all his heart. He wanted to go to the bullfight; he did not feel sure of himself remaining quietly in jail while Misitu was playing in Pichk'achuri. And in his mind, choosing the meekest words, he asked the All Holy:

"*Taytacha*, merciful Lord: you are knowing I am a citizen who does my duty; I haven't cursed you like the others; I haven't taken advantage of my fellow men nor stolen from them; I'm never anything but good! Just forget my binges for a little while, my vices with the women, my cursing Don Demetrio and Don Antenor; you are knowing that they're a pair of dogs. And get me out, *papacito*! Even if they put me back in again for a month, starting tomorrow. But now . . . no, sir!"

He tried hard not to speak aloud. He was ashamed to do so before Don Julián. But Don Julián was watching him; and by his humble face, by his bowed head, he guessed what he was doing. Halfway through the mass, when the dynamite blast announced to the town that the Sacred Host was being elevated, surely Don Pancho was praying; that's why he had such a solemn face.

"It must be for his Indians, or for himself," Don Julián said, watching Don Pancho Jiménez, who stood silently and stiffly, his head uncovered, in the middle of the room.

On leaving the high mass, all of the Indians went off in a throng to Pichk'achuri. They waited for the staffbearers, the men who fought the bull with their ponchos, and the horn players to take the lead, and behind them, all intermingling, came the K'ayaus, the Pichk'achuris, the K'ollanas, the Chaupis, and the *comuneros* from the other towns. From the Plaza de Armas to the cattlepen, the streets were full of them. At the gate to the bullring they found six armed policemen, the Sergeant, and the lieutenants from the Indian neighborhoods.

"Halt! Right there!"

And they stopped the staffbearers a short distance from the eucalyptus arena. While the Sergeant gave the order, the policemen held their rifles in their hands, and the lieutenants watched the Indian mob from the bullring gate, behind the cops.

The sun was now passing through the middle of the sky; on the whole valley the sun's rays beat directly down. The tin roofs were shimmering and blazing; on the white ground of the square and on the streets the fine gravel glared; the clean sky, bright blue and joyous, seemed to graze the mountaintops surrounding the town. The rocks on Pedrork'o's summit appeared ashen; near the rocks, several black *ak'chis* were flying, so that the mountaintop appeared even higher and more remote; the birds of prey circled, soaring slowly, as if they were looking for something on the valley floor. No wind was blowing; the air was quiet and still. Only, out of the clear sky, the sun cast its fire down onto the level fields and hillsides, into the depths of the valley.

The staffbearers obeyed and stood there, holding back the surge of the Indian throng.

"Halt! *Sáyay!*" they commanded also.

But they kept on coming in and surrounding the little eucalyptus-wood ring, leaving a cleared space at the gate, in front of the civil guards. By all four corners Indian and mestizos came in, and they began to climb up onto the walls and onto the roofs of the houses, the tower, and the chapel.

"Jesus! Señor Sergeant! They never came like this to the bullfights before!" said the Chaupi Lieutenant.

The guardsmen stared in awe at the mob of Indians that kept on growing, appearing on the tops of the walls, on the roof tiles of the neighboring houses, and on the chapel roof. From the depths of the square, an odor of filth and cane liquor spread, and a heavy, strong stench reached the policemen's faces. The Sergeant began to feel afraid. "If they move around, if they pile up, they'll crush us against the eucalyptus logs. Oh, mother! What a mob of Indians!" He called out to the Pichk'achuri Lieutenant:

"Tell them that in a little while the authorities and townspeople will get here, that behind the authorities they're going to enter the arena. Don't threaten them. Tell them in a nice way."

The Lieutenant stood up on the tips of his toes beside the Sergeant and shouted:

"*Cumunkuna!*"

He spoke to them at length, explaining that they should have patience, that the authorities would soon arrive; that as soon as the latter presented themselves at the corner, the *comuneros* should make way for them to pass.

138

"It's all right, *taytay* Lieutenant! It's all right!" answered the Chief Staffbearer of K'ayau.

The Sergeant sent the same Lieutenant to tell the Subprefect, the Mayor, the bullfighter, and the townsmen to hurry, that the policemen were in danger.

The Lieutenant made his way through the Indian mob, pleading and announcing that he was going for the Mayor, so the bullfight could begin at once.

When the Lieutenant was in the middle of the square, opening a path for himself and pleading with the people, the trumpeters from the four communities began to play the *turupukllay*, the real thing, the bullfight music for the *yawar punchau*, the bloody day. The *comuneros* stirred; their eyes grew round and they stared directly at the entrance to the bullring. The Lieutenant stopped for a while; the *turupukllay* resounded loudly in the square; it seemed to be pounding on his chest; like despair it grew in his mind.

"Make way, *taytay*! Make way!"

The Lieutenant shoved the Indians harder, and elbowed his way through, as if he were escaping from the square.

"That music again! How can they play so gloomily! And on a day like this, so sunny and hot."

The Sergeant watched the Indian throng nervously, his heart beating rapidly.

"Sergeant! If they take a long time to get here, they're really going to make it hard for us," said a guardsman.

"They shouldn't be long now."

The *turupukllay*, the music of the *yawar fiesta*, carried to every part of the town. The citizens hurried to go to the square.

"It's time now! Now the Indians are calling!"

The deep, sad song of the *wakawak'ras* that sounded every year from Pichk'achuri made the notables' hearts throb that afternoon; it was driving them crazy; they were gathering to go, and were having beer and stronger drink carried to the square. Suddenly they grew enthusiastic; they became cheerful, but in a different way, not like when they got drunk or made a good business deal; the joy that welled up from the depths of their consciousness was of another kind. They could not have explained it; it was a holiday, a big celebration in each soul. So, they liked to see blood? Since when? They called out to one another and hurried to the square, barely able to resist their desire to go running, shouting loudly and cheering the *cholos* on.

The first townspeople to reach the corner of the square stopped.

"Where're we going to go through?"

"Lord of Untuna! So many Indians!"

The ladies and girls begged to go home. They had come, as they did every year, with heavy hearts, but counting the steps, despairing, because it was a long way to Pichk'achuri. The closer they got to the community square, the tighter fear gripped them, but the same fear that discouraged them was pushing them on; they wanted to get there quicker, to sit down on the chairs that had been placed in the stands; and they wanted the bull to be turned loose immediately against the drunken men with ponchos who would enter in droves. But this time the *ayllu* square was full of Indians who were still waiting. The Vicar's arena rose up behind the Indians' heads like a huge skeleton, and it seemed far off, at the end of all the Indian heads that covered the whole field. And from the midst of the sun-scorched hats, in the fire from the sky, from the tiled roofs, from the white earth in the streets, in that clean, heated sky, making everyone's heart throb, the communities' *wakawak'ras* were dolefully singing the *turupukllay* of the afternoon of the twenty-eighth. It sounded as if the bulls in the cattlepen were bellowing, as if the wounded Misitu were lifting up his black muzzle and singing to the sky and the mountaintops.

"We're leaving! Let the men stay!"

"Let's go running!"

"Once and for all!"

"Get going, then! Why talk so much about it?"

The gentlemen did not know what to do either. They did not want to ask the Indians to let them through; and on the street beyond the corner of the square, the town's most prominent families were assembling.

"Soon the Subprefect'll get here with the authorities and the bullfighter. The guards will have to clear the way for them. Let's wait."

Finally, the officials and the bullfighter appeared, turning off of Girón Bolívar toward Pichk'achuri.

"Here they come!"

The *mistis* clustered together to look in that direction. Then the Indians also stirred.

The bullfighter was walking along in the midst of the authorities; his silk suit was shimmering from afar.

"How beautiful! He looks like a *danzak'*!"

The prominent citizens and their ladies became excited.

"All that's lacking is a band. A march for the bullfighter!"

"What must the Indians be saying?"

When the bullfighter and the authorities reached the last street, the townsmen and ladies applauded and made way for them to pass. The Corporal and the guardsmen pushed forward to clear a space for them in the Indian mob.

All the Indians turned around to look at the corner.

"Make way! Make way!" yelled the Corporal.

When the Spanish bullfighter appeared, with his cape and his suit shimmering like the clothing the saints' images and the Tankayllu wore, the *comuneros* became even more restless.

"Make way! Make way!"

Pushing and shoving furiously, they squeezed closer together. And the authorities began to enter the square.

"I think we're saved. Courage, Ibarito! Courage, *werak'ocha!*" cheered Escobar the student, and the men from the Lucanas Center. The Indians looked at the bullfighter, as if an evening star had fallen from the sky. In their minds, Escobar and the "*chalos*" were pleading: "Ibarito, you can do what only an all-powerful being would do! This afternoon!"

And they were advancing. Don Demetrio, Don Felix de la Torre, Don Jesús Gutiérrez, Don Policarpo Santos, Don Gregorio Castillo . . . all of the citizens of note came on behind the authorities, with their wives and their girls. The men from the Lucanas Center, the mestizos, and the young people followed the leading citizens. The Indians kept closing in and moving forward, behind the *mistis*. They eagerly looked for Don Julián and Don Pancho in the *mistis'* ranks.

"Make way!" the Sergeant commanded.

The Indian staffbearers, horn players, and bullfighters also opened a path for themselves. By now there was almost no cleared space between the bullring gate and the staffbearers; they had been slipping by the policemen and pushing them back.

The bullfighter and those from the Lucanas Center stayed below the box seats; the Subprefect and the authorities went up the steps on the right to the boxes that had been set up with benches and chairs. Surrounding these boxes, bleachers of eucalyptus poles, like in the circus, in twenty rows, went around the rest of the arena, for the Indians. The ring was small and round; in the center of it, the dirt was still churned up, because the lieutenants had just finished filling in the hole the Indians had dug to serve as a refuge for themselves, like the one they'd had in the big Pichk'achuri bullring. Six planks of double thickness sunk into the ground close to the *barreras*[5] would serve as a shelter for the Spanish bullfighter.

5. The fence around the ring in which the bull is fought. The first row of seats are also called *barreras*.

"It's just like a real little bullring," said the Subprefect.

"Yes, sir. They put it up in six days, the *comuneros* from K'ayau and Pichk'achuri did."

The townspeople and the authorities were busy finding chairs. The boxes were scarcely two meters above the bullring.

From the square came the noise the Indians were making as they neared the ring gate.

"Now! Let 'em go!"

They came running in, pell-mell.

"Up you go!"

The staffbearers, the horn players, and the Indian bullfighters were the first to ascend.

"Keep going, keep going! *Kuchúman!* (To the corner!)"

The lieutenants made them go to the end, by the willow palings that separated the ordinary bleachers from the boxes. Indian bullfighters, trumpeters, and staffbearers sat down in a single row, leaning over the *barrera*. They all had on completely new clothing, from shoes to hats. Behind them, the *comuneros* from the four *ayllus* and the towns were finding seats, squeezing together so as not to leave any empty space. They were clambering up all over the stands. They were seating themselves and looking off toward the mountaintops. All of the *aukis* would be able to look down from their heights; to the bottom of the ring they could see. The women from K'ayau and Pichk'achuri came in, too; like a wide red, blue, and green band, according to the colors of their shawls and *llikllas*. The women's section looked cheerful, in the midst of the Indian throng, from the *barrera* all the way to the top of the stands.

The arena was filled with song. It looked like a dark ring of Indians, solid and wide, with an ornament in the middle, because of the color of the shawls.

But on the outside, on the *ayllu*'s big field, there arose an outcry that frightened the citizenry. The shouting took a turn around the bullring; from all sides it kept coming in. And people were running pell-mell across the field by the cattlepen.

The big eucalyptus poles swayed, and everywhere the heads of the *comuneros* began to stick up from behind, over the top row of the stands.

The gate to the arena was jammed with Indians. The guardsmen and lieutenants were shouting, telling people there was no more room, but they kept on shoving. Those who were still out in the square ran; they went out into the field; judging the distance, they ran for the fence and began to climb the big logs. Group after group grabbed hold of the logs to get into the bullring, but those who had got up first pushed the others down with their feet. There was no longer any place to get in! And the guardsmen began to flog the *comuneros* in the gateway; the lieutenants also broke off sticks from the fences and helped the guardsmen.

"Out, out! Beasts!"

The whips and sticks slashed the Indians' heads. The cops and lieutenants were seized with fury; closing their eyes they flailed at the Indians' hats.

"Out, guanacos!"

And they pushed them back; little by little they made them retreat, and between the lot of them, police and lieutenants, they closed the gate to the bullring. Perspiring, exhausted, they stood there, leaning against the gate.

When they saw the bullring gate was shut and the arena full to the top of the stands, those who had been left out in the field ran from the gate to the wall of the cattlepen; from there they came back, crashing into one another; they stood by the logs, looking upwards.

"*Papacito*! No!"

Some of them began to cry.

"*Papacito*!"

They were calling as if they were lost, as if they were going drunkenly to their children's funeral. They were seized with despair, looking up at the top edge of the outer fence, all of them running back and forth.

"*Papay*! Here we are! Getting left out!"

They looked at one another as if a flash flood from a downpour had come up into the town and carried off their houses, their provisions, and the money they had saved—as if they were looking on, in fear and trembling, by the stream.

"*Papacito*!" they were shouting; they ran along the outer fence, looking for a place.

They looked at *tayta* Pedrork'o, at Sillanayok'.

And they wanted the arena to be opened so they could go in and see, to watch the foreign *danzak'* fighting Misitu.

And while they were running back and forth, the women's song arose from inside the arena; the *wakawak'ras* played "The Wak'raykuy,"[6] following the song:

Ay turullay, turo,	Ai bull, my little bull,
wak'raykuyari,	gore then,

6. "The Goring."—Trans.

| *sipiykuyari* | kill then |
| *turullay, turu!* | bull, my little bull! |

There they were, calling now, the women of K'ayau and Pichk'achuri; they were singing for Misitu's heart, asking for mercy, breaking the bulls' spirit with the bitterness of their song.

Turullay, turo,	Bull, my little bull,
wak'raykunkichu	how you must gore
sipiykunkichu	how you must kill
turullay, turo!	Bull, my little bull!

Hearing "The Wak'raykuy," Ibarito began to lose heart.

"Señor Escobar, couldn't you muzzle those women? They sing as if they were already seeing my corpse."

"Can't be done, Ibarito. And you shouldn't cower like that. Have a drink."

"The Wak'raykuy" oppressed the hearts of all the *mistis*. The Indian bullfighters and leaders were watching the faces of the girls and leading citizens, trying to figure out the place where the foreign *danzak'* would come out to fight Misitu.

By then the white ground, dry and hard, was scorching; the sun was beginning to go down toward Pedrork'o Pass; its heat rose up from the ground to the boxes and stands as if it were bouncing off the dry earth.

K'ayau's Chief Staffbearer stood up and signaled to the Indian councilman who was awaiting the order to release Misitu. They had already learned, from the lieutenants, that there would be no saddle-cloths, dynamite, or rockets, that the *turupukllay* would be held in silence. And there, in the gateway of the arena, were all the cops, with rifles in hand, watching the Indians.

The women fell silent. Then the trumpeters began to play "The Jaykuy," the entrance music, in a high-pitched key, like a cattle-branding song. The *wakawak'ras* were calling, with voices like those of human beings. The leading citizens stood up to see the bullpen entrance; the *comuneros* also looked directly at the same place. In the silence of the bullring "The Jaykuy" rose up to the sky, as if all the people in the arena were singing softly.

Misitu sprang straight out, but with the outcry that arose from all over the arena he tossed his head and remained in the middle of the ring, with his neck raised high, pointing upward with his horns. The Indian bullfighters were shaken; K'encho, Tobias, Wallpa, and Honrao

144

felt as if their hearts had cast them down; their blood was scalding them from head to foot.

"Goddamn Misitucha!"

"Goddamn! I *mak'ta*! K'ayau!"

And they began to ready their ponchos.

But the Spanish bullfighter came out through the gate where the policemen stood guard. And all of the Indians stood up. His suit was shimmering in the sun, his chest thrust forward arrogantly. He took off his hat and saluted all sides of the arena.

"Bravo!" The *mistis* clapped their hands, applauding him.

Misitu drew himself up, facing the bullfighter. Ibarito began to approach the bull cautiously, judging the distance well.

"Long live Ibarito! Long live the great bullfighter!"

The delegates from the Lucanas Center cheered loudly. But the student and the *chalos* were losing their confidence.

Misitu took off; he pawed the ground and raised dust with his hooves on the first leap.

Ibarito was waiting for him with his cape ready, his legs firmly planted on the ground. He raised his cape and Misitu passed by his body, snorting; he spun around on the spot; the bullfighter still passed his cape before him well; but on the next pass, Misitu planted himself beside the figure and, with his hind hooves prancing, began to seek what was behind the cape. Ibarito threw the cloth over the bull's head; in three leaps he had reached the shelter and hidden himself behind the planks. The bull tossed the cape around furiously; he stamped on it and slashed it everywhere, as he had the sorcerer's body.

"No, damnit!"

"Damn lazy slug!"

"*K'anra!*"

"*Atatau!* Damn queer!"

From the barrier the Indian bullfighters yelled:

"I *k'ari*! I K'ayau!"

K'encho, Tobias, Honrao, Wallpa . . . each of them indicated himself by beating his chest with his fists.

"*Atatau k'anra!*" and they pointed to the plank shelter where the bullfighter had taken refuge.

"Lazy slug! Fairy!"

Then suddenly the Mayor himself, Don Antenor, jumped out of his seat, shouting,

"Let Honrao go in, goddamnit!"

"Let Tobias go in," yelled Don Felix de la Torre.

"Let Wallpa go in!"

"K'encho!"

All the Indian bullfighters jumped down to the ground. And once again the trumpeters played "The Wak'raykuy" in the lowest key.

"K'encho!"

"Tobias, damnit."

"No, Wallpa!"

Wallpa ran like crazy, straight for Misitu. The guardsmen squeezed in where they could see, pushing in front of one another. The Sub-prefect was not able to speak: trembling, with hard eyes, he watched the ring.

Misitu charged Wallpa. The K'ayau got his body well out of the way.

"Whoa, goddamnit! Misitucha!"

And he got set again, stepping back a bit. Misitu turned around and made a pass with his horns, grazing the Indian's belly.

"Whoa, slug! *K'anra!*"

Calculating carefully, Misitu pursued him. Wallpa still held up his poncho, but by the time the bull looked for him again he was retreating.

"He's gonna kill him! Balls!" shouted Ibarito the bullfighter.

The other Indian bullfighters drew closer to Misitu, calling at the top of their voices. But Misitu knew what he was doing. He kept after Wallpa. The K'ayau saw the horns steadily coming closer to his body and with all his might he shouted:

"Misitucha! Dog!"

But the *sallk'a* found his groin; he thrust his left horn deep into it. And Wallpa was pinned to the barrier; the others had come right up to the *sallk'a*, and Honrao pulled his tail for him. Misitu turned on him furiously, ripping Wallpa's shirt. Honrao threw his poncho in the bull's face, and while the *sallk'a* was tossing the poncho around, the *capeadores* prepared themselves to confront him. K'ayau's Chief Staffbearer handed Raura a stick of dynamite.

Wallpa was still acting like a man; it was hard for him to stay on his feet, clinging to the barrier, and he stiffened his legs to keep from toppling over. He was in front of the important people's box. Almost all of the girls and *mistis* were looking at him. Suddenly his pants swelled out over his thicksoled shoes and a great jet of blood gushed out of the mouth of the pants, flowing down and covering his shoes, and it began to spread over the ground.

A dynamite blast went off at that moment, near the bull. The dust that swirled up in a whirlwind in the ring darkened the arena. The *wak'rapukus* played an attack melody and the women stood up to sing, divining where the ground of the arena was. The dust cleared, as if dissipated by the song. Wallpa still stood there, clasping the poles. Misitu was walking, step by step, with his chest destroyed; he looked blind. Honrao Rojas ran toward him.

"Well, die, *sallk'a*, die!" he yelled at him, opening wide his outstretched arms.

"You see, Señor Subprefect? This is how our bullfights are. The real *yawar punchau*!" the Mayor said into the official's ear.

Puquio: A Culture in Process of Change

THE LOCAL RELIGION

Some Data on the Agents of Change and the Social Composition of the Four Ayllus

The city of Puquio, capital of Lucanas Province in the Department of Ayacucho, is on the Pacific slope above the Río Lomas basin, at an elevation of 3,200 meters, in the widest Andean valley we have ever known. The main street follows the crest of a hill that rises nearly in the center of a horizon almost as imposing as the one around Cuzco. The *ayllus*, which the mestizos call "neighborhoods," extend on both sides of the hill. The most direct road from Lima to Cuzco passes through Puquio.

Ever since olden times the city has been divided into *ayllus*: K'ollana and Chaupi, Pichk'achuri and K'ayau. Today it is estimated to have 14,000 inhabitants, 70 percent of whom are Indians. The four *ayllus* were officially recognized as communities beginning in 1942.

Note: We made studies in Puquio in August 1952 and in September and October of 1956. The latest was with the assistance of our esteemed professor, Dr. François Bourricaud, and the collaboration of Josafat Roel Pineda, Head of the Ethno-musicology Section of the National Conservatory. It is worth noting that the author of these notes spent his childhood and adolescence in Puquio.—Author

This edition omits most of the original Quechua texts and includes only the English translation of the author's Spanish versions of them. Words in parentheses are Arguedas' addition, while those in brackets have been added by the translator.—Trans.

In ancient times the Rukanas area formed an important province in the Empire; in the pre-Inca period they created an original culture that, to judge by abundant examples of its pottery, reached a level of development as high as the most notable pre-Inca cultures.

Chaupi and K'ollana *ayllus* are considered to be "brothers" of each other; K'ayau and Pichk'achuri are also. There is a certain uniformity in the social and economic composition of the two groups. The legend of the mythical heroes, the Wachok', is evidence of the antiquity of both this difference and this similarity. Only in the past ten years has the K'ollana Indians' economic situation deteriorated noticeably. K'ollana and Chaupi are the *ayllus* with the larger proportion of mestizo and *misti* population. The class the Indians label *mistis* is the one we would call *señorial* [or aristocratic]. A *misti* is not a white person; this name designates the *señores* [or gentlemen] of Western, or almost Western, culture who traditionally, since colonial times, have dominated the region politically, socially, and economically. Naturally, by now none of them is of the pure white race, or of purely Occidental culture. They are creoles. To the mestizos the Indians have given the name "half-*misti*," or "*tumpa-misti*," which means the same thing.

It seems the Spaniards were late in making their entrance into Puquio. Some other district capitals[1] have a much higher proportion of white and mestizo people; the urban and architectural configuration of those small centers is more Spanish. Moreover, in no district of the province do the indigenous communal authorities—the staffbearer, the headman—have so much influence and jurisdiction as they do in Puquio, where they were still presiding over the Sunday council meetings until only ten years ago, and the staffbearing Indian leader had absolute authority over the allocation of Puquio's irrigation water; he himself distributed it. The *señores* and the mestizos could not take this privilege away from the Indians; it is of fundamental economic importance in an area where there is a critical shortage of water. At the present time the staffbearer's authority over the water allocation has been neutralized; the national government appoints a mestizo "controller," who assists the staffbearer on the pretext that the Indian leader is illiterate. Theoretically, the controller's only duty is to write down the names of the people to whom the staffbearer allocates water; in effect the controller is more powerful than the staffbearer. And the conflict between the two authorities is quite serious. It represents the conflict among Indians, mestizos, and *mistis* in the administration of the community.

1. These are similar to township centers.—Trans.

In K'ayau and Pichk'achuri *ayllus* the proportion of Indian population is very high. A former staffbearer from K'ayau told us that in his *ayllu* the number of *mistis* barely came to twenty. And as we asked him if in that number he had included the half-*mistis* (mestizos), he answered with a smile: "Well, with those few more." In both communities the Indian has a more solid economic independence. In Chaupi there is not so high a proportion of mestizos and *mistis* as in K'ollana, and while the Indians in K'ollana seem to have been dispossessed of their lands and transformed into share-tenants or day laborers for the mestizos and *mistis*, in Chaupi the Indians have been better able to preserve their independence. For this reason a situation of harmony between Indians and mestizos has been created in Chaupi, while in K'ollana there is a state of ill will—the Indians deeply resent the mestizos; at the same time, amongst the mestizos there is a state of belligerent anarchy, toward each other as well as toward the Indians.

Until the modern highway was built—the first one was made by the Indians as a communal effort in 1926—Lucanas Province belonged to the Huamanga area of cultural and commercial influence. The folk architecture is typically Huamangan; prominent people sent their children to school in Huamanga or in Lima. The highways to the coast have broken up the Huamanga (Ayacucho) cultural area; Parinacochas and Lucanas provinces now belong to the growing area of influence of Ica and the coast.

From a small city of landowners and Indians, the highway changed Puquio into an active trading center. Old norms are being broken with progressive rapidity. "Society," composed of the old landholding families, the *mistis*, no longer exists. The norms that ruled the coexistence of those old families with Indians and mestizos are being reformed. Merchants and stock raisers have become the dominant groups, and most of those men are newly risen from the mestizo class. Almost all of the aristocratic families have been scattered, and have migrated. Those who still remain in Puquio have had to change their ways. "Don — goes around in his shirtsleeves and you can slap him on the back. His father used to walk about wearing a derby hat and carrying a gold-headed cane; when he went down the street, you had to get off the sidewalk to let him go by," a young mestizo who owned a prosperous business told us. "Even up in heaven there are hierarchies; in Puquio there no longer are any," the elderly heir to an illustrious surname asserted bitterly.

In 1935 there were only 8 shops; now there are 137.

The culture of Puquio's four *ayllus* (Indian communities) has also felt the effects of the economic transformation of the zone. The most important result, according to our observations, is the active state of collaboration between Indians and mestizos that has been created in three of them: between the *ayllus* and some of the newly prominent citizens of the city, the modern leaders. Such a situation became possible in 1946, after the official recognition of the four communities. It seems evident that the recognition was sought by mestizos and *mistis* in the hope that the government of the communities would fall, absolutely, into their hands. But the economic power of the Indians, who are smallholders in Puquio, and the solid influence of the Indian communal authorities, which was very great before the communities were given official recognition, frustrated the expectations of the *mistis* and mestizos. Nevertheless, since the official recognition, it is the Personero,[2] rather than the Chief Staffbearer, who presides over the council meetings, the truly deliberative assemblies that govern the communities.

Another very important factor is that there is no conflict between the economic situation of the most outstanding mestizos and that of the Indians—instead, they are complementary. The mestizos live by trade, and the increase in the value of farm products and cattle has augmented the Indians' purchasing power. The fact that Indians, mestizos, and even representatives of the old families are being obliged to associate in the official administration of the community has created a new situation that has yet to be defined in a stable fashion. Nevertheless, as we have already stated, in at least one community, Chaupi, the obligatory association has infused a great deal of energy into the community, and the latter has carried out important public works projects, remodeling the urban layout of the neighborhood. This had demonstrated that the association is necessary. A Pichk'achuri Indian leader told us, quite seriously, that his community had not progressed very much because it had few *mistis* and mestizos, and for that reason the older people were striving to have their children become mestizos. This declaration is important because it shows that it is possible for mestizos to appear in Pichk'achuri and K'ayau communities as a result of conscious efforts to change on the part of the Indians, and not because of the traditional inverse process of the *mistis* growing poorer, or as a consequence of illegitimate births. And from what we have been observing in the schools and in families, the transformation will occur rapidly, probably in no more than two generations.

2. An appointed official who was a member of the council of a recognized community and was responsible for documents and land litigation.—Trans.

The old Indians from the four *ayllus* complain about how the young Indians are changing their customs—especially those who return from the coast after a relatively short stay. They also complain about the Indians of the new generations: *k'epa ñek'en*. Three clear-minded old men, leaders of three of the *ayllus*, concurred that the *k'epa ñek'en* declare the old people "speak a language they no longer understand." "They—the *k'epa ñek'en*—don't even want us to attend council meetings. They tell us we speak another way, that they don't understand us. They don't even want to give us the irrigation water. Now they're quite different, all of them," said Don Mateo Garriaso of Chaupi.

There is, then, a parallel change in the Indian population that may be just as important as the one that has occurred and is still taking place in the mestizo and aristocratic classes.

We are convinced that it is not a matter of the usual change in habits from one generation to another—a change that takes place extremely slowly in the small, isolated interior towns; instead, it is a real revolution in norms.

Such a fact can explain, in part, why the Indians of the new generations, the *k'epa ñek'en*, are not familiar with the Inkarrí myth. They know nothing about it.

The Old Gods

"Our God (the Catholic one) is separate," categorically stated Don Mateo Garriaso, the wisest old Indian in Puquio, from the community of Chaupi. In the same terms the Chaupi *auki*[3] asserted that El Condor[4] is a Wamani,[5] but "He is separate." "He does not meddle." That is to say he's a Wamani, not God; he doesn't have influence; he doesn't meddle in men's affairs.

Our Catholic God is separate. He is the first God; he's over everything. Don Mateo Garriaso took off his hat every time he pronounced his name. But he is "separate." Don Viviano Wamancha asserted, also categorically: "Our God (the Catholic one) created the cloud, the rain; we receive them as one of his blessings. And from our fathers, the Wamanis, we receive the water, because that's how God has seen fit to ordain it." However the rain and the lightning rays are the work

---

3. Name of the mountain spirit and of the priest who represents him in the community and, at the same time, represents the community during the water *fiesta*.—Author

4. A mountain.—Trans.

5. A mountain deity.—Trans.

of the Amaru, according to Don Mateo Garriaso. "With his tail alone the Amaru flings the rain and the lightning ray. The Amaru is not a snake; he's only like a cat, like a dog. He pisses the rain and scatters it with his tail." Then, after thinking a moment, he said, "The lightning is Saint James' and Saint Philip's punishment, for the animals as well as for man. Riding on a white horse, Saint James, Saint Philip hurls the thunderbolt."

Inkarrí

We collected three versions of the Inkarrí myth. Our informants were leaders, council elders (men respected for their age and good judgment) from Chaupi and K'ollana *ayllus*. They were Don Viviano Wamancha and Don Mateo Garriaso of Chaupi and Don Nieves Quispe of K'ollana. We shall refer to them again later.

Version of Mateo Garriaso, Chaupi Ayllu Leader.

They say Inkarrí was the son of a woman who was a savage. His father, they say, was Father Sun. That savage woman bore Inkarrí; Father Sun begat Inkarrí.

The Inca King had three women.

The work of the Inca is on Ak'nu.[6] On K'ellk'ata Plain the wine, the *chicha*, and the *aguardiente* are boiling.

Inkarrí drove the stones with a whip, ordering them about. He drove them to the high country with a whip, ordering them about. Afterwards he founded a city.

K'ellk'ata could have been Cuzco, so they say.

Very well. After all I told you, Inkarrí confined the wind on Osk'onta,[7] on Big Osk'onta. And to Little Osk'onta he bound Father Sun, so time would last, so the day would last, so that Inkarrí would be able to do what he had to do.

When he had bound the wind to that mountain, he hurled a golden rod from the top of Big Osk'onta, saying, "Will Cuzco

6. Ceremonial clothing or place where ceremonies are held, according to Holguín [Diego González Holguín, *Vocabulario de la lengua general . . . llamada lengua Qquichua o del Inca* (1608; Lima: Instituto de Historia, Universidad de San Marcos, 1952)]. The K'ellk'ata Plain is a plateau at an elevation of 4,000 meters, located about thirty kilometers from Puquio. Everyone declares there is a spring of boiling hot water on that plain.—Author

7. A mountain east of Puquio. There are alleged to be ruins on its summit.—Author

fit?" It did not fit into K'ellk'ata Plain. He threw the rod far down, saying, "It does not fit in." Cuzco was moved to where it is. How far off might that be? We of the living generation do not know. The old generation, before Atahualpa, knew that.

The Spanish Inca imprisoned Inkarrí, his equal. Where, we do not know.

The head is all that's left of Inkarrí, they say. From the head he's growing inward; toward the feet he's growing, they say.

He will return then, Inkarrí, when his body is whole. He has not returned until now. He is to return to us, if God sees fit. But we do not know, they say, if God is to decide that he should return.

Don Viviano Wamancha's Version, Collected by Josafat Roel Pineda.

The Wamanis exist in their own right (as beings and as original things of ours). They were created by the ancient Lord, by Inkarrí.

The Wamani is our second god, then.

All of the mountains have Wamanis. On every mountain is the Wamani.

The Wamani gives the grasslands for our animals and gives us his vein, the water. Our God put (created) the cloud, the rain; we receive them as his blessing. And from our fathers, the Wamanis, we receive the Aguay Unu, because that's how God has seen fit to ordain it. But everything was put there by our ancient Inkarrí. He created all things that exist.

Then, while he was working, he told his Father, the Sun, "Wait for me." And with some iron bands he bound the Sun to Osk'onta, to the mountain, near Wanakupampa.

And the Sun was Inkarrí's Father. Inkarrí has lots of gold.

They say he's in Cuzco now.

We don't know who could have taken him to Cuzco. They say they took his head, only his head. And the hair on his head is growing, so they say; his little body is growing downward. Whenever he is made whole, maybe then the Judgment will take place.

When Inkarrí was about to die, saying "Ay, gold and silver!" in that way he made the silver disappear from the earth. "Hide yourselves, in the seven states, gold and silver," they say Inkarrí commanded.

We do not know who killed him; maybe the Spaniard killed him. And his head they took to Cuzco.

And for that reason, on the coast the birds sing, *"K'osk'opi riy;*[8] *K'osk'ota riy!"* (In Cuzco the king; to Cuzco go ye!)," they are singing.

Version of Don Nieves Quispe, K'ollana Ayllu Leader.

Inkarrí, they say, had power over all things—whatsoever he willed was done.

I don't know whose son he might have been. Perhaps Father Sun's.

Since he was the second God, he could command.

On K'ellk'ata Plain *aguardiente*, wine, *chicha* is boiling. Inkarrí's work.

The K'ellk'ata Plain could have been Cuzco. From Osk'onta, Inkarrí hurled a rod to Cuzco. Over the plain it passed, casting a shadow on it. It did not stop. It got to Cuzco. Where could Cuzco be? I don't know.

Inkarrí was throwing stones, too. Into the stones he sank his feet, as into mud surely. He commanded the stones, the wind. He had power over all things.

He was an excellent man. He was an excellent youth. I don't know him.

He can't possibly be alive now. They say his head is in Lima. How much, how much, how much he must have suffered! I don't know anything about his death. His commandments are no longer kept nor known.

It must have been our little God[9] who caused him to be forgotten. What will be! I don't know. But now the water, the natives, everything is as God disposes.

It is clear on K'ellk'ata, the *chicha* boiling, the wine boiling, the *aguardiente* boiling. Inkarrí's work.

The Catholic religion as practiced by the Indians is separate from the local religion; it performs a different function.

The first God is Inkarrí, as Viviano Wamancha's original words inform us. The Wamanis were created by the ancient Lord (God) Inkarrí, and they are the second gods. Inkarrí is the first. Nevertheless, Don Nieves Quispe asserts, "Since he was the second God, Inkarrí could command." Second God with respect to the Catholic God, but

---

8. *Riy* means "king" and is derived from the Spanish word *rey*, meaning "king"; the second *riy* means "go ye" in Quechua.—Trans.

9. The Christian God.—Trans.

first God, creator of the Wamanis and of all things, among the indigenous gods.

Inkarrí is conceived of as a latent God rather than as a doing one. After the myth had been recorded, Don Mateo Garriaso was asked if Inkarrí had created the world. With evident discomposure, he removed his hat and answered, "It was our God (the Catholic one) who created the world; it was our God." The question was not asked of Don Viviano Wamancha. The *sullka* (lesser) *auki* of Chaupi was asked the same thing, although indirectly, in the taped interview, after the hymn published below had been recorded. He was asked what the relation between the Wamanis and the Catholic God was. Unfortunately the interview took place before many *misti* witnesses. The *sullka auki* turned pale and his expression revealed his consternation as he replied, "No sir, no; I was mistaken about that." The *auki* had just finished asserting that the Wamanis were the protectors of the lives of men and of animals. The *sullka auki* refused to answer any questions at all, and kept quiet. The *hatun* (greater) *auki*, who was a bit tipsy, agreed to continue the conversation.

With a method some might think designed to conceal the main issue, but which was in keeping with the original logic of the thought of the Puquian Indians, and probably of Peruvian Indians in general, the three informants portrayed Inkarrí as the creator God. "But everything," said Don Viviano, "was put (created) in ancient times by our Inkarrí. He created everything that exists." Don Mateo was less explicit; he said that Inkarrí had bound the Sun to Osk'onta's lower peak so that time and the day might last. So that Inkarrí could do what he had to do. The same concept appears in Don Viviano's information: "Then, while (Inkarrí) was working, he told his Father, the Sun: 'Wait for me.' And with some iron bands he bound the Sun to Osk'onta. . . ." Don Nieves asserted that [Inkarrí] had power over all things and that he was *munayniyok'*; that is to say that whatsoever he willed was done.

All three informants spoke of Inkarrí as a decapitated, suffering God who is to return. Don Nieves, a man from K'ollana, who was the youngest and most contentious of our informants, said vehemently, "How much, how much he must have suffered!" And after asserting that the *mistis* would die if the Indians did not help them, and that it would be desirable for the national government to rule that each class—Indians and mestizos—be self-sufficient and "separate," because in K'ollana the Indians were treated cruelly, he stated, on narrating the Inkarrí myth: "His commandments are no longer kept. Since he died, his commandments are neither kept nor known . . . everything is done (now) as God disposes." And although he did not refer to Inkarrí's return, he insisted, "It is clear on K'ell-k'ata, the *chicha* boiling, the *aguardiente* boiling, the wine boiling. Inkarrí's work!"

Don Viviano spoke tenderly of "Inkarrí's little body" that is reconstituting itself. And serenely, not threateningly, but almost as if fearful for those who would settle accounts, he stated: "Whenever he is made whole, maybe then the Judgment will take place." And the fact that he is considered to be latent is explicitly noted in Don Viviano's reference to the coastal birds' song: "(In Cuzco the king; to Cuzco go ye!) they are singing." And in the statement that the God's body is in process of reconstitution from the head—which is immortal—to the feet, and inside of the earth, not in the light, in which it could be discovered.

The discovery of this myth surprised us. It was Professor Roel Pineda who found it, while participating in a mission directed by Oscar Núñez del Prado, with the financial support of *La Prensa*, of Lima, to the town of K'ero, in Paucartambo Province. According to Roel Pineda, the Inkarrí myth was also discovered in K'ero, and had motifs similar to the one found in Puquio.

The myth and the God provide a necessary explanation of the origin of the universe and of man, and of the history and situation of the Puquio Indian and of his final destiny up to the beginning of the present evolutionary process of change.

The Inkarrí myth appears in Puquio, insofar as we could determine, as the exclusive patrimony of only some of the old men. The young people do not know it; the mature men, between forty and fifty years of age, who have become influential people, leaders of the *ayllus*, know only passages that are incoherent or confused with the legend of the appearance of the Child Jesus of Prague in Puquio. Don N. N. of Pichk'achuri, who had been a leader for fifteen years, had served in the army, and was a *comunero* of high standing in the council, told us that Inkarrí hurled a golden rod from the top of Osk'onta Peak, and that the rod fell on K'ollpapampa, the place where the original city of Puquio was founded. An Indian child who was then herding sheep on the hill where the present city is located discovered the Child Jesus, "a little *misti* child who came to play with him every day." The Child was taken in by the shepherd's parents and the city had to be moved from the plain to the place where the shepherd used to play with the Child Jesus of Prague.

We think that probably in a few years' time the last repositories of the myth will have disappeared. The economy and culture of the Indians of Puquio are being shaken in their foundations. The authorities, the *mistis*, and a good part of the mestizos still treat the less

158

affluent, illiterate Indians with the traditional disdain that has come down from colonial times, but the Indians who are "well-to-do" have built new houses and are accumulating personal possessions to an increasing extent, to the point of converting houses into dwellings where they have the same comforts (in the way of furniture, china, etc.) as the mestizos. The *comuneros* have built schools in their neighborhoods, and in the four *ayllus*, as we have already stated, there exists the express purpose of making mestizos—not *mistis*—out of the younger generations.

Don Nieves Quispe spoke with strong feeling when he stated that he wanted all of the children of the natives, or *naturales*, as the Indians are accustomed to calling themselves—as they never call themselves Indians—to become mestizos so that official positions of authority and management of the community could be held by them, by the mestizo sons of the Indians, and not continue to be the exclusive patrimony of the old stock mestizos. "In the hands of the mestizos, sons of *naturales*, the authority would be excellent." This is seen as an imminent possibility in Puquio.

The Wamanis, Mama Pacha, Allpa Terra

The *naturales* worship the Wamanis every day. There is no outward worship of Inkarrí; that God is considered to be still dead. He has the attributes of the decapitated Inca, of the suffering God who is to return, and of the Creator. The Wamanis are the mountains, Señor Wamani. There are greater and lesser ones. Don Pedro [10] is the greatest of the Wamanis of Puquio, but K'arwarasu is the principal Wamani of all the Wamanis of the region within the area known to the Indians of Puquio.

In our interviews with the Indians, we did not succeed in finding out whether they have different conceptions of the Wamanis and of Allpa Mama (Earth Mother) or Allpa Terra (Earth), as they also call her. . . . "The Wamani is the mountain," the greater *auki* of Chaupi asserted categorically. But the man who is both selectman [11] and *auki* of Pichk'achuri said, "The earth has a name, just as we do; it is Wamani (his name), Señor Don Pedro." The plains are also Wamanis. Fearing I might ask for more specific information on the possible difference between the mountain Wamani and the plain Wamani and Allpa Mama, a rather drunken old man who was listening to my

10. A mountain; K'arwarasu is also the name of a mountain.—Trans.

11. A traditional Indian official to whose position the Spanish term *regidor* has been applied.—Trans.

questions during the Yauriwiri water Angosay ceremony angrily exclaimed, "The Wamani is what it is," and then swore at me. As the other *comuneros* stared at him reproachfully, he added, "He is the second God. He who takes care of us, he who gives us what we eat." Chaupi's lesser *auki* said, "He—the Wamani—is the earth, as if he were God, the being of our animals. Everything comes from him. From him flows the blessing of God, the vein, the water, the vein of God."

The mountains and plains are the personification of the earth. Each one has a name. And the *naturales* worship the mountains, since they show all the attributes of the earth: its generosity and its power of destruction. "The Wamani is fierce," admonished the old man who had sworn at me. "He can suck our hearts out while we're sleeping." Then I asked the man who was *auki* and selectman of Pichk'achuri why the Wamani was fierce. "Like the powerful man, the man who has lots of money is fierce," he answered. Chaupi's greater *auki* told us that the Wamani became angry if the *naturales* did not give him what had been agreed upon: "You end up giving it to him. He gets mad if you don't pay."

Don Viviano Wamancha asserted that on every mountain there is a large door through which innocent children enter. Inside there is a sort of temple where all the figures of the Wamanis are. The temple is surrounded by a resplendent city, with many elegant shops where fine clothing, such as the mestizos wear, and sweets and splendid foods are displayed. The children are free to eat them and wear the clothing. The Wamani requires only that the children take care of the flowers. The children can leave the inner city, but only for a short time; when they do they look powerful, with dazzling garments.[12] The Wamani is also called *auki*, which is likewise a name for the priest who officiates as the community's representative during the Sequia water festival.[13]

The Personero of Pichk'achuri community, a gentleman from Puquio, told us the story of quite an interesting personal experience he had had concerning the Wamanis and their serf and priest: the Pongo.

While he was Governor of a district in the interior of the province, it happened that the people of the district capital and outlying area

12. According to Waman Poma, 500 children were sacrificed in worshiping the large mountains; he cites K'oropuna [Mountain].—Author

13. This festival is to celebrate the coming of the irrigation water at the end of the dry season, and the festival involves the cleaning and preparation of the ditches. *Sequia* is a variant of *acequia*, the Spanish word for "irrigation ditch."—Trans.

were stirred by the news that in the high country, in a cave, lived a Pongo who performed marvelous cures and could foretell the future. Since people were getting all excited and going up to where the Pongo was, the Governor decided to put an end to the Indian's hoax. He sent four men to arrest the Pongo. They brought him down all tied up. The Governor treated the Pongo roughly; he made him sleep all tied up, in the jail. People from every social class, ignorant and literate, came to beg the Governor to set the Pongo free, and to vouch for him.

Then the Governor decided to test the Pongo. The latter asked for a series of ingredients to prepare the *"mesa"*[14] and to summon the *aukis* or Wamanis. Once the ingredients had been obtained, the Governor and the Pongo shut themselves up in a room, in the dark. The Pongo laid out the ritual table and called the Wamanis, who presented themselves. They flew into the room with a great whirring of wings. The Governor told us that he was able to see one of them, since he had left a window half shuttered. The Wamani had the figure of a small eagle, and looked incredibly imposing. He said that the Wamanis spoke majestically and angrily, and that they flogged the Pongo. The fiercest and most insolent of them was K'arwarasu. The Wamanis foretold the Governor's future; they gave him prescriptions to cure all of his ailments, and spoke to him. Each Wamani had a different voice. The Governor was charmed and converted!

He became a good friend of the Pongo and, in the end, wanted to become a Pongo. But the Pongo told him that it was no job for a *misti*, that a *misti* would not be strong enough to withstand the punishments and trials to which the Wamanis would subject him. And that, while the Wamanis were flogging the Pongo they had actually said that he should tell them whether he felt he could take such ferocious treatment with absolute humility. And then the Governor renounced his aspiration to be a Pongo. And far from that little town, the district center, he continued to maintain cordial relations with the Pongo. He said that once a woman friend of his, from Nazca, had begged him to take her to the Pongo to be healed of a disease no doctor could diagnose. His faith in the Pongo inspired him to perform the errand of mercy, and he called the Indian, who was three days by road from Puquio. And they hired a fast car and traveled to Nazca. In Nazca the Pongo laid out the ritual table, prepared the Wamani's ceremonial payment, and from a darkened room, in the presence of the

14. The Indians use the Spanish term *mesa* for this "ritual table," which is actually a cloth with the offerings placed on it in a set pattern. See p. ooo for fuller description.—Trans.

ex-Governor and the sick woman's relatives, summoned the Wamanis. As he was on the coast, he also evoked the Nazca *aukis*, especially Cerro Blanco. Then a conflict arose, because Cerro Blanco spoke only Spanish and the Pongo could not understand him. The Wamanis left in a huff, all of them. The following day the former Governor begged Cerro Blanco to let him serve as an interpreter. The Wamani accepted. And the mountains were able to participate. Cerro Blanco reproached the sick woman for being a witch. He declared that the illness from which she suffered was the result of an evil spell cast upon the sick lady at the request of one of her victims. K'arwarasu then ordered two lesser Wamanis to go and get the evil charms. And the ex-Governor said that in a few moments two birds dropped two witchcraft packets on the ritual table; they were foul-smelling objects that were burned immediately. The Pongo and the ex-Governor returned to Puquio in a few days, after the sick woman felt better and was recuperating.

The ex-Governor (who is now a Personero) thought that the Wamanis actually did take care of the Indians, and that the secrets of being a Pongo could only be learned inside of the mountains, where a strange city exists. He believed his friend, the Pongo, was still alive and had remained inside of a mountain for six months. At the end of that time he had appeared asleep on a plain.

There is no precise conviction that the Wamani has a manlike form. When the informants were questioned insistently on this point, they said that he did have a human figure. Chaupi's greater *auki* said, "He is visible or seen, just as we are." Don Viviano said that he is a man. However, they all agreed that, when summoned by the Pongos, the Wamanis fly and take the form of birds. No one said he had seen a Wamani in human form. But in the Inkarrí myth Don Viviano establishes the existence of a spirit, an abstract concept of the Wamani: "All of the mountains have Wamanis. On every mountain is the Wamani."

The Aguay Unu

The common word for water in the departments of Ayacucho and Huancavelica is **yaku**. If one uses the word **unu** as the word for water in speaking to anyone at all—*misti*, mestizo, or Indian—it is not understood. Nevertheless, the name for water in the *aukis'* hymns during the Sequia *fiesta*—the festival of Water and of the Wamanis—is **Unu**, as in Cuzco Quechua. The Puquio Indians accumulate the terms *Unu* and *Aguay Unu* in the ritual language. Instead of the Spanish word, *agua*, they use *yaku* in their everyday speech; but when they refer to water in a religious sense they use the Spanish term in addition to the word *Unu*. As may be observed in the *auki* hymns, in the original Quechua texts of the Inkarrí myth and of the Wachok' legend, the Indians of Puquio have incorporated many Spanish words into their Quechua, in most cases to express concepts or states of mind the Spanish words express more completely.

The Aguay Unu is a gift of the Wamanis. "From the Wamanis flows the vein of blood, the Water [Unu]. For our children of all kinds, for all of them, then," said the selectman and lesser *auki* of Chaupi. "The water is the Mountain Father's vein, the Aguay Unu," Don Viviano affirmed. Recounting the Inkarrí myth the same man, Don Viviano, said, "From our fathers, the Wamanis, we receive the Aguay Unu, only the water." Because the rain is the work of God. The Aguay Unu is, then, the water that flows from the earth.

Only Don Viviano spoke of the Aguay Unu as having a specific form. He said that on Pedrork'o Mountain, whence rises the spring that flows down to the pond at Moyolla, or K'orek'ocha, by that spring there are three little manlike figures, who are the water spirits.

All of our informants conceive of the Aguay Unu solely as the life-giving blood of the Wamanis. They asserted unanimously that water is the common heritage: "for the native, for the townsman." We found no indication that the Aguay Unu was considered to be the exclusive birthright of the Indians. They believe that everyone—human beings and animals as well—has a natural right to the blood of the Wamanis.

The Aguay Unu receives the most valued offerings: the llama heart and the Castilian sheep heart. Don Viviano calls the sheep "Castilla"[15] and the llama "K'oyllor" (star). The *aukis* declare that the Wamanis are paid only with fruits of the earth and with the *llampu*, "Plankuchallata" (elements that are white and bloodless). But the Aguay Unu is a gift of the Wamanis.

There is a modern dam, the Yauriwiri, that was built by the Peruvian government. When the Yauriwiri irrigation water comes in September, all four *ayllus* go to worship it; they hold a simplified Angosay ceremony, and the *aukis* from each community sing hymns in a number proportional to the amount of water they receive. We were present at that Angosay, which had been simplified considerably. Only the *aukis* bore crosses decorated with *k'antu* flowers. They sang on the bank of the irrigation ditch. At the end [of the ceremony]

---

15. The Spanish Conquistadores called the llamas *ovejas de la tierra* [sheep of the land], and the sheep introduced from Spain were known as *ovejas de castilla* [Castilian sheep].—Trans.

a Pichk'achuri woman said, "We have not done the Angosay very well. What ill-fated thing will happen? Our *aukis* could have bad luck." They invited us to witness or participate in the nocturnal Pirucha. We went to the Indian neighborhood squares at night and found them empty.

The national government built the Yauriwiri Dam for Puquio and for the district of San Andrés, but because of maladministration either so much water is sent to San Andrés that the land is flooded or else it is released into the river in an apparently absurd, cruel way; the river flows down into the rich coastal valley of Acarí. The Indian neighborhoods are about to explode with clamorous resentment because of the unfair way in which water from the modern dam is distributed. According to our informants' criteria, this water, which has been dammed up by modern engineers, falls into the domain of the powerful *mistis*. It is not like that which comes directly from the Wamanis, from their blood vein, which is equitably distributed "to the native, to the town citizen, alike," as all the Indians assert.

The still-beating hearts of the sacrificial victims are not cast into the spring that flows out of Pedrork'o; they are thrown in lower down, at Pallk'a, where the water is deep. The *aukis* state that the water there devours the offerings, since they sink and disappear immediately.

The Legend of the Wachok'

The legend of the heroes, the Wachok', is directly related to the Wamanis and the Aguay Unu. We did not have the chance to collect other versions of this legend. It was our last finding. Don Mateo Garriaso told it to us and we were able to take down his version verbatim. In it we find quite a specific definition of the Aguay Unu, the rules of worship, and an attempt to explain the origin of the rather different traditional economies of the *ayllus* that are brothers of each other: K'ayau with Pichk'achuri and K'ollana with Chaupi.

In Cuzco Quechua, as in Inca Quechua, *wachok'* means "relating to fornication." Long ago it was the word for sexual delinquent; the Catholic religion kept that meaning and spread it. However, as in the case of *unu*, in Puquio the term *wachok'* seems to mean nothing more than the name of the legendary heroes, those who pierce the mountains, with the strict sense of the word unknown. Possibly, in a new attempt to study these interesting personages, we will find that the Wachok' are specifically considered to be those who made the orifices through which the mountain water flows out, since this meaning is insinuated or implied: "It was they who first came to know water. Into the heart of the mountains they penetrated."

Don Mateo Garriaso's Version.

It was the Wachok' who allocated lands to the four *ayllus.*

The Wachok' probably belonged to a generation even older than that of the savages. It was they who first got to know water. They penetrated to the heart of the Wamanis.

Through the vein of water itself, walking inside of it, they got to know the very source of the water, the Wachok' did. They were not like ordinary men.

To be able to go down that deep to the water's source, they say they always used to put a little golden drum on their head. And their garments were of gold and of silver, dazzlingly beautiful, like the altars. In sunlight, in moonlight they also shone. They had tunics and vests of shimmering gold and silver. When they came out, they did it with the golden drums.

We people from Chaupi and K'ollana *ayllus* were assigned large *moyas,*[16] and those from Pichk'achuri and K'ollana were given good warm lands: Wayrana for Pichk'achuri, and Puka Ork'o and Tinkok' for K'ayau.

In the days of the Wachok', the Napa Lake mother—the Father Creator's source of water, vein of God, for the native, for the townsman, for everyone—asked that every August they bring her two guinea pigs, a Castilian sheep heart, and the heart of a beautiful llama, saying, "Let my *naturales* bring them to me." Saying, "I shall accept them from the hands of the *aukis.*"

Ever since then, the *aukis* go up to Señor Don Pedro every August; they go up from our town. They sleep on Señor Don Pedro's summit. They spend the night embracing a big stone: there is a great big stone up there, almost the size of a plaza. There the *aukis* lay out the ritual table. Up there the *sullka campo*[17] takes the Castilian sheep and the llama. But the heart, moist seed, is thrown into the water at Pallk'a, by the *aukis*. The water swallows it up, swallows it instantly.

When the *aukis* return, they bid Señor Don Pedro farewell, singing:

16. The intermediate zone between the puna and the tillable land of warmer climate (called the *k'eshwa*). The *moyas* are rich grazing lands.—Author

17. A lesser staffbearer in charge of keeping order in the countryside.—Trans.

Señorllay agro Yaya	My lord, spring Father,
u wayli!	*u wayli!*
adios niway dispidiway	bid me farewell, say goodbye to me
u wayli!	*u wayli!*
Kausaspak'a kutimusak'ku	If I live I shall return
u wayli!	*u wayli!*
Wañuspak'a manaña	If I'm dead, then I won't
u wayli!	*u wayli!*

Wamani and Water Worship: The Sequia

There are two *fiestas* dedicated to the Wamanis: the Herranza and the Sequia—that is to say, the livestock and the water festivals. On both occasions the Wamanis are worshiped, for they are the ones who watch over human beings and livestock and who feed them.

In a council meeting, the staffbearers and *aukis* designate the *mayordomos* who sponsor the Sequia festival. These sponsors, with the help of their relatives, co-godparents, and friends, and of the staffbearers themselves, will pay all the costs of the *fiesta*.

Chaupi, Pichk'achuri, and K'ayau hold their Sequia festival around August 15;[18] the K'ollana one is a month later. We shall describe the August fiesta.

Two days before the appointed date, the sponsor, in agreement with the staffbearers, the *aukis* and the Pongo, prepares the materials for the offering, and the food and drink for the *ayllu*. The *aukis*, on the eve of the festival, prepare the *mesa* in the sponsor's house. Choice examples of all the edible fruits of the earth are donated by the community. The carnation is the favored flower for the decorations and cigarettes cannot be lacking. The *llampu* is prepared, using the choicest cornmeal, as soft as fine talcum powder. With part of the **llampu** a dough is made, and from it the *aukis* model little animal figures: the *illas*, fertility images of the domestic animals. And it is just as indispensable to take little Agua Florida bottles full of *chicha*, wine, and *aguardiente*. The products are placed in stone or clay vessels, used exclusively for the purpose, which are called *wamakas*. They decorate the principal *auki*'s cross with *k'antu* flowers. This cross, which the Chief Staffbearer keeps in his house during the course of the year, is called *k'ak'ru* in Pichk'achuri. We

18. The date of the Feast of the Ascension of the Virgin Mary in the Catholic calendar.—Trans.

have not found the meaning of this word in any dictionary, nor do the Indians give an explanation of it; apparently it is derived from K'ak'rulla, the name of one of the principal Wamanis of the *ayllu*.

In the months of August and September, the fields are scorched by sun and drought. Yet one bush, the tallest, blooms magnificently during that time in the Puquio zone; it is the *k'antu*, called *k'antuta* in the Puno region. The high zone of the Central and Southern Andes in Peru is bare of trees. The *k'antu* yields a crimson flower, in little bells that hang in clusters. It grows at an elevation of 3,000 to 3,800 meters. The principal *auki* adorns his cross with *k'antu* flowers; he covers it with them.

About nine o'clock in the evening, the *auki* leaves the Chief Staffbearer's house. He is escorted by the lesser *auki* and the Pongo, carrying the offerings. The "militia" (a musical group composed of whistle or transverse flute and a long-framed drum) plays a march. And behind the *aukis* comes the community, accompanying them to the edge of the neighborhood.

K'ayau and Pichk'achuri follow their *aukis* along the summit road to a nearby place called Siwis Pata. There they serve the *aukis* an abundant supper and bid them farewell. Looking grave, the *aukis* set off. The Pongos whistle and shriek; according to Ernesto Quispe, they are trying to imitate the wailing of the wind in the tall grass on the peaks and the "rumbling of the mountains." The farewell has the characteristics of a pathetic separation. But later, on the way back to town, the community enters the Indian neighborhoods in a festive mood. The "militia" accompanies the Chief Staffbearer to his home. The community devotes itself to drinking and dancing. Each community member, man or woman, has sent a special prayer to the Wamanis through the intermediation of the *aukis*.

According to our informants, the *aukis* rest three times on the way: in Rumi Cruz, Motilón, and Ask'omarka. There they eat the cold food, have a drink, sing, and worship the earth where they are resting.

The reports we received as to how and where the offerings to the Wamanis are placed were consistent. Don Mateo stated that on the mountaintop the *aukis* sleep, embracing a large stone on which they lay out the *mesa* [ritual table]. *Mesa* is the name they give to the spread-out shawl on which they have placed the offerings in a set order. Don Viviano, who was an *auki*, told us that the Wamani's "pay" is placed in a hole that is made in the ground. The same man, Don Viviano, stated that the heart of a sacrificial victim is an offering to the Wamani; Don Mateo said the bloody offerings are dedicated to the water and are thrown in at the place called Pallk'a, where the irrigation ditch is deep. All of the other Indians interviewed concurred in this.

The *sullka campo*—a staffbearer of lower degree—has the duty of taking the llama and sheep to the place of sacrifice. The principal *auki* tears out the victims' hearts, covering them with his hat so the Condor Wamani will not devour them with his spirit. The still-beating hearts are cast into the water. The white offerings are buried.

In 1952, when we made our first study of the festival, Ernesto Quispe, a fifth-year student in the Puquio National Secondary School, offered us some information collected from the *aukis* and elders of Pichk'achuri community. Now a law student at the University of San Marcos, Quispe is the son of Indians. According to his information, the offering to the Wamanis is put inside of a *pukullu* (an ancient tomb). It is "a construction of flat stones, a sort of Incaic *chullpas* [funeral tower] and inside it is a sort of catacomb." This secret enclosed area is in a place called Pukullu Pata. The *aukis* put down their crosses at the door of the *pukullu*, kneel and sing the following lines:

Pukullu patapi	On Pukullu summit
k'ori waylla ischu	tall golden puna grass
walpa wak'ay horalla	at the hour the cock crows
chaupituta horalla	at the midnight hour
anchuykamuni	I draw nigh to thee
celebraykok' adorayakok'lla.	to celebrate, to adore.
Tayta ork'olla	Father mountain,
ama piñakunkichu.	you must not be annoyed.

Only the *auki* goes into the *pukullu*. Quispe's precise words concerning the passage are, "The moment the *auki* finds himself inside of the *pukullu*, a hummingbird with showy plumage appears (so they say), and then disappears." The *auki* cries out:

Pukullu ukupi	Within the ancient tomb,
verde siwar k'enti	emerald green hummingbird,
chaupituta hora	at the midnight hour,
wak'ak'masillay	my weeping companion,
rogaykaysiway	help me to implore,
adoraykaysillaway	do help me to adore,
ama hina kaychu	don't hold back,

ork'opa sonk'onpi   in the mountain's heart
wiñask'aykita.   you grew.

On finishing his earnest plea, the *auki* orders the lesser *auki* and the Pongo to hand him the offerings, and they place them in the *pukullu*. They close up the entrance and go right to the spring; at the edge they sacrifice the sheep and then cast its heart, still warm, into the very eye of the pool.

Quispe learned that the offering is made at midnight, and that at the end of the ceremony, the *aukis* sleep, near the flowing spring water. In their dreams, the images of the mountains that received the offering reveal themselves and thank them; loud noises are produced inside the mountains and the *aukis* awaken. By then it is always early morning. At that time, they roast the sacrificial victim's flesh and eat it avidly, and such an act is called *castillo*. After the ritual meal, they cut stalks of *waylla ischu*, the tall bunch grass that grows on the puna. They also pick the wildflowers of those regions. From the dry grass they make crosses for the Pongos, adorning them with the flowers. Their hats are also decorated with bunches of the straw, which is quite golden. The man who took the sheep for the sacrifice covers his body with the animal's hide and personifies him. In this way the *aukis* intone the farewell hymn:

Waylillay waylillay   *Waylillay waylillay*
u wayli   *u wayli*
waylillay waylillay   *waylillay waylillay*

Adios nillaway   Say goodbye to me, bid me
  dispidillaway   farewell.
u wayli   *u wayli*
punchayllaykip   I have visited you on your day
  watuykamusk'ayta
u wayli   *u wayli*
señor cabildo suyawachkan the honorable council is
                               waiting for me

u wayli   *u wayli*
Moyalla patapi mesallapi   on Moyalla shore, by the ritual
                               table

u wayli   *u wayli*
Watapak' killapak' adios   for a year, for a month, bid me
  nillaway   farewell

u wayli	*u wayli*
kausak' runapak' purik'	so the living man, so the
runapak'	walking man
u wayli	*u wayli*
kutimunallampak'	may return, may come back
bueltamunallanpak	
u wayli	*u wayli*
kutimunallaykama tayta	until my return, father
ork'olla	mountain
u wayli.	*u wayli.*

Bearing their crosses, *aukis* and Pongos descend the mountain, resting in the places mentioned, where they sing. When the lake reservoir appears, they chant the *wayli* song of return. The *auki* sings the words, the lines, and with his assistants sings the chorus—the initial *waylis* and the intermediate ones; only the assistants repeat the *wayli* refrain. The *auki* sings in an extremely high tone, in falsetto, the lesser *auki* sings the refrain in a deep voice, and the Pongo does it an octave higher. A dialogue is set up. According to Don Viviano, the first chant is the following:

Waylillay waylillay	*Waylillay waylillay*
u wayli	*u wayli*
Señorlla Don Pedro	Señor Don Pedro
u wayli	*u wayli*
Señorlla Chok'llok'ocha	Señor Chok'llok'ocha
u wayli	*u wayli*
chayrak' chayrak'mi	whom now, just now
u wayli	*u wayli*
tariy tariykamuchk'ayki	I come upon on coming in
u wayli	*u wayli*
apasiblilla	peacefully
u wayli	*u wayli*
huchasapalla	sinfully
u wayli	*u wayli*
wawallayki	your poor child
u wayli	*u wayli*
anis kintuchaywan	with my choice anise leaves
u wayli	*u wayli*
oroypinmentachaywan	with my golden pepper
u wayli.	*u wayli.*

The community awaits the *aukis* on the shore of Lake K'orek'ocha, also called Moyalla.

On the morning of the day the *aukis* are to return, Thursday, the community is called together in the *ayllus* for the *"impesiones"* (impressions), which is what they call groups of costumed people. We found three groups: the Nakak', the Llamichus, and the Huamanguinos. The Nakak' (slashers) wear costumes consisting of ordinary army pants with leggings, pull on wide-brimmed hats, paint their faces black, and arm themselves with *kallwas*, the battens used in the old vertical looms. The *kallwa* closely resembles a two-edged sword and is pointed at both ends. The Llamichus represent the herders and the llamas themselves. Dressed in tatters, or covered with llama skins, especially with the hides from the animals' heads, they resemble the ghosts of shepherds or two-legged llamas, all magical figures. The Huamanguinos represent the mestizo and Indian pedlars who, before the highway was built, went around from Huamanga to the towns of the province selling cloth, *charangos*, guitars, trinkets, saints' images, and amulets. The Huamanguinos appear in suits hung about with lengths of cloth in diverse colors and with trinkets. They pretend to play the *charango*.

Other types of *"impesión"* seem to have become extinct only a short while ago, as little as five years, such as the Chinos and the Gañan,[19] who are still present at the Sequia *fiestas* in some of the villages near Puquio. The Chinos dress up in raggedy *misti* clothing and tattered straw hats; they carry shovels over their shoulders. The Gañan, a word never used in ordinary speech, pretend to plow, with a little plow drawn by another costumed man.

The *"impesiones"* go through the Indian neighborhoods, creating an uproar; they demand that the festival sponsors treat them to firewater. The Nakak' pretend to slit the throats of children or older people. All of the costumed ones dance and move in irregular patterns, screaming, without musical accompaniment. They go up and down the streets and fields of the rugged hillside on which the town lies, running as if they were seized with irrepressible jubilation.

In the morning, before ten o'clock, the Indians set off for K'orek'ocha Lake, or Moyalla, bearing pots of food and large pitchers of *chicha*. They do not wear festive attire. K'orek'ocha is a small, old reservoir. It's on a plain, about 300 meters higher than the city.

On K'orek'ocha Plain the *"impesiones"* perform; they are not still a moment. They are not accompanied by any kind of music. The

19. Farm hand, clod.—Trans.

"militia" play near a rectangular field marked out with stones, where ceremonies are held. The community waits, separated, though not strictly, by age and civil status. The unmarried men and women, especially, form groups apart.

When the *aukis* appear on the mountainside, rockets are set off, or dynamite is exploded near the reservoir cross, which is on a small rise. The community marches out to meet the *aukis*, who sing as they come. We were able to record the hymn of the Chaupi *aukis*. Here are the words, with a translation we have made,[20] and music that has been transcribed by Josafat Roel Pineda:

Aylillay aylillay	*Aylillay aylillay*
u wayli	*u wayli*
aylillay aylillay	*Aylillay aylillay*
u wayli.	*u wayli.*
Señor Cabildo	Honorable Council
u wayli	*u wayli*
señor comunis	worthy community members
u wayli	*u wayli*
sumak' palabra	eloquently
u wayli	*u wayli*
sumak' atención	attentively
u wayli	*u wayli*
perdunakuway	forgive me
u wayli	*u wayli*
entendiykanchiway	make me understand
u wayli	*u wayli*
rimay taytallay	speak, my father
u wayli	*u wayli*
k'ellakuychikchu	do not be idle
u wayli	*u wayli*
rabiakuychikchu	do not be angry
u wayli.	*u wayli.*
Aylillay aylillay	*Aylillay aylillay*
u wayli . . .	*u wayli . . .*

20. The English version relies mainly on Arguedas' Spanish one, with a few changes in an attempt to approximate the Quechua meaning more closely.—Trans.

Imamantacha	I don't know why
u wayli	*u wayli*
haykamantacha	I don't know how
u wayli	*u wayli*
k'ellakuchkawak'	you could be idle
u wayli	*u wayli*
rabiakuchkawak'	you could be angry
u wayli.	*u wayli.*
Ama taytallay	No, my father
u wayli	*u wayli*
k'ellakuychikchu	do not be idle
u wayli	*u wayli*
rabiakuychikchu	do not be angry
u wayli.	*u wayli.*
Aylillay aylillay	*Aylillay aylillay*
u wayli . . .	*u wayli . . .*
Ima nisparak'	Wondering why
u wayli	*u wayli*
hayka nisparak'	wondering how
u wayli	*u wayli*
mikunanchikta	our food
u wayli	*u wayli*
witurk'uchkasun	we shall be reaping
u wayli	*u wayli*
sipirk'uchkasun	we shall be slaughtering
u wayli.	*u wayli.*
Ama taytallay	No, my father
u wayli	*u wayli*
k'ellakuychikchu	do not be idle
u wayli	*u wayli*
piñakuychikchu	do not be bad-tempered
u wayli.	*u wayli.*
Aylillay aylillay	*Aylillay aylillay*
u wayli . . .	*u wayli . . .*
Señor Don Pedro	Honorable Don Pedro
u wayli	*u wayli*

Señor Mama Yaka	Worthy Mother Yaka
u wayli	*u wayli*
chayrak' chayrak'mi	now, just now
u wayli	*u wayli*
rikurimuchkani	I am appearing
u wayli	*u wayli*
usharimuchkani	I am hastening
u wayli	*u wayli*
imposiblilla	it's impossible, then
u wayli	*u wayli*
wawallaykik'a	your (poor) babe
u wayli	*u wayli*
pisi sonk'olla	faint-hearted
u wayli	*u wayli*
churillaykik'a	your (poor) child
u wayli.	*u wayli.*
Aylillay aylillay	*Aylillay aylillay*
u wayli . . .	*u wayli . . .*
Ima nisparak'	Wondering why
u wayli	*u wayli*
hayka nisparak'	wondering how
u wayli	*u wayli*
mikumurk'ayki	I ate you
u wayli	*u wayli*
sirbimurk'ayki	I served you
u wayli	*u wayli*
puka takuywan	with my red dust
u wayli	*u wayli*
k'espe misaywan	with my crystal offering
u wayli	*u wayli*
k'ori k'ollk'eywan	with my gold and silver
u wayli	*u wayli*
anis kintuywan	with my choice anise leaves
u wayli.	*u wayli.*
Aylillay aylillay	*Aylillay aylillay*
u wayli . . .	*u wayli . . .*

Señor Cabildo	Honorable Council
u wayli	*u wayli*
señor comunis	worthy community members
u wayli	*u wayli*
kayk'ay señorllay	here it is, sir
u wayli	*u wayli*
mandallawask'ayki	what you sent me for
u wayli	*u wayli*
kamachiwask'ayki	all you asked me for
u wayli	*u wayli*
k'amila taytallay	now you, my father
u wayli	*u wayli*
k'ellakuchkanki	are being idle
u wayli	*u wayli*
llullakuchkanki	are being deceitful
u wayli.	*u wayli.*
Ama taytallay	No, my father
u wayli	*u wayli*
k'ellakuychikchu	you shall not be idle
u wayli	*u wayli*
rabiakuychikchu	you shall not be angry
u wayli.	*u wayli.*
Aylillay aylillay	*Aylillay aylillay*
u wayli . . .	*u wayli . . .*
Señor llak'ta Alcalde	Honorable town Mayor
u wayli	*u wayli*
señor llak'ta Regidor	honorable town Selectman
u wayli	*u wayli*
kayk'ay taytallay	here, my father
u wayli	*u wayli*
kamachiwask'ayki	is all you asked me for
u wayli	*u wayli*
mandallask'ayki	all you sent me for
u wayli	*u wayli*
icha señorlla	perhaps, sir
u wayli.	*u wayli.*

piñakunkichu	you are annoyed
u wayli.	*u wayli.*
Amay señorllay	No, my lord
u wayli	*u wayli*
piñakuychikchu	do not be annoyed
u wayli.	*u wayli.*
Aylillay aylillay	*Aylillay aylillay*
u wayli . . .	*u wayli . . .*
Ima nisparak'	Wondering why
u wayli	*u wayli*
hayka nisparak'	wondering how
u wayli	*u wayli*
k'esperk'uchkasun	we shall be arriving
u wayli	*u wayli*
rijark'uchkasun	we shall be burdened
u wayli	*u wayli*
rijrallanchikman	at our sides
u wayli	*u wayli*
lomullanchikman	on our backs
u wayli.	*u wayli.*
Aylillay aylillay	*Aylillay aylillay*
u wayli . . .	*u wayli . . .*
Don Pedrollaway	Our Don Pedro
u wayli	*u wayli*
mama Yakallay	our mother, Yaka
u wayli	*u wayli*
chayrak' chayrak'mi	now, just now
u wayli	*u wayli*
sek'arimuchkayki	we are climbing
u wayli	*u wayli*
aysarimuchkayki	we are raising you
u wayli	*u wayli*
apasiblilla	peacefully
u wayli	*u wayli*
sierbullaykik'a	your poor serf
u wayli	*u wayli*

pobrellaykik'a	your poor man
u wayli.	*u wayli.*
Ama taytallay	No, my father
u wayli	*u wayli*
piñakunkichu	you must not be annoyed
u wayli	*u wayli*
rabiakunkichu	you must not be angered
u wayli.	*u wayli.*
Aylillay aylillay	*Aylillay aylillay*
u wayli . . .	*u wayli . . .*
Ima nisparak'	Wondering why
u wayli	*u wayli*
hayka nisparak'	wondering how
u wayli	*u wayli*
k'esperk'uchkasun	we shall be arriving
u wayli	*u wayli*
sek'ark'uchkasun	we shall be climbing
u wayli	*u wayli*
puka takuywan	with my red cornstarch
u wayli	*u wayli*
k'espe misaywan	with my crystal offering
u wayli	*u wayli*
k'ori k'ollk'eywan	with my gold and silver
u wayli	*u wayli*
anis kintuywan	with my choice anise leaves
u wayli.	*u wayli.*
Aylillay aylillay	*Aylillay aylillay*
u wayli . . .	*u wayli . . .*

To the accompaniment of the "militia," harp box, and "rolling" drum, on the town road, leaving K'orek'ocha reservoir:

Aylillay aylillay	*Aylillay aylillay*
u wayli . . .	*u wayli . . .*
Ima nichkawak'	What could you say?
u wayli	*u wayli*

hayka nichkawak'	How much could you say?
u wayli	*u wayli*
señor comunis	worthy community members
u wayli	*u wayli*
piñakuchkawak'	you could become annoyed
u wayli.	*u wayli.*
Kayk'a señorlla	Here, sir, is
u wayli	*u wayli*
kamachiwask'ayki	all you asked me for
u wayli	*u wayli*
mandallawask'ayki	all you sent me for
u wayli.	*u wayli.*
Amay taytallay	No, my father
u wayli	*u wayli*
comun puralla	among *comuneros*, equals,
u wayli	*u wayli*
rabiakuychikchu	do not be angry
u wayli	*u wayli*
sumak' atención	attentively
u wayli	*u wayli*
mana llakisk'a	not grieving
u wayli	*u wayli*
usharikuchkasun	we shall be hastening
u wayli	*u wayli*
napaykuchkasun	we shall be greeting
u wayli.	*u wayli.*
Aylillay aylillay	*Aylillay aylillay*
u wayli . . .	*u wayli . . .*

The First Angosay. When the *aukis* reach the first stone-paved part of the irrigation canal, where the water enters the lake, they sing. Then the council elders of the community and their women line up on both banks of the channel and perform the Angosay ceremony. Only the council elders participate. The Angosay consists of ceremonial libations of red-colored liquids mixed with water from the irrigation ditch. It could be simply cola, wine, or *aguardiente* colored with *ayrampu* seeds. Men and women offer each other drinks in glasses decorated with *k'antu* flowers. They go on drinking for a long time.

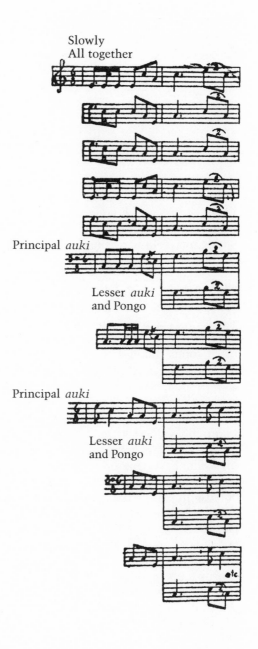

Slowly
All together

Principal *auki*

Lesser *auki*
and Pongo

Principal *auki*

Lesser *auki*
and Pongo

179

At the wheat harvest in Sicuani, capital of Canchis province, in the department of Cuzco, the word *angosay* is used for the act of heaping all of the piles of wheat together into a single stack in the middle of the threshing floor. A cross made of wheat straw is set up on top of the stack.

The Adoration of the Crosses. After the Angosay ceremony, the community files off, behind the *aukis*, to the designated field, which is near the canal intake. The *aukis* put down their crosses, leaning them against a stone. The principal *auki*'s cross, made of wood with *k'antu* flowers, is placed in the middle; the straw crosses of the lesser *auki* and the Pongo are placed alongside it. The adoration is begun by the staffbearers with the council elders and finally the young men following them. They kneel, without saying a word. The women do not participate.

The Midday Meal and the Capitana Dance; The Return. In the designated field a meal is served to the *aukis*, staffbearers, and council elders. The unmarried men eat in a group apart. The overseers of the Sequia festival, their co-godparents, and their relatives bring the thick soups and drinks.

During the meal and afterwards, a girl about five years old, dressed as a mestiza, dances *huaynos* with the members of the *"impesiones"* groups. The "militia" accompanies them. No one else dances. Meanwhile the *"impesiones"* continue to amuse the community. The Llamichus—llamas and llama-herders—shout curses and gallop about. The Nakak' imitate military marches, executions, and slashings. The Huamanguinos dance.

In the evening the *aukis* take up the crosses; the staffbearers escort them. The whole community gets ready to follow the priests and the Indian authorities down to the town. The "militia" accompanies the *aukis*. The latter change the rhythm of the hymn slightly and sing as they go down the mountain to town.

The *aukis*—especially the principal *auki*—drink with all the community members and council elders from their *ayllu* from the time they meet the community at K'orek'ocha until they get back to the Indian neighborhood. We watched them descending the steep slope, from K'orek'ocha to the city, walking rather stiffly, without stumbling, with no need of assistance. They chew coca all the while. They had drunk limitless quantities of alcohol. Many of the Indians were left by the wayside, felled by drunkenness, despite the fact that they had undoubtedly drunk very little compared to the *aukis*. The latter, attended by the lesser *aukis* and the Pongo, descended surefootedly to the hidden places of the irrigation channel, to bless them with the *llampu*. They scattered the cornmeal below the large stones, at the foot of the little waterfalls, in places that have a certain air of mystery. Until the last resting place, on some level land only a few meters from the first of the village houses, they sang. Their features were dulled, their eyes almost impersonal, lost in the void. Even so they responded in a dignified and imperturbably grave manner to the invitations to drink alcohol they kept receiving from men and women. Leaning against a stone wall, at the entrance to town, they still sang. The extremely vast horizon of Puquio, in the evening twilight, so severe in the Andes at that altitude, surrounded them. As night began to fall, some *comuneros* engaged in fistfights, at some distance from the *aukis*, who for a long while kept their faces turned toward the mountain, where the irrigation channel descends. Then they set off for the squares of their respective *ayllus*. Like the *aukis*, the staffbearers kept their feet and did not stagger on the road, despite the fact that they had been seen drinking almost as much as the *aukis*.

The chapel bells peal when the *aukis* enter the squares. The chapel doors remain closed. The *aukis* lean their crosses against them, and worship them, reciting Catholic prayers in Quechua. Finally, they take up the crosses once more and walk to the Chief Staffbearer's house.

The Indian neighborhoods are silent during this night of the first Angosay.

The Second Angosay.   The following day, Saturday, the *ayllu* communities go to celebrate the Angosay at Churulla, a small reservoir that holds the waters of a spring that flows out right there. This is an Angosay for the whole community. The one at Moyalla K'ocha is limited to the council elders. Men and women of all ages go to Churulla, wearing their best clothing. The staffbearers wear new ponchos slung across their chests. The reservoir is near the city, in a high place. No one fails to exchange libations with his relatives and all of his friends and acquaintances. They do it on the bank of the irrigation ditch where the water enters. It is deep. The water is rapidly tinged with red.

Early on, the *aukis* bury offerings beneath a stone near the spring. They do not offer sacrificial victims.

In Churulla another ceremonial meal is given, and the *"impesiones"* perform once more, as on the previous day. At nightfall they go down to the town.

At that time they begin the community dance, the dance typical of the Sequia, the *ayla*. The unmarried people form lines, with the women behind and the men in front, without intermingling. The women sing, and to that music the young people dance. At designated spots on the road they make a circle to dance. The words of the *ayla* song do not refer to the Sequia fiesta; they pertain to love. We shall cite an example. The music was recorded by Roel Pineda.

Terripelo pacha	Velvet dress
solterapa churakunan	maiden's dress
pirak' mayrak'	whoever, whichever
churakunk'a	puts it on,
chay kak'lla	that very one
yanay k'ank'a.	is to be my love.
Ischuchallay waylla	My tall puna grass
clabelinaschallay.	my little pink.

The melody, as well as the lyrics of the *ayla*, are used exclusively for the Sequia *fiesta*.

The Pirucha. We have not been able to discover the exact meaning of this word. It is the name of the folk dance held at night during the Sequia *fiesta*. Most of our informants agreed that the name Pirucha is especially used to designate a kind of circle of very tall poles that were put up in the squares in the Indian neighborhoods, and that a Peruvian flag was placed on the highest point of the timbers. "All blood, Peruvian flag,"[21] an old man of Chaupi told us. This could be a phallic symbol. No longer than ten years ago, according to our informants, the political authorities prohibited constructing those *piruchas* and banned putting up the flag there "because it was not dignified for the flag to wave as if it were providing respectability for the Indians' drunken sprees and dances," as a Puquio gentleman asserted. The place where they dance is called *pirucha*. Nevertheless, when the Indians refer to the dance, instead of telling us there is to be an *ayla*, the name of the dance itself, they say, "There is to be a *pirucha*." They invited us to go to the Pirucha.

This name, then, designates more the place where the dance is held than the dance itself, which is undoubtedly called the *ayla*. The Personero of Pichk'achuri informed us that the unmarried men organize *aylas* for nights when the moon shines brightest, even when it is not the water festival season.

21. It has vertical bands of red separated by a vertical white band.—Trans.

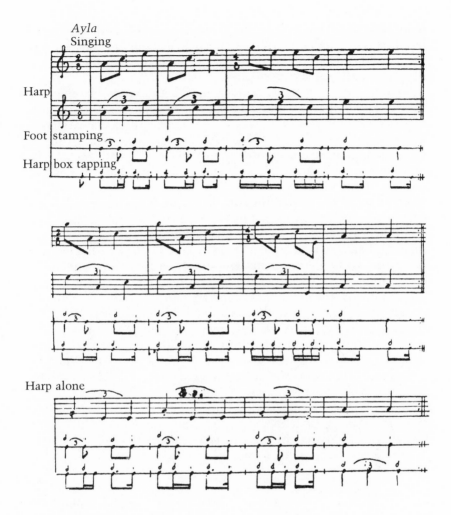

Ayla

The Pirucha begins near midnight. In the *ayllu* squares, each Sequia sponsor provides an orchestra composed of harp and violin. People can dance to the harp alone. The *cajoneador*, or "box player," who taps on the wooden part of the harp with his fingers, is indispensable. Bending over it near the low strings, the *cajoneador* beats out the dance rhythm with extraordinary skill.

Men and women dance in a circle. It often happens that there are only men in the circle; or there could be more women than men. The musicians call this dance the Sequia. Small kerosene lanterns shed their light on the harps. Women selling *aguardiente*, *chicha*, and

183

punch station themselves near the walls, also illumined by small lanterns. The Sequia sponsors offer people *aguardiente*, but many of the participants bring bottles of cane liquor or buy them in the square, and they also treat others.

Meanwhile, the married people dance in the squares to the harp music. The unmarried men go from one neighborhood to another, dancing with the women's chorus. The young girls exchange shawls and hats with one another, so they will not be recognized. It seems evident that during the *aylas* the unmarried people have sexual relations free of inhibitions. We were able to confirm that it is not true that the *aylas* invariably end in disorderly orgies. The girls are already "committed" when they go. The lines of young people disappear into the empty fields that lie between one neighborhood and another, beneath the shade of the bushes, or into the ravines on the rugged hillside on which the town is located. Or they withdraw from the urban areas. Future marriages are pledged on the night of the *ayla*; virgins who have reached the proper age offer themselves.

On Saturday, the night of the Pirucha, one is aware of nothing but music, dance, and song in the Indian neighborhood. There is not the slightest indication of a disturbing memory in anyone's mind; people are completely open to the fullest expansion of joy. It is the ceremonious welcome the community gives to the coming of the life-giving water from the springs, in this zone where every drop of water constitutes, as they say, *yawar*, or blood.

At dawn, when the daylight appears, the girls give back the shawls and hats. They regain their identity; the established order is restored. In the squares the married people dance until the first sunlight reaches them. At that time we were able to take some photographs of the Pirucha.

El Despacho.[22] The *aukis* only officiate during the ceremonies prior to the Pirucha. On their return from the Angosay at Churulla they put their crosses in the Chief Staffbearers' houses. The Despacho is a ceremony common to all kinds of *fiestas*: the house-roofing, or Wasichakuy, as it is called in Puquio; the livestock festival, or Herranza; and the Catholic religious holidays. But it is a non-Catholic ceremony. Only the Pongo officiates in it, aided by the "*serbisio*" [servant] of the Sequia *mayordomo*. This "*serbisio*"[23] is a

22. Closing ceremony.—Trans.

23. This is a local mispronunciation and misuse of the Spanish word *servicio*, which means "service" or "servants." Proper Spanish words for one servant are *servidor* and *sirviente*.—Trans.

relative, co-godparent, or well-esteemed friend whom the sponsor puts in charge of attending the guests. Dutifully, the *"serbisio"* drinks only a few drops of the *aguardiente* that is offered in the *fiesta*. He remains imperturbable for as many days as the *fiesta* lasts, which constitutes a strong proof of temperance.

The Despacho de la Sequia ceremony begins as it is growing dark, almost at night. The community comes out of the Sequia sponsors' houses dancing the *ayla* to harp and violin accompaniment. In K'ayau and Pichk'achuri the men put women's shawls over their shoulders and the women wear men's ponchos. In the streets and fields they pretend to quarrel. The "men" strike the "women" and knock them about so realistically that I saw a stranger who was unfamiliar with the custom intervene energetically in the "women's" defense and experience the strangest surprise. The long shawls cover the men's shoulders, and by nightfall it is not easy to discern immediately that they are masquerading.

The Despacho ceremony is held in the open fields, outside the urban area. The Pongo takes the elements for the ritual table already prepared. By some stone, indiscriminately chosen, he stops, to lay out the *mesa*. On a shawl, with a knife he forms a square of *llampu*, modeling it by using the knife blade as a spatula. On that delicately and carefully arranged symmetrical form he makes a cross with tiny perfect coca leaves, the coca *kintu*. In clusters of three, at almost imperceptible distances, he places the choice leaves and traces the arms and the vertical timber of the cross. Then, on each corner of this ritual table, he lights candles. He decorates the form with carnations. He places four cigarettes in the *llampu*; they harmonize with the other elements, as this is done following a preconceived design. Around the *mesa* he places little bottles of wine, *aguardiente*, and *chicha*.

Once the *mesa* is laid out, he kneels down and worships it. Then he divides it in two. He digs a hole in the ground with the knife and buries half of the offerings. The other half he throws into the stream that flows toward the southern or northern end of the city—toward whichever direction corresponds to his neighborhood.

They dance in the field until late at night. Then they return to the house of the *mayordomos*. All night long these fiesta sponsors are visited by their friends and co-godparents, who keep bringing more and more *aguardiente* to drink. Some sleep on the floor of the rooms or on the porches, without being suffocated by the dust raised by the dancing, for the *ayla* is a foot-stamping kind of dance.

Signs of Catholicism in the Fiesta. The Sequia *fiesta* has a standard-bearer (Sequia *alférez*) tolerated by the Catholic church. The sole duty of this personage is to participate in making an offering of *llampu* to the water, on the way back from the reservoirs to the city after the Angosay. He walks behind the *aukis* with the staffbearers, carrying a banner in the form of a small, silvery triangle. When the *aukis* go down to the irrigation ditch to scatter the *llampu*, the standard-bearer comes to a halt by the staffbearers, with the banner on his shoulder.

We have already referred to the crosses of the *aukis* and Pongos, and the homage paid them at Moyalla or K'orek'ocha and in the chapel doorways.

Pongo and Auki

The Pongo is the **servant**—sometimes of the *auki* and at other times of the Wamanis. The **auki** is a priest, as the community's representative and messenger to the Wamanis and the Aguay Unu, but he also personifies the Wamanis themselves; that is why he is called **auki**. The **sullka auki** is a sub-*auki* who inherits the *auki*'s position. The Pongo is the "**serbisio**" of both *aukis*. This term, *pongo*, does not have the same meaning in Puquio that it has in southern Peru and in Bolivia; in Puquio the Indians do not perform unpaid personal service, except in the case of the staffbearers' work for the official authorities, which is quite limited and is offered as a public service.

Once the *fiesta* is over, the *auki*'s prerogatives cease. He has no special privileges whatsoever within the community. He has influence, not because of the title of *auki*, but because of his wisdom, which he uses during council meetings when projects of benefit to the community are planned and decided upon.

However, in their old age many *aukis* become healers, **hampik'**, because after the age of about fifty one can no longer be an *auki*, according to what we were told. Age is revealed by one's physical aspect. The *auki* should be strong, in the fullness of his strength. No old man is an *auki*.

The Pongo, as a servant of the Wamanis, initiated into the position of evoking and communicating with the mountain spirits, is a strange personage. We did not succeed in discovering whether there were any Pongos in Puquio, whose Indian population is quite large. People told us that there were some in the "interior" towns (the districts of the province that lie deeper in the Andes), which have denser Indian populations. The Pongo is also a sorcerer. He is in league with the gods that do not need intermediaries to destroy those who offend them, but do need them to perform beneficial acts for those who solicit them. No ordinary man, then, has the ability to summon them and speak to them. Not even the *aukis*.

The *aukis* and staffbearers choose the Pongo, who is an apprentice *auki* of lower degree, because the Pongo will rise to be *sullka auki* when the latter becomes an *auki*. The *aukis* told us unanimously that the *auki*'s disciple, the *sullka auki*, is chosen to be *auki*. "We choose the one who follows us to be *auki*, not anyone else," they said. And the one who follows is the lesser *auki*, that is, the *sullka auki*. And he who follows the lesser *auki* is the Pongo. The *aukis* and the staffbearers themselves are careful to take an interest in choosing the Pongo from among the young men who have shown they have a vocation for the job.

The name **layk'a** is given to the sorcerer, who is well acquainted with the powerful destructive secrets of the elements. It is the *layk'a* who prepares evil charms. His friendship with the demon, *supay*, is the source of his power. Supay, the spirit of evil, inspires and guides him in the knowledge of the earthly elements that can cause death and injuries.

The Other Life

Don Mateo Garriaso and Ernesto Quispe informed us that the dead go to K'oropuna, saying that on top of that great, far-off mountain is the province of Castilla, in the department of Arequipa. There the dead are kept busy, at God's command, building a tower that is never finished, since it topples over whenever it has reached a great height. And the dead patiently begin the work all over again. The dead arrive at their destined place accompanied by llamas. They are nourished by eating hominy made of llama turds and a thick soup made of ashes.

Men who have committed evil deeds remain in the world, "haunting," as lost souls. They wander about howling, devouring beasts and human beings until some casual act of the Catholic God saves them. For that they have to die again, to suffer the true death, their separation from this world. The act can be an encounter with some person who redeems the lost souls [*condenados*] by offering to do penance for them, by returning the things they have stolen and righting wrongs in the lost soul's name, or by burning them alive through some ruse.

But Don Mateo frequently interrupted his version of that world by asserting, "The worst sinners burn eternally in hell. Children and honest people go to sing in God's glory, also eternally." Nevertheless, at the end of his statement, he told us the following tale in Quechua.

He said there is an immense iron cross on the K'oropuna, at the gate to the country of the dead, and that Saint Francis is the one who guards that gate. In the olden times the wife of a happy man died. The man could not be consoled for the loss of his wife, whom he loved very much. He decided to travel to K'oropuna. He went up to the foot of the cross, in Saint Francis' presence, and implored him to return his wife to him. He wept so much that Saint Francis granted his wish. But he did not restore the woman herself. He gave him a bundle of reeds and told him to carry it carefully and not to open it, because she was inside. Once he was in his own town he was to cut open the bundle of reeds and his wife would appear to him. The man was overcome with impatience on the way. He desired his wife's presence; he had gone to get her. And he opened the reeds. From inside, the fly of death, the *chiririnka*, flew out.

Don Mateo asserts that humanity was saved by that man's impatience. Because if that heartbroken man had not disobeyed, the dead would have returned to earth, and since their number is infinite, there would not have been enough food in the world for everyone, and they might have devoured each other. "They're all right on K'oropuna, the dead are," he said. "They have something to do and only show up in the world of the living on certain occasions, such as on All Souls' Day. But only when the mourners think about them."

THE FUNCTION OF THE LOCAL RELIGION

As the natives seem to see it, they receive real gifts only from their old gods: the Wamanis, Mama Allpa or Allpa Terra, and the Aguay Unu. The Inkarrí myth and that god explain the origin of the present social order that prevails, superimposed on the old one, and offer the promise that the old order can be reestablished. No very clear idea is held, to be sure, about what new order would come if Inkarrí were to return. However, it is understood, especially by the old people, that at the very least a promise exists: the possible destruction of the political and social despotism of the *mistis* and the mestizos. For there is no serious poverty in the *ayllus*, with the exception of K'ollana.

The Indian of Puquio, still unperturbed by the powerful agents for change that exert an influence upon him, appears to have the solid support of his local gods. Not only do the Wamanis feed the livestock and ordain their procreation, and offer their vein to men and animals to make the earth fruitful and so that animals and human beings may drink from it, but they are also present wherever their *naturales* are to be found, protecting them. For that reason, no Indian takes a drink without pouring a few drops of liquor on the ground or sprinkling it in the air with his fingers, so that the *wamani* may receive it as an offering.

Don Viviano Wamancha, the former *auki* and leader of Chaupi, a wise old man of more than eighty years, whom we found participating in the communal work project of building a new chapel for his neighborhood, said, in a voice resounding with conviction, "*Wamanikunak'a propiopunim, ñaupa señorpa, Inkarripa churask'an.*" *Propiopunim*: that is to say that the Wamanis really exist and belong exclusively to the natives. Their existence cannot be questioned, nor can the natives suppose they have any significance for anyone other than those who believe in their existence, that is, for anyone but the Indians. The separation the Indians accept and maintain with respect to the other religion and culture, *misti* and mestizo, is clearly expressed in those terms. "The Wamanis were put (created) by our ancient Lord, Inkarrí."

Mestizos and *mistis* do not participate in the Sequia *fiesta*. We made a survey among twenty *mistis* from the city and only one of them said he had witnessed part of the festival by chance. The rest knew nothing at all about it. Some young *mistis* and mestizos confessed to having participated only in the nocturnal *ayla*, disguised as Indians.

There is a sharply defined separation, then, between the local and the official religions. Naturally the *mistis* and mestizos do not participate in or know the fundamentals of the local religion; it belongs exclusively to the Indians: *propiopunim*, as an *auki* would say, using words taken from the Spanish and applying them with a precision valid for both languages.

The two religions perform different functions and nevertheless are components of a greater complex that takes in both of them. Each borrows from the other; there is syncretism in both fields.

The Catholic religion does not seem to have convinced the Indians insofar as its theoretical foundations are concerned. Catholicism's most notable result, or its greatest conquest, insofar as basic beliefs are concerned, seems to be confined to the conviction that God created the heavenly world and that he should be feared. As for the religion's social function—it definitely determines the ways a particular social status is acquired in the community. Social classes within the Indian groups are determined by the number and category of religious obligations fulfilled by each *comunero*. Civil duties undertaken for the community are also taken into account, but they are of a secondary order. Thus an Indian who has held all of the religious offices, who has received the sacraments, and who has also performed the duties of the civil community positions occupies the highest social rank; the lowest pertains to a person who has not held any religious or civil office. Naturally, the ability to perform those duties is directly, but not expressly, related to a person's economic wealth. An Indian can avoid these obligations, if he is greedy. There is, then, a direct relation between prestige and the fulfillment of the official religious obligations.

The local religion seems to have a very solid structure, with religious duties that are observed strictly. The local gods are present in all the aspects and important events of individual and social life; they seem to be the elements that keep the individual, and society as well, secure. Catholic worship is practiced ostentatiously. Nevertheless it appears to obey norms that are not substantially related to basic religious needs, performing functions more related to other necessities, such as recreation and social advancement.

In that regard, the attitude taken toward the two religions by mestizos who have come from the very heart of the *ayllus* is demonstrative. This attitude is the result of time spent living in coastal cities, or comes from the education they have received in the schools, or arises from both influences.

These mestizos are skeptical. We watched them observing the Yauriwiri water Angosay ceremony like spectators who wished to show their lack of participation in it. When we conversed with them they told us about the Angosay, speaking of those who participate in "those customs" in the third person. At the same time, they go around saying that the office of *mayordomo* [the sponsorship of the *fiestas*] should be abolished. Don Mateo Garriaso, whose life is now almost completely devoted to observation, told us that these young people insist that the only function of the religious holidays is to enrich the priest and the sellers of "donkey piss" (which is what they call *aguardiente*, not beer).

There is agreement, among all social groups, that the substantial expenses required to support the religious *fiestas* are what impoverish the Indians' economy. Mestizos and town citizens seldom assume the obligation of sponsoring the *fiestas* and performing the other duties involved in the religious holidays. Nevertheless, the Indians anxiously apply for the sponsorship and lesser offices; they come in multitudes, truly anguished, to the enclosed yard beside the church. There the parish priest finds it necessary to select those who will hold the *fiesta* positions "by drawing lots," and only after having admonished the job-seekers that if they are not sufficiently "comfortably well-off," the duties of office will bring them to ruin, and that they will discredit the *fiesta* if they don't celebrate it properly. The reason for this is that those who have never been *mayordomos*, or held other offices, are subjected to such overwhelming disapproval, being excluded from certain communal rights, such as the right to have irrigation water. Whoever has not discharged certain duties is publicly shamed to his face: "You are a dog!" they are told. And naturally they are dishonored in this way in council meetings.

But the influence of the skeptical mestizos is growing. We confirmed this by comparing the Sequia fiesta we observed in 1952 with the 1956 one. The Despacho of the Sequia festival we witnessed in K'ollana in 1956 was a poor spectacle because of the small number of natives we saw participating in it, and also because most of the Indians did not take part in it, even though they happened to be in the neighborhood.

The mestizos do participate in the old-style family fiestas, such as the Wasichakuy [House-Roofing], which follow a complicated ritual. The traditional-type mestizos also attend it and participate in its customs. We found no indications that modern urban dances were being introduced into the communities.

We got the impression that both local and official religions are suffering from the influence of the changes that are occurring at an ever-increasing pace in the traditional culture of the four *ayllus*. The strengthening of the family economy by trade with the coastal area seems to have now become the Indians' dominant ideal. The individual's life is oriented toward training that will make him more able to reach this goal. The whole religious complex is being shaken by this movement, which has the support of the mestizo merchant class with entrepreneurial spirit. The weakening of the old beliefs and worship (of both the official and the local religions) is shaking the foundations of communal life; they still appear firm, but are being sorely pressed by the agents of change we have mentioned.

In the *ayllus* there is the conviction that the religious *fiestas* are impoverishing the natives. Each Indian seems convinced that if the natives would stop sponsoring the festivals their household economies would be strengthened, but at the same time, since they get so much satisfaction out of the festivals as recreation, and because they hold social sway over the city during the large festivals they support, they are not really disposed to give them up, especially not to the old generation. Strengthening the family economy by accumulating savings and showing it in objective and conspicuous ways are relatively recent phenomena.[24] The construction of two-story houses with tin roofs, the establishment of shops, entrance to the National School, and the change toward a status that formerly characterized the mestizos are new aspirations for the Indians of Puquio, and they are achieving those goals. Some gentlemen and mestizos view this situation with optimism, but most of them either feel offended and threatened, struggle to maintain the traditional status, or prefer to leave Puquio, moving to the coastal cities, especially to the capital. Thus, Puquio seems like a small city in which one may observe quite clearly the phenomena typical of revolutionary cultural change.

In a few years a group of human beings—a group that is well-integrated despite the extreme heterogeneity of its elements—is set in motion and rushes to regain a cultural level that has implied centuries of labor in the areas affected by the agents that have caused the process of change.

We learned that in twenty short years the city of Puquio has been rapidly transformed from the capital of an old-fashioned, predominantly colonial-style farming and livestock area into a trading center with an active economy. As for the Indians, we observed that this process is tending to emancipate them from the despotism that the aristocratic and mestizo classes have exerted over them, traditionally and also up to the present day. However, at the same time, the process is removing the Indians from the foundations on which their traditional Indian culture rests, even though it is not clear what elements are to replace those foundations. The Indians are apparently following an open road to skeptical individualism, loosening the ties to the gods who have regulated their social conduct and harmoniously inspired their arts, in which we contemplate and feel a beauty as perfect as it is vigorous.

Inkarrí returns, and we cannot help fearing that he may be powerless to reassemble the individualisms that have developed, perhaps irremediably. Unless he can detain the Sun, once more binding him with iron bands to Osk'onta Peak, and change man; all is possible where such a wise and resistant creature is concerned.

JOSÉ MARÍA ARGUEDAS

24. Eighty percent of the houses built from 1953 to 1955 inclusive belong to Indians; most of them were built in K'ayau and Pichk'achuri *ayllus*.—Author

Glossary

agua (S): water.

aguardiente (S): various kinds of strong spirits, including sugarcane liquor; firewater.

Aguay Unu (S+Q): water that flows from the earth.

ak'chi (Q): a hawklike bird of prey; Ak'chi Mountain is the guardian spirit of the K'oñanis.

alaymosca (Q): a granitic stone thought to have magical properties.

alcalde (S): mayor; could be the Chief Staffbearer (mayor of the Indian community) or the mayor of the city of Puquio.

allinlla (Q): just fine.

Allpa Mama (Q): Earth Mother.

Allpa Terra (Q+S): Earth.

Angosay (Q): an Indian water ceremony with libations of red-colored liquids mixed with water from the irrigation ditch.

apasanka (Q): a tarantula spider.

Q: Quechua   S: Spanish   E: English

When letters are in combination the word is shared by the languages. The first letter indicates the language from which the other language(s) borrowed the word. Letters joined by + indicate a word that is a combination of two languages; Quechua often borrows a root word from Spanish and adds its own endings.

arí (Q): yes.

atatau (Q): exclamation of disgust.

auki (Q): a mountain spirit or demigod; also a priest who is the community's representative and messenger to the Wamanis and the Aguay Unu.

ayarachi (Q): a lugubrious kind of funeral music; literally it means "corpse-making."

ayataki (Q): song of the dead.

ayla (Q): a folk dance.

ayllu (Q): an Indian community.

banderillas (S): rounded dowels, covered with colored paper and with a steel harpoon point, that are placed in pairs into the bull's withers.

banderillero (S): bullfighter under the orders of the matador who helps run the bull with the cape and places the *banderillas* into the bull's withers.

bandurria (S): an old lutelike instrument, a bandore.

barrera (S): the fence around the bullring; the first row of seats are also called *barreras*.

bombo (S): a bass drum.

cabalgadas (S): in the sixteenth century these were the Spanish Conquistadores' expeditions to capture Indians and to find gold and other booty.

cañazo (S): a drink made from the first distillation of fermented sugarcane juice; also called cane liquor.

capeadores (S): amateur bullfighters who challenge the bull with their capes or, in this book, ponchos.

carcocha (S+Q): a jalopy.

castilla (SQ): Indian term for sheep.

castillo (S): a castle; (Q): Indian term for ritual act of eating sacrificial animal's flesh.

-cha (Q): a diminutive suffix that may be added to a person's name to show respect, affection, or to make the person "more one's own"; using this form in personal address is a way of drawing closer to

194

the person for whom it is used. This syllable also has religious connotations and is used as a suffix for the names of gods, spirits, and other supernatural beings, in which case it may be translated "Great." For instance, *mamacha* could mean the Virgin Mary.

chalo (SQ): a derogatory term for a person of mixed blood or an Indian who has adopted the speech and dress of the Western culture. It is the local Indian pronunciation of the Spanish word *cholo*.

chalukuna (S+Q): Lima *cholos*, a derogatory term for mestizos or Indians who go to Lima to live and adopt the speech, dress, and manners of non-Indians.

charango (Q): a high-pitched instrument similar to a mandolin.

chascha (Q): little dog.

chicha (QS): a mild alcoholic drink made from corn.

chiririnka (Q): a dark blue fly that is a harbinger of death.

cholo (S): a derogatory word meaning a person of mixed or Indian blood who has adopted the speech and dress of the Western culture; *chola* is the feminine form.

coca *kintu* (QSE): choice leaves of a South American shrub. These are chewed as a stimulant or used as an offering to mountain deities.

compadres (S): co-godparents to one another's children; spiritual relatives.

comunero (S): a member of an *ayllu*, or Indian community.

concertados (S): Arguedas defined this elsewhere as "Indians who have left their communities; they are lost souls who serve their *misti* all their lives in his house, receiving in exchange food, clothing, and a small annual salary."

condenado (S): according to Indian belief one of the damned, who are condemned to wander across the high snowfields forever, dragging chains. See Puquio article, page 187.

cumunkuna (S+Q): Indian community members.

danza (S): a type of dance.

danzak' (S+Q): a ritual dancer.

Despacho (S): dismissal; in Puquio the Despacho is a closing ceremony common to all kinds of fiestas: house-roofing, the livestock festival, and the Catholic religious holidays.

don, doña (S): a respectful title of address used before the Christian name.

girón (S): an avenue.

guanaco (QSE): a South American mammal with reddish-brown wool that is related to the camel and the llama; this word is often used as a derogatory term.

hacienda (SE): a large, traditionally operated landholding.

huayno (Q): a folk song and dance of Inca origin.

"impesiones" (SQ): groups of costumed people who go around at festival time mimicking others.

indianista (S): a person who cultivates the languages and literature of the Indians.

indigenista (S): belonging to a pro-Indian literary movement.

ischu (Q): a tall type of bunch grass that grows on the high puna.

ja caraya (Q+S): a strong interjection.

jajayllas (Q): an expression of scornful derision.

jatun (Q): great, big.

k'adihua (Q): a type of song meaning "follow me."

k'alakuna (Q): a derogatory term meaning "naked or peeled ones," used for people who have no mutual ties or obligations with the Indian communities; here Indians use it for leading citizens.

k'anra (Q): a disgustingly dirty person.

k'antu (Q): a bush bearing crimson flowers that grows at high Andean elevations.

k'ari (Q): a brave man, used in the same sense as for a North American Indian brave.

k'eñwa (Q): a low, coniferous tree with scaly red bark; a *k'eñwal* is a thicket of these trees.

k'epa ñek'en (Q): new generation.

kipi (Q): a load bundle.

kirkincho (Q): a *charango* made from the shell of an armadillo.

kiswar (Q): *Beauleia incana globosa*, a leafy bush growing in the lower areas of the Andean highlands. Its leaves resemble an olive tree's and it is used for firewood.

kúchuman (Q): to the corner.

-kuna (Q): the plural suffix.

lambra (Q): a tree with twisted, thorny branches.

liwi (Q): three stone balls connected by a thong or cord that bring down quarry by entangling limbs.

llampu (Q): a red ceremonial powder made of very fine cornmeal, special seeds, and minerals, used as an offering at ritual table and elsewhere; it is a prophylactic against contamination, capture, and illnesses caused by the Wamanis.

lliklla (Q): a rectangular cloth the Indians use for carrying food, babies, and other things.

Lucana (Q): Lucana is the name of an ethnic group and is sometimes written Rukana. Lucanas is a province in the department of Ayacucho.

mak'ta (Q): a young man.

mamacita (S): diminutive form of *mamá*, mother.

mamitay (S+Q): diminutive form of *mamá*, mother; *mama* is also used as a respectful form of address for older women, like Mrs. or Madam. Indians sometimes use Spanish diminutive suffix *-ito* mistakenly, thinking it has all the attributes of Quechua suffix *-cha* defined above.

manan (Q): no.

mayordomo (S): in Puquio article, the sponsor of a religious festival.

mesa (S): table; (Q): a "ritual table" or cloth laid with offerings in a set pattern.

mestizo (SE): a person of mixed Indian and white ancestry.

misti (Q): a term used by Indians to designate persons of the aristocratic class, of Western or near-Western culture, who have traditionally dominated the region since colonial times. Although *misti* means "white" in Quechua, by now, naturally, none of them is of the pure white race or of pure Western culture.

naturales (S): natives; a name the Indians call themselves.

papacha (S+Q): great father, a term of respect.

papacito (S): little father; similar to *papay, tatay, padrecito,* and *papituy.*

papituy (S+Q): my little father; Indians use it to mean "my great father" or "my great lord." (See *-cha* in glossary.)

pasaychik (S+Q): you (pl.) go by.

patron (S): boss or master.

perduncha (S+Q): a great pardon; term used to ask for a mutual pardon, redefining relationships.

personero (S): a person appointed by the national government to be a member of the council of a recognized community and to be responsible for documents and land litigation.

pinkuyllu (Q): a giant, five-holed flute the Indians of Peru play at community celebrations.

Pirucha (Q): place where a folk dance is held at night during the Sequia festival; also, the dance that is the reception the community gives to the coming of the life-giving water from the springs.

pisco (QSE): alcoholic drink made by fermenting and distilling grape juice.

Plaza de Armas (S): the main square the Spaniards always established in the center of the cities they founded in the New World.

Pongo (Q): in Puquio he is the serf and priest of the Wamanis and sometimes the servant of the person acting as *auki*; in southern Peru and Bolivia a *pongo* is a hacienda Indian who does unpaid labor in a landowner's house.

pukllay (Q): to play; in Puquio this term is used for the traditional bullfight, and also for the bullfight music, also called *turupukllay.*

punas (QSE): high, bleak regions of the Andes.

punacomuneros, -cumunkuna (Q+S): puna community members.

punaruna, punarunakuna (Q): puna people, those who live on the high, bleak uplands.

punchau (Q): day.

quena (Q): a reed flute with a slot in one end across which the musician blows.

ripuy (Q): go away.

riy (SQ): a king, derived from Spanish *rey*; (Q): go ye.

Rukana (Q): see *Lucana*.

sallk'a (Q): savage; wild, uncivilized people who live on the puna; in this book the term is used for wild mountain bulls.

sáyay (Q): stop, whoa; *sayachik* is the plural form.

señor (S): a title used to address an important man; used in small towns to address a notable or by Indians to describe a member of the provincial upper class in the sense of "lord" or "master."

Sequia (Q): a festival to celebrate the coming of the life-giving water from the springs at the end of the dry season; it is derived from the Spanish word *acequia*, "irrigation ditch."

Sequia *alférez* (SQ): a standard-bearer for the Sequia festival.

sok'ompuro (Q): a reedy plant.

staffbearer (E): an Indian community leader, or *varayok'*. He carries a long staff as a symbol of authority.

sullka (Q): lesser.

supay (Q): a demon.

Tahuantinsuyo (Q): Quechua name for the Inca Empire, meaning "Four Regions."

tankayllu (Q): a heavy-bodied buzzing insect that flies through the fields sipping nectar from the flowers.

tayta (Q): father; also used as an affectionate and respectful form of address.

Taytallay tayta! (Q): "Father, my father!": an expression commonly used in difficult or distressing situations.

taytay (Q): my father.

tinya (Q): a small ceremonial drum played by women.

tumpa misti (Q): a half-*misti*; mestizo.

turucha (S+Q): little bull, or great respected bull.

turupukllu (S+Q): bullfight; also special bullfight music played on *wakawak'ras*.

unu (Q): "water" in the ritual language and in Cuzco Quechua.

varayok' (S+Q): *See* staffbearers.

vecino (S): a town citizen who owns a house lot, pays taxes, and has voting rights; in this book translated as townsman.

vicuña (QSE): an Andean mammal related to the camel and llama, smaller than the guanaco.

viscacha (QSE): a rodent the size of a squirrel with ears like a rabbit and a long tail.

Wachok' (Q): in Puquio, the name of legendary heroes who pierce the mountains; in ancient and Cuzco Quechua the word related to fornication.

wak'ates (Q): those who weep like women.

wakawak'ra (Q): a trumpet made of bull's horn.

Wamani (Q): a mountain deity.

Wasichakuy (Q): a house-roofing fiesta.

waylla (Q): a tall evergreen grass.

werak'ocha (Q): the equivalent of *señor*. Werak'ocha was the name of the Inca's supreme god.

yaku (Q): common word for "water" in Puquio.

yareta (Q): a low compact plant, *zorella yarita*, that looks like a mossy rock; sometimes called "cushion plant."

yau (Q): hey.

yawar (Q): blood.

yawar fiesta (Q+S): bloody fiesta, the traditional Indian-style bullfight.

DATE DUE

1/4/91 PYM ✓			
IL: 9530594			
(Due : 2/4/91)			

DEMCO 38-297